IN DEEP WATER

Happy reading

Peter Goldsby

Peter Goldsbrough

Copyright © 2018 Peter Goldsbrough

All rights reserved, including the right to reproduce this book, or portions thereof in any form. No part of this text may be reproduced, transmitted, downloaded, decompiled, reverse engineered, or stored, in any form or introduced into any information storage and retrieval system, in any form or by any means, whether electronic or mechanical without the express written permission of the author.

This is a work of fiction. Names and characters are the product of the author's imagination and any resemblance to actual persons, living or dead, is entirely coincidental.

The views expressed in this work are solely those of the author and do not necessarily reflect the views of the publisher, and the publisher hereby disclaims any responsibility for them.

ISBN: 978-0-244-06250-7

PublishNation
www.publishnation.co.uk

Acknowledgements

With thanks to my wife Lynda for her infinite patience and encouragement.

Thanks also go to the Paphos Writers' Group, Cyprus, for their support and critiquing, but more importantly, socialising in the bar afterwards.

Chapter 1

She was naked. It was almost midnight. Her body was still damp, flushed, and tingling in the afterglow of sex. Outside, an unseasonal storm lashed rain against the bedroom window. She took a sip of chilled Sauvignon Blanc then placed the glass on her bedside cabinet. She turned down the duvet and sat on the clean, crisp, newly-laundered bedding, a stark contrast to the bed she had left just fifteen minutes ago. A bed, whose crumpled sheets had smelt of a mixture of perfume and perspiration after nearly four hours of rampant sex with her lover, safe in the knowledge her husband wouldn't return home until tomorrow.

She smiled as she recalled the events of the evening. She had been playfully restrained and blindfolded, left alone and untouched for what seemed an age. Her lover had then taken her to heights of ecstasy never enjoyed with her husband, ripples of pleasure coursing through her body all evening. Another smile lit up her face as she bent down to take out her secret diary from its hiding place in the bedside cabinet. She wrote, *May 2nd Spent four hours with Alex tonight, tied up and taken to heaven and back. I've never been so happy.* She absent-mindedly flipped back through the pages, smiling again. The sordid facts of her two-year affair were spelt out in detail.

The tome contained nothing about her deteriorating relationship with her husband whom she had met at a nightclub in Lincoln nine years ago when she was thirty. Until then, she had never enjoyed a serious relationship.

'You need to find yourself a man and settle down,' her mother had repeatedly said. At the time, her plain looks, frumpy hairstyle, and dowdy choice of clothes did little to help her cause. The lack of lighting in the nightclub had masked her shortcomings. They had both had a lot to drink and he had invited her back to his 'penthouse apartment'. They had spent the rest of Saturday night and most of

Sunday in bed. It was only when they surfaced on Sunday evening that she noticed his penthouse apartment was in fact a dirty, seedy, first-floor flat with threadbare carpets, and grimy torn curtains barely covering the filthy cracked windows. The furniture was old and mismatched; more second-hand junk shop than department store. The rented flat was all he could afford at the time, having just left university.

The following week she had changed her hairstyle and bought a new wardrobe. After four weeks they had fallen in love, and went to visit her parents in Nottingham to tell them they were going to rent a two-up two-down cottage in Market Rasen and move in together.

Within ten minutes of their arrival, her new boyfriend had upset both her parents and they had taken an instant dislike to him. Her mother had said, 'You're too good for him.' He hadn't helped by calling her father Jimmy. 'His name is James,' her mother had scolded. 'I don't like your attitude, so if you think you are sharing a bed under my roof, you're mistaken.' Absolutely fuming, he had stormed out of the house and driven home alone. It hadn't helped that they had married three months later at the local Registrar's office; neither set of parents invited to the wedding. After eighteen months, the flames of passion had become dying embers; they had married in haste and regretted it at their leisure.

Four years ago, with the aid of a crippling mortgage, quickly followed by two large bank loans for refurbishment works, they moved into a three-bedroom detached house in Wendham Close, Louth. He had hoped the fresh start in new surroundings would perk up their worsening relationship. He even agreed to her suggestion that he have a vasectomy.

'It might improve things between us,' she had lied.

It hadn't.

She had been spending most nights in the guest bedroom, often after a late night with her lover. Occasionally she had joined her husband in the marital bed. On one such night, drunk, he had tried to force himself on her. She had kneed him in the groin and pushed him away. His temper had flared and he had lashed out, his left elbow whacking her face. When she stopped crying, she went into the spare bedroom, never to return. Her right eye was black and blue. The next day he had looked at her swollen face. It was obvious he couldn't remember what had happened.

'Did I do that?' he had asked. She had merely shrugged. He became a pariah in the eyes of his neighbours. Her work colleagues labelled him a wife-beater.

Sleeping separately she saw little reason to clean his bedroom or cook for him. She didn't like housework anyway. She had also stopped washing and ironing his clothes. For a while he slept in an unmade bed and looked scruffy and unkempt, but had eventually taken the hint and started using the local laundry for a service wash and iron.

Now, she had a lover. She had decided some time ago that she was going to leave her husband. She was sick of being locked in a loveless and sexless marriage. She had sent him a text while he was away on a training course, telling him she was leaving home. *Home,* she thought, it was merely a roof over her head. She ran through her plan one last time. Once both their salaries were paid into their joint bank account she would withdraw as much cash as she could up to their overdraft limit. By the time her husband returned home tomorrow night, she would be at her parents' house in Nottingham for the weekend, only returning to Louth next week to collect her clothes and belongings while he was at work. By Wednesday she would be free. The divorce and division of the joint assets would take longer.

Her thoughts were brought back to the here and now by a flash of lightning, quickly followed by a clap of thunder. She drank the remainder of her now warm wine, and then went into the bathroom to shower. Back in the bedroom, she paused in front of the full-length mirror on the wardrobe door. Her skin was pink and tingling from the hot shower, shining after the application of body lotion, the smell of coconut filled the room. Her short razor-cut, spiky hair was damp and smelled of jasmine. She turned sideways and examined her lithe and supple body in profile. Her pert breasts were still firm and her stomach flat. Nine years ago, her husband had been able to press all the right buttons. He had been able to turn her into a lustful, wanton woman. Now, rapidly approaching forty, she no longer felt anything for him except contempt. He was obsolete, superseded by her lover.

She picked up her journal and carefully replaced it in its hiding place.

Cheryl Bishop would never write in the diary again.

In Deep Water

Chapter 2

Alan Bishop had not enjoyed a happy childhood. Born to working class parents, the family had lived in a block of high-rise council flats on one of the roughest and most notorious estates in Sheffield. Squatters and drug dealers soon occupied any flat that became vacant. Alan's strongest memory of that time had been the broken-down lifts, or when they were working, the overpowering smell of urine and vomit. Fortunately they had lived on the fourth floor so compared to some, it had been a relatively short walk up the staircase. Alan, a small, stocky lad, was well capable of looking after himself amongst kids his own age. However, his elder brother Tom was a pale, lanky boy who was bullied mercilessly. As a result, Alan became involved in fights with boys two or three years his senior as he fought off his brother's bullies.

In the early-1990s, the residents had been relocated to a newly-built estate, a mixture of terraced and semi-detached houses. The high-rise flats were demolished but the people hadn't changed to match their new environment. The council had merely relocated the wife beaters, junkies and deadbeats into new houses. The estate had started its decline almost immediately the families moved in, scruffy kids and uncontrolled dogs once again roamed the streets. The workshy still continued to enjoy a reasonable lifestyle on benefits, and satellite dishes sprung up at every corner. Rusty, broken-down, or burned-out cars with flat tyres, or no wheels, appeared on the streets and in the front gardens, alongside abandoned supermarket trolleys and prams. Gable ends were sprayed-painted with obscenities, and the white picket fences around the gardens had quickly disappeared, either used for firewood or as weapons by squabbling kids. The drug dealers reappeared to find old customers; now using flash cars as their base, with under-age runners stalking around street corners and in bus shelters, making sure nearby street lights were broken to hide their illegal activities. Only the bravest, or the fool-hardy, ventured out at night.

Some residents, mostly in the minority, were decent folk trying to make an honest living, and Alan's parents were one such couple. His father worked in a local steel mill which produced some of the largest steel forgings and castings in the world. He wanted no more than have his two sons work alongside him. Working class nepotism.

'What's good enough for me, is good enough for thee lad,' he frequently said. Alan's mother worked full-time in a local bakery and bread shop, and ambitions for her children were just as limited as her husband's.

Alan Bishop had been determined to get away from the estate, and from Sheffield, as soon as he could. He worked hard at the local comprehensive school, aiming to be top of the class. Most of his peers seemed content to head in the opposite direction, considering reading and writing to be unnecessary skills. Surrounded by mediocrity, Alan's desire to better himself meant he was ostracised by all and sundry. Home life had not been conducive to studying either, if it wasn't the TV on full volume distracting him, it was the sound of fighting and squabbling kids outside. All his schoolwork was either done at school after hours, or in the local library. He had done extremely well and obtained a bucketful of GCSEs. Against his parents' wishes, and following several family arguments, he was eventually allowed to stay on and take his 'A' levels.

'It's not natural, spending so much time in't school,' his father often said. 'Tom's working in't steelworks with me, earning a decent wage, and you should be doing't same.'

Alan's reply, 'But it's a dead end job,' had earned him a clip round the ear, followed by several days of silence and withering glares. In the sixth form, unknown to his parents, his paternal grandfather had driven him around the country for various university interviews. When he obtained his 'A' levels, he told his parents he had gained a place at Newcastle University. They were devastated and he was never truly forgiven for leaving home. He helped subsidise his college life by holding down several part-time and summer vacation jobs. If he ever returned to Sheffield between terms, he always stayed with his grandfather.

During his time at university, he had little spare money, what he earned was spent supplementing his accommodation and food bills. His grandfather would occasionally visit him and give him what extra cash he could afford.

'Thanks Pops, that's another twenty-five chip butties,' Alan would say after a quick mental calculation. There was no surplus money for girlfriends or beer. After seven years of study and two degrees, he had joined Lincs Water at the age of twenty-five as a Design Engineer, recruited for his expertise in sewage treatment. He quickly gained a reputation for designing innovative and economical solutions to engineering problems put before him.

His gruff Yorkshire attitude and accent had been softened by the years spent away from Sheffield. However, it would occasionally resurface when angry. At five-foot-nine tall, with a stocky build and short thick black hair, his naturally ruddy looks, tanned skin, and rosy cheeks gave the impression he spent a lot of time outdoors. He would have looked more at home in the farming community than in a boardroom. His favoured choice of an old and well-worn Barbour jacket, a charity shop purchase during his university days, seemed to emphasise his love of the outdoors. With his broad shoulders, muscular forearms and biceps, and chiselled jaw, some folk unkindly likened him to Popeye. Although he could never be described as an Adonis, there was a ruggedness to his looks that many women found attractive.

Chapter 3

Four years ago Alan Bishop was summoned to the boardroom by Lincs Water's Chairman, a verbose and forgetful man in his late-seventies.

'Come in Bishop that was quick. I've only just put the phone down.'

Alan merely nodded, but thought, *When the Chairman rings and asks to see you immediately, you don't hang about.* His race up the stairs meant his heart rate would take a while to return to normal.

'Sit down, sit down,' was emphasised by a waved invitation. Alan sat at the opposite end of the boardroom table which was larger than a full-size snooker table, and capable of seating sixteen with more than enough elbow room for everyone. The table was solid mahogany, with a circular green leather inlay, and smelt of recently applied polish. Around the table, the chairs were covered in matching green leather.

It was not the first time Alan had been in the boardroom. He and several audacious colleagues often popped in after-hours to see if the infamous drinks cabinet had been left unlocked. Today was his first visit in an official capacity. The room itself was large and rectangular with three windows along one side, overlooking the car park. The vertical blinds had been partially closed to keep out the bright sunlight.

The Chairman sat at the other end of the table, his green-checked suit, so favoured by the county's hunting/fishing/shooting fraternity, hung loosely on his shrunken frame. His matching checked shirt seemed several sizes too large, and the brown worsted tie disappeared under a woollen waistcoat. His thin grey hair was neatly trimmed and combed. He peered at Alan over his reading glasses, an open file, telephone, and walking stick on the table in front of him.

'Well, you're probably wondering why I asked to see you.' Alan hadn't really had time to think while bounding up two flights of stairs. 'As you know six years ago we recruited you for your expertise in sewage treatment.' He paused. 'Sorry, perhaps a little background would help.' Alan nodded again, still short of breath.

'Well, cutting a long story short,' *I hope so,* thought Alan, the Chairman's reputation for waffling was well known, 'Lincs Water was formed in 1854 as a "water supply-only" company and, in that regard, it has served the people of Lincolnshire with a clean and wholesome water supply ever since. However, somewhere between the 1974 Local Government re-organisation and the privatisation of the water industry fifteen years later, Lincs Water ended up being offered the sewage function on a 300 year lease. Don't ask me how or why it happened, but my predecessor jumped at the chance. Within the industry it was, and still is, an unusual and unique arrangement.

'Turnover nearly doubled overnight but we didn't have a clue about sewage treatment. Eventually the penny dropped and we started recruiting qualified staff. You, with your PhD in anaerobic sewage treatment, whatever that is, were seen as a key player. And I have to say, I'm told you haven't let us down. We promoted you three years ago to Senior Design Engineer. I now want you to consider applying for the post of Northern Area Manager based at Grimsby.'

'But I thought we already had a Northern Area Manager,' Alan stammered.

'Yes we do, and this is entirely confidential, but he is taking early retirement.' Alan had met and worked alongside Will Johnson many times and he didn't think he was old enough to retire. However he had heard rumours of Johnson's extra curricula activities with numerous female members of staff. He decided not to pursue the matter. What Alan didn't know was that the Chairman had received an anonymous letter stating that Johnson was using his company debit card to entertain women, a card which should have only been used for legitimate company expenses. An investigation had shown that, in the last year, expenditure on local hotel rooms and restaurants had exceeded £9000.

'But I've no operational experience,' Alan replied. 'The northern area has a huge water supply network, with separate supplies for domestic and industrial use, whereas my experience and expertise are both in sewage.'

'Alan . . .' the Chairman paused, pushed his glasses up his nose, and looked down at the file in front of him. 'You are thirty-one years old and already you have a first-class Masters Degree in civil engineering, a PhD, and you are also a double Chartered Engineer, both in civil and structural engineering. You can't tell me you don't have the capacity to learn. You will have five District Managers, eighteen Superintendents, together with other area staff and nearly 200 blue-collar workers, all there to help you.' The enormity of the task stunned Alan. He was unable to speak. The Chairman went on, 'You'll be fine, let me have your application by Friday, and we'll go through the motions of a formal interview at the board meeting next Thursday. Major Wiltshire, our HR consultant, will also be present but purely as an observer. And don't worry about references; I've already spoken to your departmental head.'

At the subsequent board meeting, Bishop was the only candidate to be interviewed for the post. The Chairman was pleased to note that Alan's reservations had disappeared, and he was offered the job. A new Ford Mondeo hatchback and a huge hike in salary, together with private medical healthcare, had gone a long way to persuading him. The rusty and dented Saab he had bought after leaving university was almost on its last legs, and had recently cost a small fortune to get through its latest MOT test.

As Alan was leaving the boardroom, the Chairman said, 'You'll report directly to the new Managing Director whom we hope to appoint later today.'

Following Bishop's departure from the room, the Chairman looked around the table at his fellow directors. 'Well gentlemen, now that Sugden has finally left the company, we have an opportunity to appoint a new and dynamic Managing Director.'

§§§

In Deep Water

Since taking over the sewage function, Lincs Water had failed to translate the extra workload into bottom-line profit. Turnover had leapt to £175 million, but profit had stagnated at £500,000. James Sugden, the MD, had been an acerbic and tetchy man, plagued by illness. His increasing absences from the workplace over several years did little to help the company's dire financial position. An ill-health retirement would have given Sugden an enhancement to his years of service, and an increased pension. However the correct terminology was 'ill-health dismissal' and none of the directors had had the courage to approach Sugden using such insensitive language, never mind suggest that a medical examination would be required. Every board member was relieved when he had applied for early retirement.

§§§

'This chap Young seems to be the best candidate on paper,' the Chairman said.

'But he's only a Public Relations Manager. Surely he can't possibly be a serious contender,' the Company Secretary retorted.

'Let's not pre-judge the situation; we'll see how he performs.'

It was nearly four-o'clock before Ian Young was invited into the boardroom.

'Yes sir, that's true,' he said, in reply to the Company Secretary's sarcastic question, 'but as Press and Public Relations Manager with Yorkshire Water, I have needed to have a thorough insight and understanding of every aspect of the business when facing journalists. You will see that I bring with me a glowing reference from my Chief Executive, and in two of my previous jobs I gained valuable experience in company turnarounds.'

It was after five-o'clock when the Chairman said, 'Well I think that's about all we need to ask you. Do you have any questions yourself?'

Young replied, 'No thank you sir, but I would just reiterate that with a wealth of knowledge in company recoveries, an unrivalled experience within the water industry, together with my three excellent references, I feel I am the ideal candidate for the job.

Efficiency will improve immediately, and I can confidently predict that profits will double in a year.'

After Young had left the room, the Chairman scanned the directors, most of whom were nodding their agreement. Major Wiltshire had tried to ask a couple of questions during the interview, but had been politely and firmly informed his was an observational role. Wiltshire looked around at those present and thought, *out of the frying pan and into the fire.*

The Company Secretary said, 'I'll follow up those references first thing tomorrow.'

'No,' the Chairman retorted firmly, 'I don't want any delay in this appointment. The sooner we get him on board, the quicker our profits will increase. I'll ring him later and offer him the job.'

Major Wiltshire, his elbows resting on the table, dropped his head into his hands. Then he straightened his back and looked around at the board members. He got the distinct impression that they all wanted to go home. Today's meeting had been a marathon session. He said, 'Chairman, if I may . . .'

'I'm sorry John, I must dash, I have a dinner engagement tonight, and our board meetings normally don't go beyond lunchtime. Ring me tomorrow will you?'

'But tomorrow might be too . . .' He never finished the sentence. The Chairman had already left the room. John Wiltshire slumped back in his chair. *What a useless bunch of blubbering old buffoons,* he thought.

It would take two years of steadily falling profits before the directors of Lincs Water eventually discovered that Young's company turnarounds had both failed, and the Chief Executive of Yorkshire Water had written a glowing reference just to get rid of him.

Chapter 4

While Cheryl Bishop was packing her case for the weekend trip to see her parents, ninety miles north-west of Louth her husband Alan was slowly regaining consciousness. The hazy oblivion only alcohol can provide meant he remembered little about the previous night. His head pounded mercilessly and his mouth felt like old dry leather. He rolled over in the bed and looked at the now familiar paintings on the wall. The room had been his home, on and off, for the last nine months. When he eventually stood up, his vision was blurred and his temples were throbbing. As he walked naked and unsteadily towards the bathroom he noticed his clothes, a pair of scruffy old trousers, black and white hooped shirt, and a black beret, neatly folded on the chair. He vaguely remembered a party the night before. His memory stirred. 'French onion seller,' he muttered to himself.

It had been the farewell dinner, themed on fancy dress, of the water industry's prestigious Senior Management Development Programme, or SMDP as it was known by everyone involved. The course had been run annually for nearly twenty years in the training centre at Tadcaster Hall. Each year twenty-four of the industry's brightest managers were selected to attend the course, and last year Alan's name had been put forward by his Chairman. Competition for places was fierce as it was ranked in the industry as a fast track to the boardroom. Six in-house modules of three weeks each were spread over nine months, with short breaks in-between for the delegates to spend some time back at their workplace.

Pressure on participants was enormous, as much of the time they were removed from their comfort zone. Media training, including television interviews and public speaking, covered two of the modules. Some of the country's top politicians and television presenters came to give advice. The third and fourth modules were entirely centred on the planning, management, and control of major emergencies, while the last two focused on a specialist subject chosen by the delegates themselves. Of the thirty-seven courses on offer at the training centre, participants on thirty-six of them looked upon a spell at Tadcaster Hall as a bit of a holiday.

Last night Alan had drunk a couple of large whiskies from the bottle hidden in his locked suitcase, before hanging strings of onions and garlic around his neck, then going down to the bar. Beer, followed by copious amounts of wine with the meal meant he couldn't remember anything. His boxer shorts were in the shower tray, soaking wet. He frowned, wondered, but couldn't remember. As he looked in the mirror and tried to focus, his worst fears were proven. His eyes were bloodshot and puffy, he looked extremely hung-over. Even *he* now realised that his drinking was completely out of control.

'Shit, why do I drink so much?' he asked himself aloud, even though he knew the answer. He showered, but decided against shaving, his hands were shaking too much. Trembling hands after a heavy drinking session had become a regular occurrence. After gulping down four paracetamol, he dressed and sat on the bed. He looked at the two paintings again. The first depicted grey, red, and blue skyscrapers at a waterfront, their reflections distorted by the water's movement. The other was a painting of a landscape with vivid flowers in the foreground. He was unable to bring either of them into focus for any length of time.

His love affair with alcohol had been going on for two reasons. Firstly, his marriage to Cheryl was on the rocks, and secondly, he and his boss, MD Ian Young, shared a seething mutual hatred of one another. Young had joined Lincs Water shortly after Alan had been promoted to Northern Area Manager, and Alan quickly realised that Young had a scant understanding of the water industry, having bluffed his way into the job with hollow promises. Young, however, had become aware that Alan Bishop had an encyclopaedic knowledge of water and sewage treatment and felt threatened because of it. Young made no secret of the fact he wanted rid of Bishop who was now handing him the ammunition with which to sack him. Even though he couldn't remember what had happened

In Deep Water

last night, someone would, and word would surely get back to Lincoln.

§§§

As Alan entered the now spotlessly clean dining room at Tadcaster Hall, his mind again went back to the previous night. He had a vague recollection of a bun fight followed by a scuffle between two of the delegates. Was it Elvis and Batman? A solitary figure sat at the far end of the room, engrossed in a Friday newspaper, an empty cereal bowl, cup and saucer, on the table in front of him. His heart sank when Bill Waites looked up. Alan nodded a hello, but Waites didn't respond. Waites was in his late-forties, five-foot-ten tall with a head of thick blonde hair. He kept himself in shape with regular visits to the gym. After leaving Cambridge with a degree in civil engineering, he had joined a medium-sized engineering consultancy in London, before being sent to Hong Kong to open an office there. After five years, the Hong Kong office was the largest in the company. Brought back to London and made a partner, he was then head-hunted by Severn Trent Water to become the youngest Chief Executive in the water industry.

Waites had been invited by the training centre to be the part-time principal and head mentor of this year's SMDP. It was the third time he had been asked to lead the programme. Last night had not been the first time Alan had been drunk and incapable during the course, and although Waites hadn't been present on the other three occasions, Alan was sure he must have been informed.

Alan chose a different table and slumped in the chair, unable to hide his hung-over aura. A waitress appeared at the table, ready to take his order. 'Just black coffee thanks.'

'Would you like a cooked breakfast?' she asked. Alan shook his head slowly, the thought of fried food immediately made him feel nauseous. After the coffee arrived, he waited several minutes for it to cool before picking up the cup. His hand trembled so much he spilt coffee on the fresh white tablecloth. He tried again using two hands with a little more success and took a sip. Bill Waites, who had been watching his every move, came across to the table and sat opposite him.

'What the hell were you playing at last night?' he hissed. 'This isn't the first time you've been drunk during the course, is it? In the beginning, I didn't believe the reports about you, but now . . .' He left the sentence unfinished. An uncomfortable silence followed before he went on, 'Delegates on SMDP are supposed to be the *crème de la crème*, but you're a bloody disgrace to the good name of the industry. You were completely comatose last night. It took Daisy Powers and four waiters to get you back to your room. She had to stay with you most of the night until she was satisfied you weren't going to choke on your own vomit. She even had to point Percy at the porcelain a couple of times. You need to apologise to her, and thank her. What the hell is your problem?'

Alan turned crimson and his mouth fell open in shock. Daisy Powers was the training centre's Food and Beverage Manager. She was a short stocky woman, married, in her mid-thirties, with dark hair, cut in a page-boy style. She always seemed to have a smile on her face which accentuated her dimpled cheeks. Until last night, Alan had only passed the time of day with her. His face reddened more as his thoughts went back to the times at home when he had been too drunk to make it to the toilet, and peed all over the en-suite floor. *Was that why his boxer shorts were wet?* he wondered. His eyes filled with tears and he blinked to try and stop them, but they ran down his cheeks unchecked.

Waites paused for a minute allowing Alan to compose himself, before taking a more conciliatory attitude. 'Alan, we know SMDP is tough, that's the whole purpose of the programme. It pushes you to the limit. The course is designed to help you find your own strengths and weaknesses, so that you can then better understand those of your peers and subordinates. I even agreed to let you study finance, against my better judgement. I thought it would be a step too far for you, but you sailed through with flying colours.'

During the first week of the course, the delegates had been split into three groups in which they would remain for their specialist training. This took place over the final two modules. Alan felt he had more than enough knowledge in water and sewage treatment, so it should have come as no surprise when he asked to study finance as his specialist subject. Initially Bill Waites had refused the request.

'There's not a lot you can teach me about water or sewage,' Alan had stated confidently.

'But what financial experience do you have?' asked one of the tutors.

'I'm a graduate of the Mr Micawber School of Economics,' he had replied.

Waites had guffawed when he was told what Alan had said, and finally agreed to the request, allowing him to study finance.

Bill Waites' thoughts came back to the here and now. 'This is the first year we have introduced psychologists to help anyone who needed it. I was pleased to hear you have been in regular discussions with Sarah Steadman who has made me aware of your marital problems and the battles with your MD. You need to sort yourself out before it's too late.'

Alan nodded. Waites then took out his mobile phone and pressed the screen several times before sliding it across the table. 'That's how bad you were last night.' The photo showed Alan slumped over the arm of a high-backed chair, unconscious. His forehead, cheeks, nose, and chin were covered with kisses from someone who had a penchant for bright red lipstick. His hair was badly in need of a trim, and someone had ruffled it mercilessly. He looked like the wild man of Borneo. 'Now go and make your peace with Daisy.'

Alan slowly rose from the table. 'Will you be reporting this to my Chairman?'

With sadness evident in his eyes, Waites replied, 'Alan, your employers have paid over £30,000 for you to attend this course. I have no choice but to tell them.'

Alan, his head bowed in shame, walked out of the dining room, tears once again streaming down his cheeks. The words *bringing the company's good name into disrepute* rang in his ears.

Chapter 5

Alan walked around the gardens of Tadcaster Hall, trying to clear his head of the thumping hangover. The grounds were cloaked in silence, only an occasional chirping bird breaking the stillness. The thunderstorm which had raged for most of the previous night had abated, but the evidence of the storm was strewn around the grounds. Broken twigs and branches were everywhere; leaves were piled high against the base of walls, and a young horse chestnut tree was leaning at a precarious angle. The sun was trying to break through the heavy grey clouds which still scurried across the sky.

Tadcaster Hall was over 300 years old. Once a large and opulent residence set in twelve acres of gardens and woodlands, more recently it had been a derelict and failed country hotel. It had been purchased by the ten major water companies of England and Wales in the late-1980s when the industry was preparing for privatisation. The government of the day had been encouraged by the 'Tell Sid' campaign to privatise the gas industry, and was hell-bent on selling more of the family silver. When the five-man working party tasked with setting up a training company first saw the building, they were dismayed. Only the architect who accompanied the team saw the potential. Although the Hall was dilapidated and neglected, overgrown and unloved, it was architecturally impressive.

As he came round to the front of the Hall, Alan looked up at the entrance, unimpressed by the building's beauty or heritage. He muttered, 'I fucking hate this place.' He couldn't shake off the image of himself, unconscious, his face covered in lipstick kisses.

Alan had arranged to take Daisy Powers to lunch. He needed to know about the events of last night, no matter how embarrassing it might prove. There was a chill in the air after the storm, so he headed for his car, and its heater, to wait for Daisy. He took out his mobile and scrolled through the contact list to *Sam*. The call went unanswered so he left a message.

§§§

'I have to say Sarah, I'm *so* disappointed. Part of the reason I come to oversee SMDP is to see if there are any high-flyers I might, one day, tempt to join me at Severn Trent. Bishop had been the first.' He paused. 'Until last night.'

Sarah Steadman raised her eyebrows in question. She sat opposite Bill Waites in the still-empty dining room. She had just delivered her reports on the eight delegates for whom she was responsible and they lay on the table between them. Like every other report already in Waites' possession, seven of them barely covered a single sheet of paper. The account on Alan Bishop ran to four closely-typed pages. Sarah had ordered a full English breakfast; she felt she deserved a treat after nearly nine months at Tadcaster Hall.

Waites took out his phone and brought up the photo of Bishop. 'That's how he ended up, out for the count. It took five people to get him back to his room.' Sarah shook her head in disbelief; last night she had gone to her room early to complete her reports.

Bill Waites looked closely at her. Nine months ago, when the course had started, he had seen a fresh, newly married, vibrant young woman with shining black hair and a bubbly personality. Now sat before him was a woman slumped in her chair, the tiredness caused by lack of sleep showing on her face. Her skin was sallow and her damp hair, fresh from a shower, did little to improve the image.

'To be honest Bill, there's really only one problem. I know he whinges about his MD always looking for excuses to carpet him, but he's more than a match for Ian Young. The main problem is his relationship with his wife. As you'll see from my report, he says she's never at home. He can't remember the last time they ate a meal together.'

Sarah Steadman's breakfast and coffee arrived and Waites invited her to start with a wave of the hand. The smell of the hot food tempted him to order something more himself, but instead he returned to the Daily Telegraph until she had finished, during which time a few of the other delegates had started to drift into the dining room. He leaned closer to her, his voice little more than a whisper.

'Do you think she's having an affair?'

'I asked him that early on, and although they sleep in separate bedrooms, he didn't think so. The whole situation has just driven him to drink. He admits he can't stop, he told me he yearns for a drink *every* waking hour.'

'Did you suggest he leave his wife?' asked Waites.

'Yes, but he says he can't afford to, they have a huge mortgage and two bank loans taken out when his wife insisted on a new kitchen and bathroom. He even has some student loans still outstanding.'

'What do you think will happen when he leaves here?'

'Well, he does have a colleague he describes as his "best friend and confidante". He showed me a photo of her. I have to say, she is *absolutely* gorgeous.'

'Married?'

'No, she's a single parent with a daughter, just turned eight.'

'Well why doesn't he shack up with her?'

'He says he's not good enough for her.'

'Oh come on Sarah, he's got a Masters degree, a PhD, double Chartered Engineer and she's what, a typist who had a fling and is now paying the price of bringing up a child alone?'

'It's not quite that simple. She went to a public school and Trinity College, Oxford. He compares his formative years growing up in the slums of Sheffield and his inner-city comprehensive school education to her privileged upbringing. He certainly has a crush on her but he feels, in his own words, "outclassed".'

Waites sighed. 'Do you have her contact details? Perhaps we could enlist her help.'

Sarah shook her head. 'No I don't, but from what I've gathered, she knows everything about him, apart from last night, obviously. I hope she can help him before he presses the self-destruct button.'

A silence followed before Waites nodded. 'Well I don't think there's anything else *we* can do to help. I'll put a copy of this photo in his file and speak to his Chairman next week.'

Chapter 6

Samantha Hyde had enjoyed a sheltered upbringing. Three years younger than her brother Piers, she had grown up in what she believed was a normal family. Her father had worked abroad in the Middle East for many years, and as a result, she had rarely seen him. When he came home on leave he had seemed cold and distant, but not unkind or cruel. Her mother had tried to compensate for her husband's absences but the strain of bringing up two children alone, and holding down a part-time job had taken its toll, and she had had insufficient time to give Samantha the affection she yearned. As a result Samantha's uncle, who didn't have children of his own, had stepped in to give her the love and attention she had craved. By the time she was ten everyone knew she was going to become an attractive young lady. She became particularly close to her uncle who, having taken on the role of surrogate father, had wanted nothing but the best for her. He paid for her to go to prep school followed by an all-girls' public school.

She was academically gifted and it came as no surprise to anyone when she won a place at Trinity College, Oxford, to study chemistry. Again her uncle had footed the bill. At the end of the four-year course, after the farewell party, she had slept with a fellow student and had become pregnant. Her mother had been mortified and demanded she have an abortion.

'You're throwing away everything you've worked so hard to achieve,' her mother had frequently said.

Her uncle, who had married late in life, and his new wife, had been more sympathetic. Samantha would never forget their words. 'Whatever you want to do, we'll support you, both financially and morally. Whether you want to have the baby or abort it, we will respect your decision. At the end of the day it has to be *your* decision and *your* decision alone.'

When Emily was born, Samantha's mother still hadn't accepted the situation, embarrassed what the neighbours might think. Eventually Samantha left home, and, with her uncle's help, moved into an apartment. At first, Samantha had found it hard being a single parent. Emily cried and screamed incessantly. The piles of dirty washing seemed to grow by the hour. If it wasn't vomit over her clothes as well as Emily's, it was food hurled in every direction when a tantrum occurred. She had no help or support from her parents and she struggled, particularly with the lack of sleep. She never seemed to have a minute spare for herself. However, after a year, things became easier. Although she had occasionally worked part-time, her uncle and auntie had still supported her financially during this difficult time. Emily was three before Samantha's mother had held out the olive branch.

Samantha was an inch short of six-foot tall with shoulder length blonde hair, usually worn in a pony tail, and an hourglass figure. She did nothing to try and camouflage her height, often wearing high-heeled shoes. Whether dressed to kill, or merely strolling down the High Street in jeans and jumper, men would crane their necks as she passed. There was an independence about her which was a challenge to many men. Her public school accent was softened by her smooth silky voice.

As soon as Emily started pre-school, Samantha decided to apply for a full-time job. She didn't want to rely on her uncle's generosity forever. She had yearned to put her chemistry training to good use and four years ago, when a job was advertised at Lincs Water for a laboratory assistant based at their Riverside House HQ in Lincoln, she decided to apply. There were nearly forty candidates but she was the only one who had a Masters degree in chemistry from Oxford. She was the best qualified and most attractive candidate.

Game over.

§§§

Within a week of starting work, Alan Bishop walked into Samantha's life. He too had just started his new job as Northern Area Manager, and had brought a sewage sample into the laboratory for analysis. As they sat on opposite sides of the work-bench, a bottle full of sewage between them, they had chatted briefly as Samantha completed the necessary paperwork for the sample analysis.

She had looked down at the bottle of sewage, and smiled. 'Hardly the most romantic gift I've ever received.' They both laughed.

As it was nearly one-o'clock, Alan suggested they go for lunch and an hour later, driving back to Grimsby, he couldn't stop thinking about her. The more they met, the more infatuated he became. As far as Alan was concerned, she was the complete package. The things that attracted him most were her large saucer-shaped sky-blue eyes which seemed to hypnotise him, and her smile which would light up the room. She appreciated the fact that Alan was one of the few men who wasn't constantly ogling her large breasts.

Over the next year they had become friends, sharing little secrets with each other. They both seemed to want the friendship to progress to something more. However, the more Alan learnt about Samantha's background, the more he realised he couldn't match her privileged upbringing. Coming from a working class household, in his early years he had suffered from self-doubt and a lack of confidence. Success at school and university had partially dispelled those misgivings, but they suddenly came flooding back. He had clear-cut views on his place in life. His rule of thumb was simple. Working class people had one forename, middle class two, and upper class three. A double-barrelled surname trumped everything. He was just plain Alan Bishop but her full name was Samantha Charlotte Angela Hyde. Added to the fact she had attended a private prep school, had then gone to an all-girls' boarding school, followed by Oxford University, and it was game over as far as he was concerned. His council estate upbringing and inner-city comprehensive school education were no match. He decided she was way out of his league.

Although Alan had taken a mental backward-step in terms of a possibly more intimate relationship, they remained close friends. Romance may have been struck off Alan's agenda, but it didn't stop him dreaming. Samantha, however, was in love. She found him funny and spontaneous, but vulnerable. He had confided in her about his marriage problems, and as time went by, he also admitted his increasing dislike of his MD. Samantha also shared her secrets with him. She wanted to protect him, nurture him, mother him, but he always kept her at arms' length. There was nothing she wanted more than to make love to him.

Last year he had told her his drinking was starting to get out of hand.

'There's not a day goes by when I can't find an excuse for a drink,' he had said. 'At first it was restricted to popping out to the local pub, but recently I've been drinking more and more at home.' He now saw Samantha as his best friend and confidante, not someone he had to impress. He told her everything. 'I hide bottles behind the boxes of cereals so Cheryl won't find them. I pre-load with booze before going to the pub so I would only be seen to drink a couple in public, rather than a skin-full.' He even admitted to her that every night, on the way home from work, he bought a half-bottle of vodka, and drank the spirit neat after parking the car in the garage. He had reached the point where he couldn't get through a single day without a drink. He admitted to her he had concerns about being over the drink-drive limit some mornings and when going into town for a takeaway. Then one day he broke down and cried in front of her for the first time.

'The marriage is a sham,' he said. 'We haven't had sex for nearly eighteen months. To be honest Sam, we are like two strangers living under the same roof.' The more he divulged to her, the more she wanted to help. She was deeply in love with him, and was determined they would be together soon.

Whatever it took.

Chapter 7

During a leisurely lunch with Daisy Powers in a non-descript run-down tea room in Tadcaster, Alan finally plucked up the courage to talk about last night. They sat on mismatched tubular-steel chairs on opposite sides of a small, round, water-stained wooden table. The overpowering smell of greasy fried food emanating from the kitchen had forced them both to order nothing more adventurous than a sandwich.

'I know this is going to be embarrassing, but I'd like to know what happened last night.'

'Are you sure?'

Alan hesitated then nodded, the pain in his head now reduced to a dull ache. 'Yes, I'm sure. Bill has given me a hint of the night's events.'

She looked directly at him, took a deep breath and seemed to find the courage to start. 'Well apart from you peeing in your underwear, pissing all over the floor and filling the bath with vomit, it was a quiet night.' Alan felt his face redden as he looked away. 'Look Alan,' she went on, 'the only person present was me; I'd sent the four waiters back downstairs to clean up the dining room. The only thing you have to worry about are the photos everyone took of you while being carried out unconscious.'

'Yes and my bloody face covered in lipstick kisses,' he said, raising his voice, causing two old women to turn round and stare at them. His headache flared up again as the realisation that those images would soon go viral and someone at Lincoln would see them. 'Shit,' he muttered to himself, then suggested they head back to the Hall having decided he didn't want to hear any more. After strolling round the grounds, arms linked, they gave each other a friendly hug and a kiss on the cheek. Alan thanked Daisy for all her help, then they said their farewells and promised to keep in touch. Alan sat in his car for a further hour, deep in thought. He was brought back to the present by his phone pinging with an incoming text.

Sorry, flat phone battery. I'll be home by five. Ring when you're five minutes away and I'll open the garage doors. Lancashire hot pot OK for supper? Sam xx.

Samantha didn't feel guilty about her little white lie. As soon as she had picked up his message about wanting to talk, she saw an opportunity to hopefully spend the whole night with him, alone. She had contacted her mother and arranged for Emily to stay with her for the weekend. Her mother wasn't too pleased, she always wanted three or four days notice, although Samantha had no idea why. Her parents didn't have any sort of social life and rarely went out. She also knew that Emily wouldn't be too happy as nowadays she constantly complained that her Gran was always shouting at her.

Samantha didn't care. A candle-lit dinner followed by a night making love to the man of her dreams would more than make up for the whingeing from both her mother and daughter. She had dreamed of this day for more than four years.

At lunchtime she had rushed home, packed an overnight bag for Emily and put clean sheets on the bed. She had done the weekly supermarket shopping the previous evening so there was plenty of food in the fridge. She took Emily's bag round to her mother's then picked up some wine on the way back to the office. It was after half-past-two before she sent him the text. All she had to do after that was leave work at four-o'clock, have a shower and dress in something subtle yet provocative then allow nature to take its course.

§§§

With plenty of time to spare, Alan decided to take the cross-country route via York and the Humber Bridge, rather than hammering down the A1. As he drove out of the car park his mind was in turmoil. He had a job he loved but a boss he loathed. Moving from the engineering design office into operations had been the best thing he had ever done. If he hadn't been asked to apply, then he doubted if he would have considered the move. As a child he had always lacked confidence. He had been able to temper those self doubts as he grew

In Deep Water

older, university had been an eye-opener for him, it made him realise he was often equal to his peers, and sometimes better than them. His job, as Northern Area Manager, meant he was one level below the board members. Five years ago there had been an Operations Director to whom both Area Managers reported, but when he retired, he had never been replaced. Charlie Swanson, the Southern Area Manager, had been asked if he was interested in the job, but had declined the offer as he wasn't prepared to relocate from Boston to Lincoln so late in his career.

The two Area Managers were now directly responsible to the Managing Director and neither of them liked or respected him. As an operations manager, Alan enjoyed the freedom of the outdoors, the hours were long and unpredictable, the workload heavy, but extremely satisfying. Man management had come easily to him, and every one of his staff appreciated the fact that he would never ask them to do anything he wasn't prepared to do himself. In his first year as Area Manager, he had spent many days going round with his crews, learning and understanding the difficulties they faced. Now heading back to Lincolnshire, next week meant renewing his battles with his MD and possibly being dismissed for drunken behaviour.

The other problem was his wife. He and Cheryl had been drifting apart for years. After their hastily arranged marriage nine years ago, things had been fine to start with but it hadn't taken them long to realise that they didn't love each other. After the initial sexual high of a new relationship, they had both realised there was nothing left to keep them together. Now, they slept in separate bedrooms and last week she had texted him to say she was leaving home.

When Alan was promoted to Northern Area Manager, based at Grimsby, they had moved from their rented cottage in Market Rasen, and bought a three-bedroom two-bathroom detached house in Wendham Close, Louth, with the help of a very large mortgage. The move to Louth made no difference to their relationship; in fact, it seemed that they were drifting further apart. Cheryl went out socialising with friends several times a week; he spent an equal amount of time alone in the pub. Safe in the cocoon a pub provided, the outside world, containing all his problems, was on the other side of the door. His friends John Smith and Johnnie Walker were his constant companions.

Now, he was heading back to renew the clashes with his abusive MD and discover whether Cheryl really was going to leave him. At least that might be better than the constant caustic comments and sarcasm of an ever-worsening relationship. Alan thought *Life couldn't get any worse, could it?* He had a mental picture of a sailing yacht crashing onto rocks in a storm.

§§§

A blaring car horn brought him back from his daydream, just in time for him to swerve onto his own side of the road before a collision occurred. Shaken by the near miss, he pulled into the next lay-by to let his heart rate return to normal. A caravan selling teas and coffees beckoned and he decided to risk a bacon sandwich as well, having skipped breakfast and eaten very little at lunchtime.

A squally shower sent him scurrying back to the car with his coffee and bacon butty, which he quickly demolished and felt a little better for it. The car clock showed three-thirty. He pulled out his mobile, scrolled down to *Sam*, and dialled.

'Hi Bish, everything OK?' He started crying, quietly at first, then louder. 'Bish, what's the matter? I've never known you like this, talk to me.'

He couldn't speak for nearly a minute, and then he told her. 'Sam I've really fucked up big time. I'm in for the chop when I get back.'

Samantha hated bad language, but she bit her tongue and let the moment pass. 'What happened?' She waited patiently through another silence.

'I've just nearly crashed the car.'

She'd been worried for some time about his drinking, and she knew it had worsened over the last few months. It seemed to her that SMDP may have something to do with it, but she wasn't sure.

'Do you want me to come and get you?' she asked.

'No, just make sure you've got a bottle of brandy and two packets of paracetamol.'

§§§

Although it was only five-o'clock, the black overcast sky and rain meant the motion-sensitive lights came on as Alan drove into the underground car park beneath the apartment block. Samantha had opened the roller-shutter door, and was waiting for him by the lift. He parked in the bay next to her black Audi A3. They hugged tightly for several minutes, until the spell was broken by another car driving in. They held hands in the lift, and when she looked at him, she was shocked.

'Bish, you look like shit,' she said as she gently stroked his unshaven face. He was taken aback. It was the first time he had ever heard her swear.

'You should have seen me this morning,' was all he offered.

Once in the apartment, Samantha poured two glasses of red wine and sat next to him on the sofa. He had visited the apartment many times, mainly to take Emily swimming or ice skating at weekends, but it never failed to amaze him how Samantha could afford a three-bedroom three-bathroom penthouse apartment with concierge service, in one of the best locations in Lincoln. His thoughts were broken as she shuffled closer to him, her short cheer-leader skirt riding up her tanned thighs as she pulled one leg under the other. He was also surprised at the thin low-cut top she was wearing. He had never seen her dressed like that before.

It took him nearly four hours to tell her everything. As far as he was concerned, Samantha was his best friend and confidante. He didn't feel the need to impress or woo her. She was there to listen, a problem shared. He knew she would never judge him even though she would be upset by some of his actions. It didn't take Samantha long to realise that tonight wasn't going to go as she had hoped. He was too upset, too wound-up, as he related his discussion with Bill Waites and everything that Daisy had told him about the previous night. He held nothing back, including peeing in his underwear and on the bathroom floor.

A tremor of embarrassment engulfed him when he told her about the photo, his face covered in lipstick kisses.

'That photo is going to be all over the social media sites . . . if it isn't already. And to cap it all, last week Cheryl texted to say she was leaving me.'

Alan didn't notice a smile briefly appear on Samantha's face. 'What you need is to be smothered in love,' she ventured, but he didn't react to her words. She put her arm around his shoulder, pulled him close, and kissed him on the cheek. Still he didn't respond.

Several times he had mentioned he was going to resign rather than be dismissed. Nothing Samantha said could dissuade him. By the time he had finished, they were both in tears. She hugged him tightly and they seemed to sob in unison. He was cold and distant. She had never seen him like this before, he was totally despondent. When he left, Alan hadn't even noticed Emily's absence, or the fact they hadn't eaten. Samantha had no idea what she could do to help. She cursed the day he had started the course.

When he got home Alan found a hand-written note from Cheryl on the kitchen table. Little did he know the following week would be the most traumatic of his life.

Chapter 8

It was Sunday evening and Alan was sat at home, in his favourite armchair, his third glass of malt whisky next to him on the nest of tables. The evening sun was streaming through the picture window, striking the cover Cheryl had always insisted on placing over the sofa to stop the sunlight bleaching the furniture.

'What's the point of paying a fortune for a leather suite only to hide it under a dust sheet?' he had frequently argued. In fact he struggled to think of anything they had ever agreed upon. Now she was leaving him. If the text and the letter hadn't been enough to convince him she was serious about leaving, the empty bank account was.

Samantha had rung him on Saturday morning. With Emily still at her Gran's, Samantha saw an opportunity to resurrect her hope of ensnaring him. 'I've still got this Lancashire hot pot which needs eating,' she had said, and on the way to Lincoln he had tried to buy some wine. After an embarrassing episode in the supermarket with both his debit and credit cards failing, he had gone to an ATM only to find Cheryl had withdrawn everything right up to their overdraft limit. Samantha had saved the day, when he had told her what had happened, she went out and returned within half-an-hour with three bottles of wine and £4000 in cash.

'Don't ask,' was all she had said as they sat down to eat. The bottles of wine which had accompanied the meal had resulted in some serious snogging until the telephone rang, Emily demanding to come home because her Gran was shouting at her all the time. Alan shuddered and blushed slightly at the memory of how quickly he had removed his hand from under Samantha's jumper when the phone had rung.

Banging car doors and raised voices brought Alan's thoughts back to the present as he looked out of the window across the cul-de-sac. A group of twenty-something's were leaving No 5, a semi-detached bungalow rented by a couple of nurses working at the local hospital. Over the past couple of years, Alan had talked to, and knew more about Nancy and Ruth, than he did about his wife. He gave them a wave as he stood to top up his whisky.

Alan had just replenished his glass when the duty officer rang from Lincs Water's emergency control room, informing him of a tanker spillage in Immingham. His spirits were lifted when he was told the standby crew were on their way, but no duty staff had yet been mobilised. He volunteered to manage the situation himself, glad to get out of the house and back doing what he did best, and enjoyed most. Within minutes he was speeding towards Immingham, never giving a second thought to the fact he was probably well over the drink-drive limit. It was only when he missed the turning at Ludborough that he realised the state he was in, completing the remainder of the journey at a more sedate pace.

The spillage had been from a tanker transporting diacetyl peroxide, and much of the load had drained into the road gullies, which in that area of town, were connected to the foul sewers. After a discussion with the Fire Brigade, Alan asked his standby crew to go to the nearby sewage pumping station and switch off the pumps, thus containing the spillage in as small an area as possible. Diacetyl peroxide was a potentially explosive chemical and the Fire Brigade would arrange for it to be safely tankered out of the pumping station when the situation was under control. Because of the danger of explosion, nearby properties had been evacuated. As well as the emergency services, a film crew from the local TV station and a reporter from the Grimsby Telegraph were also on site. Like members of the public, they too were kept well away from the area.

It proved to be a busy night and by midnight Alan's head was throbbing again. After taking four paracetamol washed down with a bottle of water, he headed for Immingham Sewage Treatment Works to park up and sleep it off. He still hadn't got used to the new terminology of Waste Water Treatment Works. He was only woken when sunlight came streaming through the car windscreen at dawn. On the drive home he realised that his decision to attend the spillage had been ludicrous. Too drunk to think straight, he had rushed out

In Deep Water

without a thought, the standby officer had been denied a call-out and overtime, and the low-key event didn't warrant the attendance of an Area Manager. Today would be his first day back at work after completing SMDP, and already he had some bridges to build.

'Bloody SMDP didn't do me much good,' he muttered to himself, then the image of his face covered in lipstick kisses came floating back again, making him shiver.

Alan watched breakfast news on EMTV, the local East Midlands television company, whose sole aim was to advertise the owner's chain of second-rate supermarkets and report on local issues, trying wherever possible to talk them up into a *cause célèbre*. Their chief reporter, Vanessa Redfern, had crossed swords with Alan many times. Redfern was a short, feisty, middle-aged woman, mid-way between chunky and fat, with bottle-blonde hair and thick makeup. She always wore ridiculously high-heeled shoes and tight skirts. A couple of years ago Alan's whispered comment 'mutton dressed as lamb' had somehow got back to her. It had been daggers drawn ever since. Now she was telling the whole of the East Midlands region that the spillage of chemicals at Immingham had been made worse by Lincs Water's slow response.

§§§

'Glad to be back?'

Alan looked up from his desk, Cheryl's letter open in front of him. Jane Hamilton was standing in his office doorway, two mugs of coffee in one hand and a bundle of papers in the other. The northern area's corporate structure did not include a Secretary for the Area Manager but Jane Hamilton did the job anyway. She had trained as a PA and spent many years in the role before leaving to start a family. Now that her twin sons were teenagers, she had returned to work to build up some savings to help them through university when the time came. Jane's official job title was Customer Services Assistant.

'Yes and no,' he replied as he carefully folded the letter and slipped it into his briefcase, next to the four bundles of twenty-pound notes, each containing £1000. Jane often pulled up a chair and sat next to Alan at his desk as they went through the post, but seeing him hide the note, she discreetly sat on one of the seats at the table abutting his desk.

'So what's happened since you got back,' she asked, trying to make conversation.

Alan often took Jane into his confidence, initially with business matters but more recently on a personal level. Jane knew he and Cheryl were having problems. However, he had already decided he wouldn't tell her about his drunkenness on Thursday night, or the lipstick kisses, at least not until the inevitable happened and someone saw a photo. He wasn't going to tell her about the tearful night with Samantha on Friday or that Cheryl was going to leave him. He wasn't going to tell her about the luncheon invitation from Samantha on Saturday.

Neither was he going to tell Jane about the money Samantha had lent him. Money he couldn't put in the bank or leave at home in case Cheryl found it and stole that too, money that was needed to pay his mortgage and utility bills. Nor was he going to tell her about his time with Samantha on Sunday. They had gone to Doncaster ice rink, and while Emily showed off her skills on the ice, he and Samantha had sat watching. Samantha had rested her hand on his thigh, her warm breath tickling his ear and her subtle perfume sending his mind spinning and his excitement rising again. He had tried to apologise for his behaviour the previous night, but she had replied, 'You've nothing to apologise for.' After a pause she had added, 'It was a close call though,' and they had both laughed.

'I took Emily ice skating on Sunday morning,' was all he said.

Chapter 9

Since the weekend Samantha couldn't stop thinking about Alan. She had sat in her tiny office for more than a day now, in a dream. Her new job as Press and Public Relations Manager was hardly onerous and she was beginning to regret the move. She had been offered the position a few months ago and the near doubling of her salary had been the deciding factor. Alan had tried everything he could to dissuade her from accepting the position, but she had ignored his advice. Her desire to wean herself away from her uncle's constant generosity and subsidy of her lifestyle had been the overwhelming factor. The only task she had been given up to now had been to organise the forthcoming AGM, but so far, Ian Young and the new Finance Director, Gordon Reed, couldn't agree on a date. In fact, judging by the heated arguments coming from the second floor, it seemed to everyone in the building that they couldn't agree about anything.

With little to do, Samantha's mind wandered back to the first time she and Alan had been out socially together. It had been four months ago on a cold, wet and windy January evening. They had gone to Luigi's Italian restaurant and spent four wonderful hours together. Samantha was a regular customer at the restaurant, and she introduced Alan to Luigi as a work colleague. Luigi had only ever seen her with her parents and Emily; she had never brought a man to the restaurant before.

It was well past eleven-o'clock, all the other customers and staff had left, but Luigi was too polite to ask them to go. He had stood discreetly near the bar, watching them enjoy each other's company, a slight smile occasionally creasing his wrinkled face. Normally a quiet cough or a query about coffee and a complimentary brandy would have been enough to make most customers look at their watches then ask for the bill. Luigi didn't want to break the spell, despite the fact he was dead on his feet and had a busy weekend ahead. Alan's left hand rested on the red-and-white checked tablecloth next to his empty wine glass. Samantha placed her hand on his for the third time that evening, tingles of excitement ran through her whole body like pin pricks of electricity. It was Alan who made a move to leave, diplomatically lifting his hand, kissing the back of hers and looking at his watch at the same time.

'It's getting late, we ought to go,' he suggested. Even Luigi could see the cloud of disappointment appear on her face.

'Yes OK . . . I've had a super evening . . . thank you.'

'Me too,' he replied. As Alan half-turned, Luigi nodded subtly and moved towards the till.

The invitation to dinner had come out of the blue. As Samantha was thinking of leaving work that Friday evening, Alan had popped his head round the door of her office and suggested dinner.

'As a thank you,' was all he had said. She had shivered with excitement at the thought of having dinner, then coffee at her apartment, and then . . . hopefully, sex. Since meeting him she had always dreamed of ensnaring him with her discreet promiscuity and now she would have the opportunity. Reality had quickly kicked in. She grabbed her mobile and shot off to the ladies toilet. She had called her mother asking her to have Emily for the night.

'Darling I can't tonight, its Burns night, and we're all going out for supper,' her mother had replied. Samantha cursed silently at her mother's insistence in maintaining her Scottish roots. 'Can't you rearrange something for the weekend?' her mother had added, trying to be helpful. The second call was to her neighbour's teenage daughter who sometimes babysat for Samantha. This had been quickly arranged, the only downside was Samantha couldn't invite Alan back to the apartment later as Emily would be there. Although Samantha had talked to Emily about Alan, and vice versa, they hadn't yet met. The last thing Samantha wanted was a chance encounter in the hallway as Emily padded off to the toilet.

As they had walked back to his car, arms linked, the rain had stopped but the roads and footpaths were still wet, reflecting the street lights, giving the impression of lighting the street from both above and below with pools of orange light. The temperature had dropped since they had arrived at the restaurant, so they hugged each other to keep warm.

He had turned towards her. 'Cheryl's gone to see her parents in Nottingham for a few days; she won't be back until Sunday.' Her heart had skipped a beat; she stopped dead in her tracks, put her arms around his waist, and kissed him on the lips for the first time, albeit just a peck.

Outside her apartment Alan had been conscious of his thirty mile drive home, worried that the drop in temperature might cause icy roads over the Lincolnshire Wolds.

'We must do this again sometime,' he had suggested.

'Tomorrow,' she had replied too quickly. 'I'm sure Luigi will squeeze us in, and then we can come back here for a coffee afterwards.' She had more than coffee in mind.

Alan had sat quietly for what seemed an age but couldn't have been more than fifteen seconds. He nodded his agreement.

They had gingerly kissed each other again several times, shivers running through Samantha's body, and then she got out and closed the car door.

She had whispered, 'I love you,' through the closed window, hoping he had heard.

He blew her a kiss. 'Until tomorrow,' he had said as he drove off. Samantha had hardly slept that night. He had broken her heart the following day when he rang to say Cheryl had come home unexpectedly.

Samantha's thoughts then turned to last weekend. She had been so close to achieving her dream. They had been lying on the sofa on Saturday evening, kissing. Those same tingles of excitement and pin pricks of electricity had run through her body again until the phone had rung. At first she had cursed Emily.

'The joys of motherhood,' she had said, her voice dripping with sarcasm. However, half-an-hour later when Emily arrived home and Samantha saw how happy her daughter was to see Alan, she had relented. On Sunday at the ice rink, she had teased Alan, watching his excitement grow once more. She knew then it would only be a matter of time.

Above Samantha, on the second floor, Alan sat outside Ian Young's office knowing he would be kept waiting. He had received a blunt phone call yesterday. 'Come and see me first thing Tuesday. Just try being late and see where your bollocks end up.' Alan had flipped the bird in response. He guessed that it would either be about his escapades on SMDP or the chemical spillage at Immingham on Sunday night which had been widely reported on the local TV news. Whichever it was, Alan was prepared for an argument. However, he shuddered as his mind drifted back to Daisy's prediction. *The only thing you have to worry about are the photos everyone took of you.*

As he waited, Alan studied his MD's secretary, Margaret Vardy. She was a dour woman, about five-foot-six, her mousey-coloured hair always pulled back in a tight bun. She usually wore a tweed pleated skirt and matching jacket which she never removed. Her white blouse was buttoned to the neck, and today she wore a matching pearl necklace and ear-rings. It was difficult to put an age to her. Her unsmiling face was not wrinkled, her chin firm and unlined. Her face could belong to a thirty-five year old, but she dressed as if she was sixty-plus. She and Alan shared an intense dislike of Ian Young.

Initially, the one thing that had impressed Alan was her capacity for work. Whenever he saw her, she was always hammering away at the keyboard, at first he had wondered what she was typing. She never had a note book or a Dictaphone on her desk. Last year Alan had concluded that she had little work to do, and was merely typing for show. A couple of months ago she had told him what kept her busy, and he had bought the book. It was a collection of short stories about outdoor sex masquerading behind the cheesy title *Wood I?* Margaret had used the pseudonym Kate Williams to publish the book, ashamed of what family or friends might say. She sensed Alan looking at her and glanced in his direction.

'My latest book, another Kate Williams' special,' she whispered, then winked and smiled.

In his office, Ian Young sat in the comfort of a huge leather chair behind a large mahogany desk, secure in a place where his scant knowledge of the water industry could not be tested. The desk had a row of pens and pencils neatly laid out in a line, together with a family photo in a silver frame, and a desk lamp. There was no evidence of any files, papers, computer, or anything else normally associated with a working environment. It was the desk of an under-employed man. Behind him, the wall was filled with what Alan described as meaningless certificates, and photos of Young with local D-and E-class dignitaries. When Young had first joined Lincs Water four years ago, one of the photos showed him with a young Prince Charles. In the photo, Young had bright ginger hair and staff took to calling him 'carrot-top.' The picture was taken down when he got wind of the derogatory nickname.

Young's jacket button looked fit to burst, and he had recently taken to wearing his tie with the shirt collar undone, because it was too tight. His stomach overlapped his trouser belt and his shirt gaped open between its buttons. His face told another story, he had the beginnings of a third chin and the deep crevices across his face were the result of many years heavy smoking. The fingers of his left hand were stained brown with nicotine, his teeth uneven and yellow, and his clothes stank of cigarette smoke. His fat rubbery lips always seemed to be in motion, and when angry, which was often, would spray spittle over his adversaries. Young was nearing sixty years old; the hair on his head now white and receding rapidly, barely covering his liver-spotted scalp. Dandruff showered down onto the shoulders of his jacket and, like many elderly men, hairs were sprouting from his ears and nose unchallenged. He picked up the phone and rang his secretary.

'Send Dr Shit in now.' Young had taken to calling Alan that name when he discovered he had a doctorate in sewage treatment, hoping it would wind him up. Just the opposite; it was like water off a duck's back.

'I'm sorry Mr Young; Mr Bishop has gone down to reception. The police wanted to see him.'

Chapter 10

It was eight-thirty on Friday morning. Samantha and Jane Hamilton had agreed to meet in a lay-by on the A16, close to the outskirts of Louth. They had spoken to Alan numerous times over the last three days and they both knew he was on the booze big time. When Samantha saw the silver Fiesta pull in behind her, she got out and walked to Jane's car. The light drizzle made her hurry. Samantha was wearing denim jeans, white trainers and a dark-blue puffa jacket. Her blonde shoulder length hair was tied back in a pony tail. Samantha's moist eyes and sullen expression told Jane she wasn't coping. Jane swung the passenger's door open and Samantha climbed in. An awkward hug was followed by a long silence.

'Are they still saying it might be suicide?' There was no small talk, no hello, how are you? Jane's blunt question took Samantha by surprise.

'I don't know. The post-mortem results should be available today.'

'Bob and I were talking last night and he says it was probably a mechanical failure. He says if someone wanted to commit suicide they would drive into a vehicle head on. Crashing into a lorry going in the same direction is not the way to succeed.' Cheryl had been returning to Louth from her parents' house early on Tuesday morning when her car veered under a lorry she was overtaking on the A46 close to Newark. She had been taken to the Queen's Medical Centre in Nottingham where she was pronounced dead.

'He's blaming himself,' Samantha said, 'says he should have tried to talk to her when he first got the text.' She sighed heavily as another silence enveloped the car. 'Come on, let's get this over with. Heaven knows what we'll find; he was incoherent when I rang last night.'

Jane squeezed Samantha's hand then let go so she could return to her own car.

Wendham Close was a tiny cul-de-sac of six properties, four detached houses and two semi-detached bungalows, on a small housing development behind The Plough in Louth. The cul-de-sac had a miniature traffic island at its head rather than the more usual hammerhead and every property faced onto the island. This meant that everyone could see everything that went on in the Close, and as soon as Samantha and Jane pulled onto Alan's drive in separate cars, the lace curtains at No 6 twitched.

When Alan opened the front door, the smell of body odour, stale food and whisky forced them both to take an involuntary step backwards. The dirty washing from his last three weeks' spell at Tadcaster was still bundled by the front door. His clothes bore the crumpled and creased effects of being slept in and there were traces of vomit on his shirt and trousers. The fatigue caused by lack of sleep showed on his face and in his sagging posture. He was unshaven and his hair uncombed.

'Bloody hell Bish, just look at you,' Samantha snapped.

He looked at her sheepishly. 'I'm fine, just a bit tired.' At least he was semi-coherent. She bundled him upstairs towards the shower, made a quick appraisal of the state of the house, and set off for the supermarket for cleaning materials, leaving Jane to start the tidying process.

By the time Alan came down from the shower, Samantha and Jane had cleared away all the empty takeaway and pizza cartons, crisp bags, beer cans, and empty bottles of wine and whisky. They had vacuumed the lounge, washed all the dirty crockery and cutlery piled in the kitchen sink, but were struggling to get rid of the smell of stale food and beer, despite the best efforts of two cans of air freshener.

By lunchtime the women, needing a break, sat at the kitchen table with a cup of tea. Jane had looked in on Alan in the lounge but he was asleep, the mug of coffee next to him untouched. Samantha shook her head, her dishevelled blonde hair swinging across her face. Preoccupied with her thoughts, she re-tied her hair loosely.

'I just can't believe it Jane, last week after he got the letter it was like a huge burden had been lifted from his shoulders. Now look at him.' Jane raised her eyebrows questioningly. Samantha realised she didn't know. She leaned forward, lowered her voice, only just audible above the spinning washing machine. 'While he was on SMDP Cheryl sent him a text basically saying she was moving out. When he got home last weekend she had also left a letter asking for a divorce.'

'He hasn't said anything to me but I gathered something was afoot, I saw him reading a hand-written note on Monday.'

'Not only that,' Samantha went on, 'she cleared out their joint bank account and I've had to lend him some money for this month's bills. All he's done so far is spend it on takeaways and drink.'

'Don't be too hard on him; it must have been an awful shock.' They sat in silence until the spin cycle finished. 'Look why don't we all go out for lunch on Sunday? Bob would love to meet you and Emily; you're his idea of a perfect woman.'

'What's that?'

'Tall, blonde, and buxom.'

Their laughter was cut short by Alan walking into the kitchen, a tumbler full of whisky in his trembling hand. Samantha stood up and gently took the glass from his grasp, hugging him with her free arm. Jane went to refill the kettle as Samantha guided him towards one of the chairs. 'You can't go on like this Bish. What's the problem?'

As he opened his mouth he took a couple of noisy gasps of air, as if he was about to cry, but composed himself when Samantha squeezed his hand.

'It's my fault, she wouldn't have gone to see her mother if we'd been happy.'

'Bish, you can't blame yourself, things haven't been right between the two of you for how long?'

Alan looked up into Samantha's eyes, his own moist and red with crying. He nodded slowly. Just then the doorbell rang, and Jane, being closest to the kitchen door, went to answer it.

After a few seconds she shouted, 'It's just Billy.'

'He promised to come as soon as he knew the post-mortem results,' Alan said. He explained to Samantha that Sergeant Billy

Benson lived next door. He had joined the police force in Glasgow and moved to Lincolnshire about twelve years ago. Married to Dorothy, a true Yellowbelly, born and raised in Lincolnshire, they made an unlikely couple, she was barely five-foot tall and Billy was six-foot-eight. Jane and her husband Bob had met Billy and Dorothy at a disastrous barbeque at Alan's house last year, ruined by the weather and the fact that Alan ended up with broken ribs. He was explaining to Samantha how Billy had thrown him across the crowded garage and cracked two of his ribs on the workbench leg, when Billy walked into the kitchen with a glass of whisky in his hand.

'Ye'll no be calling her Potty Dotty again, will ye laddie?' said Billy, picking up on the story, his deep voice perfectly matching his huge frame. After introductions Billy confirmed he had details of the post-mortem results and suggested they all sit down around the kitchen table. 'It's not straightforward,' added Billy. They all looked at him, then at each other, wondering what was in store.

Billy explained that the cause of death had been an aortic rupture, describing, as best he could, how the aorta had burst and explained that Cheryl would have lost consciousness within seconds which may have accounted for the collision with the lorry.

'One thing that puzzles us is the fact she had over £3500 in her handbag.' Alan explained where the money had come from and Billy suggested that when he had corroborated the story, the money could be returned. An uncomfortable silence followed as Billy seemed to compose himself. 'Laddie I'm sorry to have to tell ye Cheryl was two months pregnant.' The two women looked at one another, then at Alan. Jane got up and went over to him, bending down to hug him.

'I'm so sorry Alan, that's awful.'

'Why? It wasn't mine.'

Jane stood up, a hand resting on his shoulder. 'How can you be so sure?'

Alan turned to look up at her. 'Simple. We haven't slept together for nearly two years, plus the fact I had a vasectomy four or five years ago.'

Chapter 11

On a warm, balmy Thursday evening in the spring of 1974, fourteen year old Bertie Campbell and sixteen year old Moira McDonald were behind the village hall in Pitlochry saying goodbye. Inside the hall, the weekly chess club was starting to break up. They had joined the group three months earlier, but recently they had preferred to study anatomy behind the hall, albeit fumbling through several layers of clothing. Tonight was different. Moira was determined to get her hands on a male erection, and as a trade off, she had allowed Bertie to put his hands inside her bra. Both their heads were swimming with thoughts and pleasures, never before experienced.

'I love you Moira, I'm going to marry you.'

'I love you too,' she panted.

'I'll come back every school holiday to see you,' he promised, not sure of the logistics. The Campbell's were, in the words of Bertie's father, 'emigrating' to England.

Their ardour was interrupted by cries of 'goodnight' as the chess club members spilled out into the car park in front of the village hall. They slowly disentangled themselves, knowing they might never see each other again. Neither would admit it, but their vision was blurred, their eyes moist with tears. As they rounded the hall they saw Bertie's father in the car park, leaning against his battered pick-up truck, smoking a cigarette. He was not a tall man, but was feared by many in Pitlochry, especially when he had had a bellyful of whisky. He had a bushy flame-red beard, greying pony tail, a weather-beaten face, and his stomach protruded several inches beyond his straining leather belt.

The teenagers quickly attempted to re-arrange their dishevelled clothing as they approached him. Moira politely refused a lift, preferring to walk the half-mile home. Bertie wearily climbed into the truck for their four mile trip.

In Deep Water

'She seems a nice lassie; I guess you are going to miss her.' Bertie didn't reply, turning his head towards the side window to avoid his father's tobacco-laced breath. 'Never mind son, there are plenty more fish in the sea.'

'Yes, but fish don't have tits like Moira McDonald,' Bertie wanted to say, but didn't.

For as long as Bertie could remember, the Campbell family had lived in a three-storey, turreted stone castle which stood on a small and unprofitable 150 acre estate four miles from town. The land was a mixture of forest and heath-land, and Bertie's father had eked out a living breeding sheep and Highland cattle against all the odds. The castle was crumbling, damp, cold, and draughty. Even in summer, the children often needed several layers of clothing to keep them warm. The main source of heating in their home came from open fireplaces; a large inglenook dominated the lounge, other rooms had smaller fires. Electric storage heaters did little to help. Pine and spruce logs were cut from the surrounding woods to feed the fires, but there was never enough fuel to keep more than three going at any one time. The softwood logs burned quickly, most of the heat going straight up the chimney.

Earlier that year, Bertie's parents had decided to put the estate and castle up for sale. Surprisingly, there had been a lot of interest and an investment banker from London snapped up the property at a knock-down price. Bertie's father had secured a job with a small builder near Lincoln, and until the family got back on its feet, they would rent a cottage in Navenby, ten miles south of the city.

The following day as Bertie, his sister, and parents headed south along the A9 towards England, Moira McDonald was already dreaming about her next chess partner.

§§§

Not long after the Campbell clan arrived in Lincolnshire, the owner of the building company where Bertie's father worked put the business up for sale. The family was devastated.

'Why has he done that? He knew we were coming down here for work. What will we do now?' Bertie's mother was close to tears.

'He's got a job with the local council as a building inspector. Apparently all the councils have been reorganised and there are hundreds of jobs being advertised.' His wife picked up a tissue to dry her eyes. 'Don't worry hen, he's told me I can have first option to buy the company.'

Bertie's father's words did little to comfort his wife. She loved her husband dearly, but she knew his strengths and weaknesses better than most. He was a resourceful man, could turn his hand to anything, and she felt sure he would be able to master the intricacies of the building trade. However, she also knew he had a fearsome temper, and a strong Scottish accent which many in Lincolnshire struggled to understand. Worse, his physical appearance reminded many locals of a Scottish warrior, the sort who would slay a dozen Sassenachs before breakfast, just for fun. Bertie's mother was deeply worried, but despite her misgivings, her husband took out a hefty loan to buy the business.

The company did little more than house extensions, loft conversions and patios, and the family soon learned that they had jumped out of the frying pan into the fire. To try and help the situation, Bertie left school at sixteen to assist in the running of the family concern. His father immediately sent him to college to train as a bricklayer. A plastering course followed, and it wasn't long before Bertie had a sound knowledge of the building trade. Although Bertie took over the customer liaison role, they struggled to make the business viable. Bertie realised that they had to move away from building small extensions, and into the new-build housing market. He pestered his father to buy a plot of land and start building new houses, but he wasn't keen to take on more debt. Eventually the strain took its toll, and his father died of a heart attack when Bertie was in his early-twenties.

Unsure whether to continue in house-building or try something new, he backed his intuition and borrowed nearly £250,000 to buy a large plot of land. Delays in the purchase, and planning approval, meant that building work didn't start until mid-winter, but despite these set-backs, the houses sold quickly when they were completed. Encouraged by this, Bertie borrowed more money and started to build up a small land bank. The company, renamed Campbell Homes, made a small profit for the first time.

The business continued to make a modest profit each year until Bertie had a seminal moment while driving past the local Jaguar car dealership. He wondered why anyone would pay so much for a car, when they could buy one from another manufacturer at a fraction of the price. The seed was sown. He decided to evolve the company into one which provided high specification, bespoke houses, with a high degree of customer input into the design, for those who wanted something different. He figured if customers were prepared to wait for a prestige car they would wait for a house of distinction. He decided to buy small packages of land, never building more than ten or twelve houses on any plot. Instead of cramming between fifteen to twenty houses on each acre, he would reduce the number to four or five.

Still living with his aged mother in Navenby, Bertie decided to call a family meeting. His sister, now married with two children, had no interest in the business and told him in no uncertain terms, 'I refuse to follow you into the bankruptcy courts.'

His mother had little business acumen but offered encouraging words, 'If you think that's the right way to go, then follow your dream.'

Bertie said, 'Whatever it is, people will be prepared to wait and pay a premium for quality. What we need to do is employ a top-class architect, make sure every house enjoys large gardens, oak-framed garages, and never repeat a house design on the same plot . . .' His mother's snoring stopped him. 'Looks like I'm on my own,' he said quietly to himself. It was then his thoughts turned to Moira McDonald, his childhood sweetheart. Perhaps, at the age of thirty-six, it was time to find himself a life partner.

§§§

Pitlochry, with a population of less than 3000, was a small and friendly town. However, in the summer it was a tourists' paradise with two distilleries, a theatre, stunning scenery, unlimited hiking, and for the less energetic, numerous gift shops and pubs. As a result,

Bertie Campbell decided he wouldn't book accommodation as there was a plethora of choice. The journey from Lincoln to Pitlochry was more difficult though. By train, it would take between six and seven hours. However, at weekends there was a limited timetable. It would leave him little time in Pitlochry if he travelled north on a Saturday and returned on Sunday. Taking time out of the working week was out of the question. In the end, although not relishing the 700 mile round trip, he decided to drive. It was a spur of the moment decision.

He didn't find Moira McDonald, now Moira Douglas, recently bereaved, until his second visit.

Chapter 12

The twenty-first century was only two weeks' old when Bertie Campbell went missing. He had been courting Moira Douglas for nearly four years, driving up to Pitlochry once a month and spending time together. During his visits, he had been the perfect gentleman. At first Moira had been grieving for her late husband, but after two years Bertie felt enough time had passed and he had proposed. She refused. Not an outright refusal but a 'let's wait and see' type of rejection. She was unsure whether she wanted to leave Scotland but more importantly, she was unsure about Bertie. He had told her he had never had a close relationship with a woman, and it started her wondering. Not an alarm-bell type of concern, more a niggling doubt. She would often reflect on the fact that, unlike their parting behind the village hall in 1974, he had never tried to touch her intimately. Not even a hand brushing her breasts, whether accidental or not. And now he was lost. Bertie had phoned her as usual at four-o'clock on Friday afternoon, just before leaving Lincoln for the journey north and she had heard nothing since.

She recalled their last conversation. Bertie had said, 'I'm really looking forward to sharing my fortieth birthday with you. I've booked two single rooms at the Atholl Palace Hotel for two nights and a table for two on Saturday for a celebratory lunch.'

'Why not a double room Bertie?' she had asked.

'Sweetheart, Pitlochry is a small town; would you want everyone to know that Mr Campbell and Mrs Douglas shared a room?'

'Yes,' she had wanted to say, but didn't.

There had been a moderate snowfall in Pitlochry, but that wasn't unusual in winter. Bertie had one of the latest mobile phones with a built-in stub aerial, but it was over twenty-four hours since she had heard from him. As she sat waiting for news, she started to blame herself. Now the wrong side of forty, why had she rejected his offer of marriage? It was her fault that he had to continue driving up to Pitlochry to see her. The television news had reported heavy snowfalls over northern England and many roads were blocked. She watched, hoping she would see a black Mercedes, but every car seemed to be unrecognisable under a pile of snow.

For a second night, she had tried to sleep in the armchair, the television volume turned down but still loud enough to hear any breaking news. From the street outside, the light from the TV could be seen flickering through the curtains. She couldn't stop crying. She couldn't stop blaming herself. Her eyes were red and puffy, stinging whenever tears welled up. She was still dressed in the clothes she had worn for work on Friday. By Sunday afternoon she was beside herself with worry. Why hadn't he phoned? What had happened to him? She dreaded a knock on the door in case it was the police with bad news. But they may not know he was coming to see her. Would he have her address on him?

The ringing doorbell startled her. It was late Sunday afternoon. She sat frozen to a chair in the kitchen, looking out onto the backyard. The decking area was still covered in snow, but the lawn and flower beds were starting to reappear from beneath the two days of snowfall. Her mind started to race. She didn't want to answer the door. An insistent knock followed by the bell ringing again pulled her out of her thoughts and she headed for the front door. When she saw him, she flung her arms around him, smothered him in kisses, and dragged him inside the house. Seconds later she was leading him upstairs.

Afterwards, as they lay naked in bed, sweating and sated, he said, 'I suppose that's a yes then?' She nodded. After he had told her about the horrific details of the journey and the flat phone battery, she rolled over on top of him and they made love again. Three months later, they married, a simple church service followed by a week's honeymoon touring the highlands of Scotland before heading south to their new life in Lincolnshire.

Chapter 13

Alan had always promised Samantha he would cut down on his drinking when he finished SMDP. The weekend he came home and had told her about Cheryl's text and letter asking for a divorce, she had again pressed home the point.

'There's no better time to give up drinking than now. SMDP has finished and Cheryl wants out. That's a double incentive to stop,' she had said.

In Alan's mind, stopping drinking meant giving up whisky. It was only when he drank beer with whisky chasers the worst hangovers occurred, beer and wine didn't really count in his mind. Cheryl's death had changed everything. He hadn't stopped at all; in fact his drinking had got worse. Samantha had suggested he go back to work while waiting for the coroner's inquest into Cheryl's death, in the hope it might reduce his daily intake of alcohol.

He wasn't looking forward to the funeral, if for no other reason than having to see Cheryl's parents who blamed him for her demise. Last weekend he had started clearing out Cheryl's clothes and personal effects and had discovered her secret journal. If Gertrude and James Smith kicked off at the funeral it would give him great pleasure to tell them about their beloved daughter's infidelity. During an hour long telephone conversation with Samantha they had concluded that Alex was responsible for Cheryl's pregnancy and she had persuaded Alan there was little to be gained trying to find out who Alex was, or where he lived.

'We'll see,' had been his reply.

The main reason for Alan's brighter mood had been the fact that Cheryl's death had sheltered him from any fallout over his indiscretions on SMDP. Bill Waites would surely have spoken to the Chairman but nothing had been said. He was secretly hoping it would stay that way.

§§§

'Morning boss, can you spare a minute?'

Alan always tried to operate an open door policy at the office and he looked up to see one of his sewage Superintendants, Andy Potts, standing in the doorway. Potts was not yet thirty and looked as if he hadn't yet started to shave. A tall gangling chap with a mop of rusty-coloured curly hair and wire-rimmed glasses, he had joined Lincs Water straight from university, unable to find a job where he could utilise his degree in modern art. Some of his colleagues thought his qualification was in bluntness, but coming from the same county himself, Alan recognised the Yorkshire trait. After a shaky start he had proved to be a valuable asset, and Alan was keen to promote him before he decided to move on to pastures new. With a wave of his hand, Alan beckoned Potts into the room.

'Mind if I shut the door?' Potts asked, but didn't wait for a reply. 'We've got a problem.'

After half-an-hour a plan had been agreed. They had decided to use Potts' own car as a Lincs Water van and Alan's white Ford Mondeo were too conspicuous.

The following Friday Potts returned to the area office in his dark blue Vauxhall Astra to pick up his Area Manager. Alan handed him a pocket-sized tape recorder and suggested Potts dictate the events of the afternoon when he got back to the office whilst it was fresh in his mind. By four-o'clock they were parked in a lay-by near the Healing Manor Hotel when a white Lincs Water Transit van appeared at the end of the lane and drove out of the village.

Alan said, 'Don't get too close, he mustn't see us.'

'Don't worry boss, I know where he's going. It'll be The Black Swan, then The Greyhound followed by The Durham Ox.'

At The Black Swan the driver stopped the van and took out a full carrier bag and went into the pub. 'Cabbages by the look of it this week,' whispered Potts. At The Greyhound two trays of eggs accompanied more vegetables into the premises. By the time they got to The Durham Ox they were ready to spring their surprise.

'He usually parks the van in the rear car park and stays about an hour,' Potts explained.

'We're not waiting that long, give him a chance to get into the building then we'll go round and block him in.' After five minutes had elapsed, Potts drove into the car park and hemmed in the van. 'Right Andy, you go into the bar in your high-vis coat and tell him I want a word. Remember just a soft drink yourself.'

'OK boss,' he replied as he put on his bright yellow coat and, having an idea, slipped the tape recorder into his pocket. Alan got out of the car, leaned against the van's bonnet and waited. Five minutes later they both came out of the pub.

'Hello Jack, fancy meeting you here.'

Jack Lumley's face dropped when he saw Alan. "Er, hello Mr Bishop, I was just having a quick one on my way home.'

'Bullshit Jack, give me the keys before I call the police and have you breathalysed. We followed you here from Healing via The Black Swan and The Greyhound. A pint in each was it?' Alan held out his hand and waited. Eventually Lumley handed over the keys. 'Anything you want out of the van before we lock it up for the weekend?' asked Alan.

Realising he might lose his stock, he nodded and Alan opened the back door to allow Lumley retrieve his produce. Once it was all unloaded, Alan took a photo of the eight trays of eggs and five boxes of vegetables with his mobile phone.

Potts, determined to get his revenge for the verbal abuse he had suffered in the pub, said, 'Boss, before we go perhaps you'll want to hear this.' Alan nodded, and Potts fiddled with the tape recorder until he found the relevant section, and then pressed play.

You lot are a load of wankers and you can't touch me 'cos I'm a shop steward. As far as I'm concerned you can all go fuck yerselves.

'Oh Jack,' said Alan, 'if only. Drink-driving *and* unauthorised use of a company vehicle? The union could well be looking for a new shop steward soon. I'll see you back at the office Andy.'

Alan climbed into the Transit van and started the engine. Lumley suddenly realised his dilemma. 'What about me and all this stuff?' he shouted at the reversing van.

'Not my problem, see you at the disciplinary hearing,' came the reply.

§§§

At seven-o'clock on Monday morning Alan had what he called a half-hangover. After a heavy session the previous night, if he could remember, he would drink two or three bottles of water. This would have the combined effect of reducing the dehydrating effect of the drink, and make him visit the toilet frequently during the night to flush out the alcohol. It meant his demeanour was more akin to a lack of sleep rather than a hangover. It hadn't improved by the time he got to the office, even after a hot shower and a shave with his newly acquired electric razor. Alan was stood in the office kitchen waiting for the kettle to boil when Andy Potts walked in.

'Boss, sorry to trouble you, did you see the Grimsby Telegraph on Saturday?'

'Morning Andy, do you want a coffee?' Andy's acceptance meant Alan could leave him to make the coffees and carry them up to his office. Even with a half-hangover, his hands would still shake. 'See you upstairs then.'

Potts told Alan that the article was about Jack Lumley selling vegetables and eggs from the back of a 'sewage van' highlighting the potential health hazards, including the possibility of faecal contamination.

'Jack's bloody furious, reckoned we tipped them off. They turned up at the pub before his wife got there to pick him up. I have to tell you boss, it wasn't me.'

Alan raised his eyebrows and smiled. Potts wanted to ask, but he knew there was little point.

Chapter 14

Alcohol did three things to Alan. It made him maudlin, stopped him dreaming, and gave him a terrible hangover the next day. He wasn't sure if being drunk meant he didn't dream, or he just couldn't remember. Either way, when he had tried to moderate his drinking he had suffered some awful dreams, dreams about lipstick kisses all over his face, or worst of all, dreams about catastrophes at work. One night he dreamt that Cheryl had returned home dressed in a green smock, the scars from the post-mortem examination clearly visible all over her body. It was more of a nightmare than a dream. He had woken up in a pool of sweat, the bed-sheets clinging to his damp body. The night before the funeral he had made a conscious decision to get drunk. Easy enough, he'd had plenty of practice. He could be forgiven for being weepy, people would assume he was grieving for his wife; he would also get a decent night's sleep, and a hangover on the day couldn't make things much worse.

The day started badly. When he woke his body seemed to be confined in a straight jacket. His legs were bent beneath him and the arm he was lying on was cold and numb. His head throbbed mercilessly and his mouth felt like soggy velvet. He didn't know whether it was the bright sunlight streaming through the open curtains or the noise that woke him. Eventually he crawled out of bed to answer the insistent doorbell.

'Ey up lad, you'd better get ready, the cortege is due in't forty minutes,' his father said.

After that, Alan could only remember three things about the day. Bill Waites and his wife Sheila had attended the funeral, Samantha had hugged him tightly outside the church and whispered, 'I love you,' and a woman with ginger hair in a green two-piece trouser suit had cried throughout the service. The rest of the day was a blur. Now sat outside The Splash at one of the many picnic tables with a pint of real ale and whisky chaser, his hangover had long gone. He was beginning to relax, Samantha next to him, with his brother Tom and father opposite.

Situated in the village of Little Cawthorpe two miles south of Louth, The Royal Oak, known locally as The Splash, was accessed by driving through a shallow ford. Originally a farmhouse over 400 years old, the pub had been modified and extended and was one of the area's most popular establishments. Alan had arranged to hold the wake there as it was his favourite watering hole, the conservatory cum restaurant well capable of holding 100 people.

'Small talk had long since changed to no talk,' Alan explained to his father. 'In the end we were like two strangers living under the same roof.' Alan hadn't confided in his father for years and was enjoying the opportunity to share his feelings. Their discussions were cut short by Alan's mother fretting about the two hour journey to Sheffield, so Samantha agreed to take them back to Wendham Close to pick up their car.

'Can you pop back and give me a lift home?' Alan asked.

'Yes, but I must leave by six-o'clock to pick up Emily.' As Alan watched them head for the car park, a woman moved across his line of sight.

'Mind if I join you?' She was dressed in a black pencil skirt and matching jacket, her light-brown hair hung loosely tied over her left shoulder. She had just enough eye liner and mascara to draw his attention to her eyes, but it was her bright red lipstick which made him shudder, his thoughts immediately returning to SMDP.

'Bloody hell Margaret, I didn't recognise you. You look . . .'

'Years younger?'

'I would have said . . . different. Wow.'

'I'll take that as a complement then,' she replied. 'And please call me Mags.' Alan nodded in agreement.

Margaret Vardy quickly realised that to step over the seat in such a tight skirt would entail some unladylike manoeuvres so she sat next to Alan, shoulder to shoulder with her back to the tabletop. They turned to face each other. He couldn't take his eyes off her. After a short uncomfortable silence, so typical at a funeral, she asked, 'What did Cheryl do?'

In Deep Water

There was another awkward pause before he answered. 'She was a Chartered Legal Executive working for a solicitor in Louth.'

'Seven weeks is a long time to wait for a funeral isn't it?'

'Yes, it was the coroner who held things up. A ruptured aorta is extremely rare, more so in a forty year old.'

Another silence enveloped them. Wanting to change the subject he said, 'How's the book coming on?' Anything was better than talking about Cheryl, particularly today.

'Oh it's finished and published.'

More relaxed now, he said, 'Gosh, the term prolific springs to mind.'

'Well working for someone like carrot-top I have a lot of time on my hands. He doesn't do a lot you know.' Alan nodded again, wondering if drink had loosened her tongue.

'So what's the latest book called and what's it about?'

'Same old thing. Sex. I've written it under my pseudonym Kate Williams again. You know she can be a very naughty girl, but as long as I do the proofreading and copy-editing, I can tone it down a bit. It's called *Hotel Erotica*.'

'Oh.' Alan thought the conversation was beginning to get out of hand. He was becoming embarrassed at her forthright attitude towards the subject matter. He glanced nervously around to see if anyone was within earshot.

She ignored his obvious discomfort. 'This time I've published it in both paperback and ebook format. Next time you're in Lincoln I'll give you a signed copy. Come round to my place for a chat and a drink. I know what it's like to lose someone you love.'

If only she knew, thought Alan.

Then she stood up, pecked him on the cheek, gave him her card, made her excuses, and left him to his thoughts.

Thoughts about still waters running deep.

He looked at the business card she had handed him. It showed her home address and both her landline and mobile numbers. In the place where the job title was usually printed, it said 'Author'.

When Samantha returned she used a tissue to wipe the lipstick from his face. '*Déjà vu* all over again,' she sniggered, much to his embarrassment.

§§§

It was after ten-o'clock when Alan was thrown out of The Splash. He had slapped Samantha so hard it had knocked her to the floor then screamed, *'Fuck off and mind your own business.'* The owner of the pub had no hesitation in immediately banishing Alan from the premises.

Billy Benson, still dressed in his best Sergeant's uniform, had helped Samantha get Alan into the car, and when home, up the stairs to bed. After stripping him down to his boxer shorts, Billy had put Alan in the recovery position, with a pillow behind him to stop him rolling onto his back and choking on his own vomit. Hardly a word had been spoken by either Billy or Samantha since leaving the pub.

Against her better judgement, Samantha decided she couldn't leave him until she was satisfied he was going to be alright, so she went into the spare bedroom, stripped down to her underwear and lay on the single bed. At five-thirty she heard him go to the toilet so she dressed, moved her shoes and handbag to the top of the stairs and quietly walked into his bedroom. She found him sat on the edge of the bed, his head in his hands. She walked towards him and was stood in front of him before he realised she was there. The landing light cast an ethereal glow behind her. A look of shock followed by a furrowed brow appeared on his face.

'How are you feeling?' she whispered. He merely shrugged his shoulders. 'You can't remember can you?' He shook his head. 'Then let me remind you,' she said, half-a-second before she slapped his face so hard it knocked him sideways and off the bed all together. Samantha then bent down over him and grabbed a handful of hair and jerked his head back. Alan did nothing to stop her. 'If you ever raise a finger to me again or tell me to fuck off one more time, it will be the last thing you ever do. Understand arsehole?'

Alan wanted to nod his understanding but she still had his hair in a vice-like grip. Then she let go and walked out. Picking up her shoes and handbag, it was only half way down the stairs that she realised how much her hand was stinging. She slammed the front door for effect, and drove off, engine revving and tyres screeching.

Alan sat up against the bed and put his head in his hands, feeling the heat in his left cheek.

'Holy shit,' he muttered as tears welled up in his eyes. Then he felt his stomach churning and his bowels became fluid.

Chapter 15

Three years ago, Sir Bertie Campbell was sitting in a third-floor office at the Lincolnshire Police Headquarters in Nettleham. The message on his voicemail had been curt. *Can you come to Police HQ at nine-o'clock tomorrow? The Chief Constable wants to discuss your statement.* No please. No thank you. As usual Sir Bertie was impeccably dressed, today he wore a light grey Savile Row suit, a white cotton shirt with gold cufflinks, a red and blue striped tie, and black leather hand-made shoes. Outside, he could hear the intermittent muffled sound of gunfire; Sir Bertie presumed that a firearms practice range was located somewhere close by. In front of him, on the rectangular mahogany coffee table was his empty coffee mug and a plate of chocolate digestives. He reached out and picked up a third biscuit. Starting to get impatient, he stood up and walked over to the window, looking at the grounds around the building. Despite the fact there were several car parks, most of the roads on the site had cars parked along them as well. Sir Bertie had been pleased he had come in Moira's Mini which he'd managed to squeeze into a vacant spot.

Since marrying Moira, Campbell Homes had gone from strength to strength, partly by organic growth and partly by acquisition. Sir Bertie now ran the largest family-owned house-builder in the Midlands. In recognition of his achievements, he had received a knighthood. The only project which had not turned out as planned had been his purchase of Foxton Manor, a large derelict house set in eighteen acres of land. Sir Bertie had planned to demolish the old house and build on the land with several small and separate developments of new houses. Moira had other ideas. As soon as she set eyes on the old Manor, she decided it should be totally refurbished and become their home. It had taken two years with Moira assuming the role of project manager.

The Chief Constable burst into the room, full of apologies.

'Bertie I'm so sorry to keep you waiting, I hope they've been looking after you.' The two men shook hands and Sir Bertie sat down again as the Chief Constable poured himself a coffee and refilled Sir Bertie's mug.

'Tell me again what happened,' asked the Chief Constable, 'from the very beginning.'

'Oh William,' Sir Bertie sighed in exasperation but realised the quickest way out was to comply with the request. 'Yesterday Moira and I were taking a morning stroll along the Viking Way near Horncastle before heading to The Crafty Fox for Sunday lunch. Unfortunately we bumped into one of Moira's acquaintances from the Women's Institute, I can't remember her name. She went on and on.' Sir Bertie changed from his soft lilting Scottish accent to a high-pitched plum voice to imitate the woman. 'She said, "Oh Sir Bertie, how pleased I am to meet you at last. You must come for Sunday lunch soon; all my friends are dying to meet you both." To cut a long story short, it was nearly twelve-thirty when we got to the pub.'

The Chief Constable nodded. 'And you tell me the owners of The Crafty Fox don't take bookings for Sunday lunch.'

'That's right. We're normally there at twelve-o'clock prompt to get into the dining room. Yesterday both the dining room and bar were packed. The only free seats were at a small table squeezed in next to the inglenook fireplace where one chap sat alone.'

'George Thomas?'

'So you tell me now, but we didn't know that at the time. You've seen how he was dressed, quite scruffy, pony tail, biker's leather jacket, worn jeans and dirty scuffed boots. He had a tobacco pouch, Rizla cigarette papers, and a lighter on the table next to his empty glass. Moira had stayed by the door and wasn't keen to share the table, but I had bought us all a drink and so she had to join us when I waved her over.'

'Why did you buy him a drink?'

'Simply as a thank you for letting us have a seat. He was just leaving but I insisted I buy him another half.'

'In her statement Moira said he looked quite shifty, watching everything and everybody. What was your impression?'

'I have to agree, nothing escaped his attention.'

'Hardly surprising, it turns out he's ex-special forces. And don't be fooled by his cockney accent, he was born and brought up in Wales. Despite his shabby appearance, he's a very intelligent chap, fluent in four languages, including Welsh.'

Sir Bertie nodded then went on to explain that Thomas had left them after a few minutes to have a cigarette in the beer garden at the rear of the pub. 'He had just walked out when four armed men wearing motorbike leathers and helmets burst in through the front door, fired a shot into the ceiling and demanded everyone's wallets, watches, bank cards, jewellery, mobile phones etcetera.' Sir Bertie continued his detailed account of events, describing how Thomas, obviously alerted by the gunshot, somehow appeared behind the gang, disarmed them with some force, chased after one of them into the car park when more shots were heard. He had dragged the robber back into the bar, dumped him next to the other three, and then calmly walked back to their table.

'He placed the knives and meat cleaver on the table in front of us, removed the magazine and a round from the gun and said, "Eastern European shite, kicks like a mule," as he put it down. Then he lit a cigarette, asking if anyone objected to him smoking indoors. Everyone just shook their heads.'

'Well he's certainly in a lot of trouble now,' said the Chief Constable.

'What, for smoking in the pub?'

The Chief Constable sighed and shook his head. 'There is the possibility that he was an accomplice.'

Sir Bertie snorted in derision.

'William, the guy's a hero, and if you play your cards right you might get another gong out of this before you retire.'

The Chief Constable smiled inwardly; the thought had already crossed his mind. 'Have you read the morning papers?' He pushed the Daily Mail across the coffee table to Sir Bertie.

ONE HAND GANG CAPTURED

Yesterday Lincolnshire's infamous One Hand Gang finally met their match. The gang's notoriety came about after they had

In Deep Water

previously attempted to sever a woman's fingers to rob her of her rings. The Sunday lunchtime crowd in The Crafty Fox, on the outskirts of Lincoln, were horrified when the gang burst into the pub. One of the four gang members fired a shot into the air and demanded their money and valuables. What they didn't know was that one of the customers, George Thomas, an ex-SAS soldier, had just gone outside for a cigarette.

On hearing the shot, Thomas rushed round the building and burst through the front entrance. He immediately disarmed the gangster brandishing the gun, and then shot one of the others who charged at him with a knife. Customers reported hearing a crack of breaking bones as the third gangster was disarmed. The fourth gang member fled but was pursued into the car park by Thomas who shot the man in the shoulder, and fired several shots into the Harley Davidson as he attempted to escape.

"It was incredible," said Shelly Watson, one of the bar staff. "One minute we were staring down the barrel of a gun and the next minute, when it was all over, he (George Thomas) came back into the pub and lit a cigarette, calm as you like. When one of the robbers tried to crawl away he just went across and broke his arm. The screams made the others think twice before trying to escape."

A spokesman for Lincoln County Hospital said that the list of injuries included two gunshot wounds, two broken arms, a dislocated elbow, a crushed larynx and a broken collar bone. What is even more incredible is that these injuries were inflicted when the gang members were all wearing motorbike helmets. None of the injuries are thought to be life threatening.

George Thomas was a sergeant in the SAS but left under mysterious circumstances. He then worked overseas as a security adviser and bodyguard for several years before returning to this country in September. He is currently looking for work.

The One Hand Gang's previous robberies include . . .

Sir Bertie pushed the newspaper back to his friend. 'Rather a dramatic description of events,' he said.

'Either way Bertie, he'll need a damn good lawyer, particularly when those clowns decide to sue for excessive force, or even attempted murder. We also have to consider the discharge of a firearm in a public place.'

'Don't be so bloody stupid William, there was no collateral damage, and if he needs a good lawyer then I'll get my chaps onto the case.'

'Why are you so interested in helping him? He can't be of any use to anyone in this county with his skills set. Espionage, covert surveillance, unarmed combat, lock-picking, explosives expert. Who do you know who needs a sniper around these parts?'

Sir Bertie, keen to leave, rose to his feet, 'Actually I need a gardener cum chauffeur. I want to help him as Moira and I were both wearing our Rolex watches, a tenth wedding anniversary present to each other. Irreplaceable.' He pushed his left arm forward to reveal the Rolex and tapped it to emphasise the point. The two men shook hands again, and as Sir Bertie headed for the door, he turned. 'Where is he now? I'd like to say thank you again.'

Chapter 16

Margaret Vardy lived alone in a large Victorian terraced house in one of the nicer areas of town, just north of the city centre. As an only child, she had inherited the house when her mother had passed away ten years ago. Her father had died eight years previously. The house was three storeys high, with five bedrooms, two reception rooms, and unusually for such an old property, three bathrooms. There was a long narrow little-used garden at the rear which had pedestrian access to the woods beyond. A short block-paved driveway at the front had sufficient parking for three cars. It was the sort of house which, years ago, would have been converted into a doctors' or dentists' surgery. Nowadays, many of the neighbouring houses had been converted into flats.

When she was fifteen, Margaret's mother was knocked down by a hit-and-run driver. A car mounted the pavement and killed a young woman and her child, and crippled Margaret's mother, leaving her wheelchair bound. Her father converted one of the downstairs reception rooms into a bedroom with an en-suite. Margaret and her father continued to use bedrooms upstairs. That was when her problems started.

Margaret was seventeen when her father died; no-one realised that the tears she shed at his funeral were tears of joy. At first it had started with a goodnight kiss, but soon went through the groping stage to sexual abuse, twice a week. She used to dread Tuesdays and Fridays when he would come home from the pub, drunk. She prayed that she would become pregnant then he would be stopped, and hopefully sent to jail. Before he died, the family received a seven figure anonymous donation as compensation for her mother's injuries.

Margaret's mother had said, 'Mags, I want you to have this. If your Dad finds out he'll just piss it against the wall. Use it to look after me then keep what's left.' Margaret could see the sorrow in her mother's eyes. She knew what her husband was doing and was deeply ashamed, but said nothing. Shortly after that, he died of a heart attack on the way out of Margaret's bedroom late one Friday night. Margaret had looked out of her room and seen him lying on the landing. She would always remember his pleading eyes, hands clutched to his chest, unable to breathe or speak. She telephoned for an ambulance the next morning. When she told her mother the paramedics were on their way, they hugged each other tightly. Again, no words were spoken, but they were both relieved the ordeal was over. To rid herself of his memory completely, Margaret threw away all her bedding and nightdresses.

Because of her mother's situation, Margaret had to forgo university and become a full-time carer, doing so without complaint. However, she blamed her father for the way her life unfolded. After his death, she became sullen, angry, and bad tempered. She hated men and everything they stood for. At seventeen she was a pretty girl with an attractive figure but she was repulsed by men. She dressed in the hope that men would find her unattractive. She changed her whole wardrobe, buying dowdy, old-fashioned clothes from charity shops. Eventually she agreed to attend therapy sessions, but she was so ashamed of her involvement in an incestuous relationship, she refused to reveal the source of her anger. Unable to help any further, the psychiatrist ended the treatment sessions with a parting shot.

'Margaret, I'm sorry we haven't been able to help you much. Can I suggest that you unburden your problems onto paper? Vent your anger into the written word, then as a final act, tear the paper to shreds.'

It had worked. It took several years but it worked, and her love of writing was born. She joined a local writers' group and her writing skills flourished. The group set varied tasks every month but she soon tired of the boring topics. She asked the group's leader what sold books.

'Margaret,' he had said, 'Sex sells, it's not guaranteed but it's your best chance. The American market is prolific.' She started to research sex and what drove men to do what they did. Embarrassed about writing sex novels under her own name, she used the pseudonym Kate Williams. Margaret saw Kate as a shameless, lustful woman, her complete antithesis. Margaret liked the idea, and overnight Kate Williams, her alter ego, was born. She took to the pretence so enthusiastically that, shortly after her mother's death, she bought another set of clothes, dressing as Margaret at work and Kate at leisure. One bedroom was full of Margaret's boring 'stay well away' spinster-type clothes, whereas Kate took over another bedroom and filled the cupboards and wardrobes with sexy lingerie, low-cut tops and short dresses. Her clothes said 'look what you're missing'. Margaret even bought Kate a new car, choosing an open-topped Mazda MX5 for such a fun-loving woman.

§§§

Margaret was sat writing at her desk in the study. After her mother's death she had cleared out the downstairs bedroom and converted it into an office. Situated at the front of the house, the room had views towards the cathedral, at one time the tallest building in the world until its central spire collapsed during a storm in 1549. Margaret could just see the top of the western towers in winter when there was no foliage on the trees. The chiming doorbell gave her a start. Not used to visitors, she scurried to the front door.

'Kate Williams?' A very attractive and smartly dressed young woman stood on the doorstep.

Margaret froze, her face reddening as hundreds of conflicting thoughts raced through her brain. 'No, no, may I ask . . .?'

'I'm sorry, my name's Erica Bland from K D Brown Associates.' She held out a business card which Margaret took and studied. Literary agents with a London address. 'I've been in Lincoln on business, and one of our associates asked me to try and locate Kate Williams while I was here.'

'I think you had better come in.'

'And you are . . . ?'

Fifteen minutes later, both women were sat at the bottom of the garden on the recently built decking. Margaret had a G&T in front of her on the table, Erica Bland a straight tonic. Margaret had explained everything to her. Erica had already made her decision.

'One of our associates has read your book *Hotel Erotica* and would like to meet you. Do you think you could spare the time to see him?'

Margaret couldn't believe a literary agent would be interested in such a tacky book as *Hotel Erotica*. However, she wasn't going to turn down a chance to meet him. 'I could come down to London; have a mini-break at the same time,' she enthused. Contact details were exchanged and after Erica Bland left, Margaret fist-pumped the air then quickly followed that with another much larger G&T.

§§§

It was now three weeks since the funeral and despite trying numerous times, Samantha had totally ignored any attempt Alan had made to speak to her. Weekends were the worst. He missed taking Emily swimming or ice skating. Cheryl was no longer around to argue with, and Samantha wouldn't talk to him. The house was like a morgue. To pass the time he had gone out for a drive.

'What would you like to drink?'

'I'll just have a beer thanks, I'm trying to cut down.' Alan had called at Margaret's house to collect the promised signed copy of *Hotel Erotica*.

When she returned with a glass of red wine and a bottle of beer she asked, 'How are you coping? You know, after the funeral.'

'Like you Margaret . . . sorry, Mags, living alone in a large house is not much fun. Fortunately one of my neighbours does the housework for me, she's such a sweetie.'

'Actually tonight I'm Kate.'

It should have been obvious to Alan. The woman sat opposite him was not the Margaret Vardy he knew. At work she was shy and demure, her clothes camouflaging her figure. Tonight she was wearing a short, black mid-thigh-length skirt which was close to indecent when she sat and crossed her legs, and her white blouse had been unbuttoned to mid-way between sexy and exhibitionist. Alan struggled to avert his eyes from the lacy bra and expanse of flesh on show. He had rung twenty minutes earlier to check if she was at home, and he wondered if she had changed in that time, just for him.

It should have made him feel uncomfortable, alone in her presence, but with Samantha now stonewalling his attempts to contact her, he needed someone to talk to.

'How's Samantha?' she asked, trying to make conversation.

He simply shrugged.

They sat in silence for a while, both lost in their thoughts. With nothing else to do, he opened the book and read the inscription, written in gold ink. *Enjoy. With all my love. Kate Williams XXX.*

As he sipped his beer straight from the bottle, to make conversation Margaret told him about her upbringing. She called her father a 'beast' but that was all she said. She told him how her mother had been injured in a hit-and-run accident.

'Did they ever find out who the driver was?'

'Oh yes, it was Tommy Taylor, known locally as "Tearaway". His yellow Ferrari was found further out of town, wrapped around a lamp-post.'

'Isn't he one of the Taylor Transport family?' Alan had read recently in Lincolnshire Life that Joe Taylor, owner of the largest transport operation in the county, had just retired and his two daughters had taken over the business.

'Used to be. After the accident, Joe Taylor disowned his son and he's never been seen or heard of since.'

'That turned out to be an expensive mistake.'

'Not half, Joe Taylor gave my Mum an "anonymous" seven figure sum as compensation,' emphasising the word with her fingers. 'He even came to her funeral, put his arm round me, the way a father *should,* and asked if I was OK.'

Alan had detected a bitterness in her voice, but she suddenly changed the subject, leapt up and grabbed his arm.

'Come on, let me show you around.' Not knowing why, he meekly followed her. At the top of the first flight of stairs, there were three doors, all closed.

'This one's Kate's bedroom, it's full of all her sexy gear,' she said opening the door, 'and that one's Margaret's,' she added, pointing to a door along a short corridor.

'And this one?' he asked, of the door behind him.

'That's where . . .' then she started to cry. Not knowing what had upset her, he gingerly hugged her, aware of the warmth of her supple body in his arms, the smell of her perfume arousing him. Feeling uncomfortable on the landing outside her bedroom, he broke away and made his excuses to leave.

'I'm going to London in a couple of weeks, but when I get back maybe we could meet up,' she said hopefully.

Not knowing why, he nodded in agreement.

Chapter 17

The bar of The Plough was full of the usual Sunday lunchtime crowd. Situated on one of the main roads out of Louth, it was less than 400 metres from Alan's house. The pub's football team had just played their first game of the season and the players and supporters were noisily crowded around Tracey, the landlady, exchanging ribald jokes. The shouts and laughter were enough to completely drown out the irritating background music that the bar staff always played. Tracey was the archetypical landlady, an expansive chest plenty of which was on show, and bottle-blonde hair. She and her husband had rescued the pub from insolvency and turned it into one of the best drinking establishments in town, much favoured by the younger generation.

From the road, the building looked like a double-fronted detached house, which is exactly what it had been thirty years ago. When it was converted into a pub, a flat-roofed extension had been added to one side. The painted pub sign was pealing, and weeds were a constant problem in the gravel car park. Its appearance did little to attract passing trade. Inside was similar; the central bar had been built around the staircase to the apartment above, the snug to the left had a well-worn lino floor, and mismatched tables and stools. The formerly white walls were stained with cigarette smoke before the ban was introduced, and hadn't been painted since. The lounge was little better. The fact that the only food available was either crisps or pork scratchings did little to deter the in-crowd. It was the sort of pub where men congregated to escape from their wives or girlfriends. In that respect, it had served Alan well over the years.

As far as most customers were concerned, Tracey was enough to attract them to pub. Often coarse, lascivious, and licentious, she could also be extremely charming and polite. No one really knew whether her signature phrase, 'Time for a quickie?' simply referred to a last drink before leaving.

Alan sat at the end of the bar on a four-legged stool, alone. The smaller stools around the tables only had three legs and frequently tipped over when an unwary customer had had too much to drink. Alan was wearing an old fleece jacket over a scruffy T-shirt full of holes, tatty paint-stained denims, and a shabby pair of trainers. Three days of stubble added to his unkempt appearance. Occasionally he would give a nod of recognition to one of the customers, and he knew most of them.

At half-past-two the pub began to empty. Customers didn't realise that, sub-consciously, the smell of a Sunday roast drifting down the staircase from the flat above made them aware of the time. The smell of a cooked meal made Alan think of Samantha. In the seven weeks between Cheryl's death and the funeral he had been a regular visitor to Samantha's home for Sunday lunch, and often a weekday meal as well. He had enjoyed the long chats, sometimes well into the early hours. However, in the six weeks since the funeral, not a word had passed between them.

It wasn't for his lack of trying. Even now, he was sub-consciously twiddling his mobile phone in his hand. The first week he had texted every day begging forgiveness. The second week he had started pleading to speak to her. By week three he changed tack to 'enough is enough'. During week four there had been a glimmer of hope. He had taken flowers to her apartment, leaving them and a note with the concierge. He got a text that evening. *Thank you* was all it said; those two words were enough to increase his optimism, but nothing since. Even a cheque returning the £4000 she had lent him had not received a response. He had toyed with the idea of texting now, but knowing she would probably be at her parents' house for Sunday lunch, he decided against it.

He hadn't realised until now how lonely it was living alone. For the last two years, he and Cheryl had hardly spoken, but at least there was occasionally some noise in the house, even if it was just a slamming door or a flushing toilet. Nowadays the house was cloaked in silence; he hardly spoke a word to anyone from leaving work in the evening to going back the next morning. How he missed his nightly chats with Samantha. Some nights they used to talk for up to an hour about anything and everything. He now realised how much he longed to rebuild their friendship. Once again, his violent temper had been the cause. Two years ago he had hit Cheryl giving her a black eye. It must have been him, how else would she wake up with a bruised face. Six weeks ago he hit Samantha, knocking her over in The Splash, following it up with a mouthful of expletives. The locals had confirmed that when he next visited the pub to settle the bill for the funeral wake. His hair-trigger temper had lost him a promised ten percent discount.

The only good thing to come out of all this was that he was now eating more healthily. For most of their married life, if Cheryl had been cooking, he always knew when dinner was ready by the pinging microwave. If he had to cook for himself he preferred the easier option of takeaways. However, for the last few weeks he had been trying to master the art of slow cooking. At least the food preparation filled the evenings. Initially, the meat was tender but the vegetables rock hard. Jane Hamilton had solved the problem at a stroke.

'Dice the vegetables really finely and they will cook through,' she had advised. She had also suggested he freeze any surplus food for another meal.

He had thanked Jane for the advice, but had said he was, 'Still more Gordon Blue than *cordon bleu.*'

He had even tried batch cooking chilli for freezing but hadn't realised how many onions, tins of chopped tomatoes, and kidney beans were required for the four kilos of mincemeat he had bought. Fortunately the local corner shop, conveniently situated opposite The Plough, was always open until ten-o'clock. How he missed Samantha's home cooking. He had eaten at the apartment many times, and he fondly remembered her effortlessly preparing meals as he sipped wine looking out of the kitchen bi-fold doors, across the veranda, towards the city below.

'Got time for a quickie before you go?' Tracey's words brought him out of his daydream. She was keen to shut the pub and have her lunch.

'There's more to life than a knee-trembler against a damp cellar wall Tracey,' he replied, and then ducked as she took a playful swing at him as he headed for the door.

As he strolled home, the brisk wind clawing at his clothes and the boredom and loneliness weighing heavily in his thoughts, he made up his mind to finish clearing Cheryl's 'detritus', as he now called it. Her clothes had gone to various charity shops, her jewellery to the local goldsmith and that had given him enough money for a night out. He was trying to stop himself calculating how many pints or bottles of whisky the money would have bought. The £3500 the police had returned meant he had some financial security again, together with the promised £1750 insurance payment for Cheryl's written-off car. There was even talk that the life insurance company might soon pay out on a whole life policy in Cheryl's name, something they had both taken out when the mortgage had been arranged. He would e-mail them again to try and speed up the payment. The final job was to clear out a wooden box which Cheryl had always kept locked. He hadn't found the key since her death, so he decided he would break it open.

Chapter 18

Vanessa Redfern and her husband were at a friend's house in Mablethorpe when the illegal radio, tracking the police frequencies, sprung into life in EMTV's head office in Nottingham.
All units, all units in the Louth area, we have a report of an attempted murder in Wendham Close, Louth, over.
Tango Alpha Two Zero responded and before the conversation between them and the Force Control Room had finished, a call had been made from EMTV's HQ to Vanessa Redfern. With holiday traffic, it would be an agonising forty-five minutes before she got to Louth.

By the time Sergeant Benson arrived at the scene, PCs Donaldson and Lampton had the situation under control. PC Donaldson took Sergeant Billy Benson aside and they both stared at the trashed black Mercedes in the drive of No 4. Every single body panel was dented; all the windows and lights smashed. A sledge hammer lay embedded in a hole in the boot-lid of the car.

'Some neighbours you've got Sarge, the guy from No 2,' Donaldson glanced at his notebook, 'Mr Alan Bishop, is alleged to have attacked the front door of your other neighbour,' another look at his notes, 'Mr Gerald Smith-Etherington. When he couldn't get in, he turned his attention to the car.' PC Donaldson looked up and pointed at the Mercedes. 'Exhibit A.'

'Have ye spoken to Bishop?'

'Tried to Sarge but can't get a word out of him.' Donaldson nodded towards Alan's front door. Billy hadn't noticed Alan sat on the doorstep, head in hands, sobbing quietly.

'Right,' said Billy as he spun round to look down the street. Donaldson followed his gaze and they both saw an old man peering through the window of No 6. 'That's Nosey Parker, real name Herbert, never misses a thing. Ye can't even scratch yer arse without him seeing.' Billy raised one hand; fingers spread wide, indicating five minutes. Nosey Parker's face lit up as he gave a wave of acknowledgement.

It pained Billy to pour a large malt whisky for Alan without one for himself, but Donaldson *was* from Traffic. Five minutes later they had the full story. Yes, Alan had wanted to kill Smith-Etherington, yes, he would have, had the uPVC front door not been so strong, and yes, he had damaged the car.

'Why laddie?' asked Billy. Alan gulped down the remainder of his whisky, got up from the chair to retrieve a note and book from the coffee table.

'I found these this afternoon.' He gave Billy the hand-written note first.

3 April
Cheryl
Rape is such an emotive word but at the end of the day it would be your word against mine. As a gesture of compromise I enclose, as promised, a cheque for £10,000 for your lifetime of silence.
Gerald

Alan then handed Billy a building society book showing a deposit of £10,000 dated the eleventh of April. When he finished examining the note and book, he passed them to Donaldson.

Sergeant Benson explained to his colleague, 'Alan's wife was pregnant when she died three months ago. Smith-Etherington is a local solicitor, and was her employer.'

PC Donaldson whistled quietly through his teeth as the realisation hit him.

Smith-Etherington had been taken to Louth police station for questioning before EMTV arrived.

§§§

David Hyde was dozing in front of the television after his Sunday lunch, not really taking much notice, when the name Alan Bishop was mentioned. It woke him from his reverie. Samantha had not mentioned Alan recently, but it was obvious to David that because she was now coming for Sunday lunch again, things must have

In Deep Water

cooled between them. Emily, however, had never stopped talking about him.

'I haven't been allowed to see him for weeks Grandpa,' she had frequently said. 'I think Mummy has sent him to the naughty corner, but I don't know why.'

Samantha was summoned to the lounge and the whole family sat expectantly for the news item to be repeated. They didn't have to wait long; it was a slow news day, and this was breaking news.

I am standing in Wendham Close, Louth, where today an attempt was made to seriously injure a well respected local solicitor, Mr Gerald Smith-Etherington. A witness, Mr Herbert Parker, who lives at No 6 was looking out of his window when the incident occurred. Mr Parker suffers from severe arthritis and spends most of his days watching the world pass by in this normally quiet cul-de-sac. Today was different. Mr Parker has suggested that he heard Mr Bishop, an Area Manager for Lincs Water, threatening to kill Mr Smith-Etherington. He watched as Mr Bishop stormed across to his neighbour's house with a sledge hammer, screaming, "I'm going to kill you, you bastard." Unable to gain entry into the house where Mr Smith-Etherington was hiding, Bishop turned his attention onto the car in the drive and you can see the result.

The camera, operated by Vanessa's husband, panned away from her and focussed on the car. He slowly walked around the vehicle. The camera then swung back to concentrate on Vanessa again.

Dr Bishop, to give him his full title, was seen returning from The Plough public house shortly before the incident. It is believed that Mr Smith-Etherington has been taken to the local police station for his own protection.

And now we are returning to the studio for a short commercial break. When we come back we hope to interview Mr Bishop. This is Vanessa Redfern for EMTV in Louth.

After the commercial break, Vanessa Redfern was seen outside a door with the No 2 in full shot.

Welcome back, we are now hoping to have a word with Mr Bishop.

She turned and rang the doorbell. Eventually Alan appeared, still in his scruffy T-shirt and tatty denims, a glass of whisky in one hand and his three days of stubble clearly visible.

Oh fuck off Vanessa . . .

Seconds later the television screen went blank as Samantha's mother hit the off button on the remote. 'Just as well you're not talking to him anymore,' she snapped, the rising inflection emphasising her anger. 'He's a complete and utter waste of space. He's nothing more than a drunken yob. Did you see him? Did you see him drinking whisky?'

As she stood up to leave the room, a smile creased Karen Hyde's face. She felt totally vindicated in her views about Alan Bishop.

The moment her mother had turned off the television, Samantha felt an overwhelming urge to phone Alan. They had not spoken for six weeks and she knew he would be desperate to talk. He would need to explain, he would need to be comforted and reassured. However, Samantha wasn't going to let her parents see her talking to him. Even if she went into the garden for some privacy she knew they would be watching her. Instead she decided to wait until she got home and Emily was in bed. When they *had* been speaking to one another, it was usually late evening, but when she did eventually get home, she had talked herself out of the idea. She decided Alan needed to stand on his own two feet; he had to get on with life and its traumas without her being available to hold his hand every time. Instead she would seek her uncle's counsel.

Chapter 19

It was Kate Williams who had gone to London, leaving Margaret Vardy at home. Her latest book, *Hotel Erotica*, had been selling well. In paperback form, the book had sold less than 150 copies but in the ebook format it had sold over 3000. As ebooks were much more lucrative for the authors than paperbacks, she was very happy indeed. Not that she needed the money. The compensation the family had received for her mother's accident had been invested wisely. Margaret had been very fortunate, meeting an extremely good financial adviser who had suggested she should 'get rich slowly' and not be greedy. Since the accident nearly twenty years ago, the money had grown and was now approaching £2 million.

Kate had decided to treat herself during her trip to London. She had booked a room at Claridge's and had spent a couple of days sightseeing and shopping. She would probably need to buy another suitcase to get all her new clothes and shoes back home. The only thing missing was the man of her dreams. How she wished he was here with her, if only she had had the nerve to ask him. If only. Last month, being comforted by him on the first floor landing, would have been an ideal time to ask. She had already decided to tell him the truth when she got home, in the hope he could help her forget her past, and in the hope he may start to love her. After all, what more could a man want, a sex-mad woman with £2 million in the bank?

She felt empowered as she climbed the stairs to the first-floor offices of K D Brown Associates, just off Oxford Street. She had been told that Samson Mills, the associate she was due to see, would be away in America, but she had already booked the hotel and was happy to talk to Erica Bland. After all, she still couldn't believe a London-based literary agent would want to be associated with anything as tacky as *Hotel Erotica*.

'Wow, look at you,' exclaimed a surprised Erica Bland, referring to the transformation in appearance from the last time they had met. Kate was wearing stone-washed skin-tight denims, red high-heeled shoes, a skimpy white jumper showing just a hint of midriff, and her hair in a pony-tail sticking out of the back of her baseball cap. Over her shoulder she had a large shopping bag.

'In London I'm Kate Williams,' she said as a way of explanation.

The two women chatted amiably for about twenty minutes, sharing an already open bottle of warm white wine. Kate was surprised how much noise came through the open windows. She could hear delivery drivers shouting, car doors slamming, horns blaring, and pedestrians scurrying along in the street below. Her working environment was like a morgue by comparison.

Eventually Erica said, 'I suppose we'd better talk shop. The truth is Margaret, sorry Kate, we've read your book and like it. Not so much the storyline, more the way it's written. Tell me how you came up with the idea.'

'The idea was simple. I'm hopeless at working out a plot so like my first book, it's a series of unrelated mini-stories. Customers come to the hotel, choose a member of staff they would like to have sex with, then select what they want to do from the room service menu.'

'And the waiter or waitress arrives at the room with a trolley full of . . .'

'Exactly,' replied Kate.

'As I said, the storyline is, not to put too fine a point on it, crap. However, some of the stories are so erotic, it's amazing. That last chapter, *wow*, is it called Room Nine?'

Kate nodded. 'To be truthful, that's my own personal fantasy.'

Changing the subject, Erica asked, 'When did you start writing?' The room went quiet. Erica could see Kate was trying to decide what to say, so she went to get another bottle of wine, this time chilled. Kate drank a full glass before she answered.

'To be honest, and you must understand I am telling you this in total confidence,' Erica nodded, 'I started writing when I was seventeen after my father died. He abused me.'

Erica's hand shot to her mouth, trying, but failing, to stop the gasp which escaped. Kate went on to explain that her father started the abuse when she was just fifteen; her mother was wheelchair bound and lived downstairs.

'After he died I went for therapy but never told the psychiatrist what had happened, so he sent me away and told me to put all my anger and hatred on paper. It eventually worked. That's how I started writing.'

'Do you remember much about it all now?'

'Every last detail. At first it was just his probing calloused fingers, and then on my sixteenth birthday he raped me. I will never forget his metal belt buckle digging in my belly, his stubble scratching my face, the stink of stale beer on his breath, the smell of cigarette smoke in his hair and on his clothes.'

'What did your father do, job wise?'

'He was an HGV driver.' She paused, then with bitterness in her voice, added, 'A typical long distance lorry driver, eighteen stone and a fry-up every day.'

Erica could see the seeds of a book forming, a true story of abuse and rape. She topped up the empty wine glasses and waited for Kate to continue. With half the second bottle gone, Kate soon started talking again.

'Then just after my seventeenth birthday, he made me do other things.' Kate took another swig of wine, but didn't elaborate.

Erica could only guess. 'Oh my God, that must have been awful,' she whispered.

Kate was silent for a while. She finished the wine in her glass and Erica topped it up again. 'I hated him for what he did to me and I hated myself because I began to enjoy it.' Erica was stunned, but Kate was determined to cleanse herself of the guilt and self-loathing that had been with her for over eighteen years. 'It got worse and worse. The more he did it, the more I enjoyed it. The more I enjoyed it, the more he did it. It was a vicious circle, spiralling out of control. I was so full of hatred towards him and ashamed at my own responses, several times I thought about ending it all. Seriously, I had even decided how to do it. I was that ashamed of myself.'

'What happened? How did it stop?'

'After one really hectic session, he had a heart attack and died on the way back to his bedroom.' Kate had to stop herself from telling the whole truth.

'Did your mother have any idea what was going on?'

'Oh yes, I was what you would call a screamer.'

Following another silence Erica asked, 'Can you remember all the details from so long ago?'

'Yes, I've still got all my diaries.'

All Erica had to do now was persuade her to write this book. 'Let's meet again tomorrow and talk some more.'

At the second meeting they both made a promise. Kate promised to write a 3000 word outline of a book describing her years of abuse. Erica promised to show the synopsis to various publishers, with a view to securing an advance against the royalties.

§§§

'Do you want to pop round on Friday after work for that drink I promised you? There's something I'd like to share with you, something I want to explain. I've got a spare room if you want to stay.'

If only it had been Samantha who was asking, but it wasn't. It had been seven weeks now and she still wasn't speaking to him, and may never do so again. He had all but given up hope. His violent temper on the night of the funeral, fuelled by his excessive drinking, had spoilt everything. His thoughts turned back to Mags, last time they met, holding her supple body in his arms. As he had nothing else planned for the weekend, it was an easy decision.

With the promise of a bed for the night, Alan was on his third glass of wine. 'I've read your book; I couldn't put it down, and that last chapter, hell's bells Mags.'

'There's something else I want you to read.' She had finished her 3000 word outline of her life of abuse and already sent it to Erica Bland. Normally when writing, she would put a manuscript down and leave it for some time before revisiting the words, checking, editing, changing, and improving them. The story of her life's experiences, however, had been going round in her head for eighteen

In Deep Water

years. She knew the narrative word for word, letter by letter. No editing was necessary. She figured the easiest way to explain to Alan why she was like she was, was to let him read it.

He put the last sheet of typed paper on the nearby coffee table. Kate, provocatively dressed again, had snuggled up to him on the settee, pretending to read over his shoulder. The warmth of her body and the smell of her perfume were having the same effect again.

'Can you understand now, why I'm . . .?' She left the sentence hanging.

'Yes.' A long silence followed. 'There seem to be two people living in the same body.'

She nodded. 'Margaret hates men, and . . .' She struggled to get the words out. 'Kate is exactly the opposite.' Then she burst into tears.

Alan sat in silence for several minutes, Kate quietly sobbing on his shoulder. His curiosity got the better of him. He shouldn't have asked. It was none of his business. He hardly knew her.

'Have you ever . . . you know . . . since . . .?'

She looked up at him and shook her head. Tears, mingled with mascara, ran down her cheeks. He instinctively put his arm around her, wanting to console her.

Two days later, on Sunday morning in Sainsbury's car park, Alan and Kate were loading groceries into the boot of her Mazda MX5, when Samantha and Emily drove past. Emily had her head buried in a book and Samantha was pleased that neither Alan, nor the woman he was with, had seen them. She drove straight past and out of the car park.

She said, 'We'll get the milk on the way *back* from Gran's.'

Seven weeks, she thought, *seven bloody weeks.*

Chapter 20

It was nearly three-o'clock when Alan got back to the office. The monthly operational meeting had overrun thanks to Ian Young turning up two hours late. It couldn't have happened on a worse day. Tonight at seven-o'clock Alan was due to speak to the Keelby Parish Council meeting and answer questions about sewage smells. Or odours, as the Chairman of the Parish Council, Major J W S Bolton (retired) called them. Complaints about the odours had been received regularly for nearly a year. Alan thought he had picked up a pattern. The complaints were often received towards the end of each month, and he wanted to check the dates of the Parish Council meetings. Alan had also discovered that Major J W S Bolton (retired) lived two doors away from the sewage treatment works in a new housing development which had been built right next to the site.

At the meeting, Alan wanted to use the latest term, waste water treatment. It sounded less offensive than sewage. Across Lincolnshire, many of the sewage treatment works had been built in the early 1940s to serve the large number of wartime RAF airfields which had peppered the county. Over the years, the grass runways and rows of Nissen huts had long since disappeared, and in Keelby, housing development had expanded towards the site. The sewage works pre-dated the houses by over seventy-five years. How he would love to turn up and say, 'We were here first.'

Alan had arranged for everything possible to be done to alleviate the smell which, in reality, was not very much. Firstly, he had asked that the tankering of sewage sludge offsite and spreading it on adjacent fields stop for a week. The last thing he wanted was the stink of sewage in nearby fields. The spreading of sewage sludge as a soil conditioner on farmland had been carried out for years, a free service to the farming community. Modern day thinking was now moving towards using it to produce energy in biomass plants, but that idea had yet to reach Lincolnshire. He had also asked that the grass on site be cut that afternoon. There was nothing like the English countryside smell of newly mown grass. Other than that, there was little that could be done. The one thing he needed to check was how many complaints had come to Lincs Water direct from members of the public, and how many had come under the signature of Major J W S Bolton (retired).

'Alan, can you spare half an hour?'

Alan inwardly groaned but was smiling when he looked up. 'What is it Jane?'

'The interviews for a new water operative working out of Caistor. Peter didn't come in today because of a stomach bug and Warren could really do with a bit of help.'

Peter Warcup, the District Manager, would normally have conducted the interviews with Warren Croft, a relatively new Superintendant at Caistor, but Warren was possibly nervous about interviewing prospective employees alone.

'OK tell Warren to start without me, I'll be there in twenty minutes.'

When he got to Caistor Depot, the first interview was just ending. Warren shook his head as the chap walked out. The next two were just as bad. Things didn't improve until Gail Swift walked in. She was an attractive petite young girl; she didn't look as if she would say boo to a goose.

'Why?' was Alan's first question.

'Simple,' she replied. 'I want a job. I stayed on at school, got three 'A' levels but can't afford to go to university.'

'What do you know about water supply, treatment and distribution?'

'To be honest, not a lot. I've obviously researched it on the internet but no doubt you could make me look really stupid if you asked me some technical questions.'

The interview went from good to better, particularly when Alan fired questions at her about working in a man's environment. Her replies were confident.

'If three elder brothers and Andreas Demetriou can't boss me, then I'm sure I'll manage the rest.'

Andreas Demetriou was a huge Greek Cypriot who worked at Caistor. Huge in terms of girth, not height, but still the sort of chap, if you didn't know any better, you'd give a wide berth to. Alan made a mental note to talk to Andreas later.

The final interviewee also impressed Alan. Saul Hendry West.

Aware that the name Saul was that of the first king of Israel, and therefore may have religious connotations, Alan had to tread carefully.

'Is Saul a family name?' he asked.

'No, nothing like that. When I was born my mother told my dad she wanted to call me Paul Henry but because he's dyslexic . . .'

Alan and Warren Croft chuckled and they took an immediate liking to the lad.

Warren asked, 'Are you still talking to your dad?'

'Yeh, it's not his fault. Everyone calls me Paul anyway.'

At the end Alan said, 'Well Warren, who would you choose? If anybody.'

Warren liked Paul West but said nothing about Gail Swift. Alan knew that another vacancy was coming up at Caistor but on the sewage side of the business. He would think it through before talking to Peter Warcup. He also had to talk to Andreas Demetriou.

§§§

When Alan arrived at Keelby village hall at six-fifty-two, the car park was almost empty. Either very few people were attending the meeting or they had walked to the hall. Alan parked next to an old Rover 45 which he assumed belonged to the Chairman. When he entered the hall, the Parish Council meeting was already in progress. Three people sat on the top table, situated on a raised stage at the end of the badly lit room. It was obvious who the man in the centre was, green and brown checked suit, blue shirt and regimental tie, complete with a handlebar moustache and bald head. Obviously Major bloody J W S Bolton (retired). To his right was a mousey-haired woman who reminded Alan of an older version of Margaret Vardy. To his left was a tall skinny man who looked to be asleep. Next to the sleeping man were two empty chairs.

'Yes?' barked the Chairman.

Alan's hackles rose immediately. He had already formed an opinion about Major J W S Bolton (retired) after reading his letters of complaint, and it wasn't favourable. The Chairman may be used to bullying the people of Keelby, but Alan would relish the challenge.

'Yes,' he replied loudly from the back of the hall and started walking towards the stage.

Only when he was halfway did he add, 'My name is Dr Bishop from Lincs Water. I've been asked to address the meeting tonight. My invitation informed me the meeting would commence at seven-o'clock.'

'Edith? You knew this month's meeting was starting at six-thirty,' the Chairman snapped.

The timid woman next to him cowered in fear. She looked like she might burst into tears.

Alan jumped to her aid. 'The letter was signed by a Mr Bolton, perhaps he made the mistake.'

The Major went bright red and puffed out his cheeks. Alan thought he might explode. Eventually he said, 'Well, now you're here, you might as well sit down.'

Alan had already decided he wanted to speak from the top table, not the floor of the hall. He climbed the four steps onto the stage and sat down next to the sleeping man. The scraping chair legs woke him. Alan surveyed the body of the hall. Five people sat in the front row, possibly other councillors. He had often wondered why folk wanted to be Parish Councillors. It was either to serve the community and improve their quality of life, or make sure a new bus stop wasn't sited outside their own front door. Behind the front row, there were three other people. Alan, thinking he would be late, at times had driven at over eighty miles an hour from Caistor. Just to address an audience of eleven.

The Chairman called the meeting to order and continued with the important matters which concerned the residents of Keelby village. Until tonight, Alan hadn't appreciated how big an issue car parking in Manor Street was. Nor did he realise how many tractors drove through the village, or how slowly they went.

Whilst he waited, listening to the Chairman's soliloquy, Alan idly toyed with his phone, which had been set on silent since he started the interviews at Caistor. One of the missed messages had been from Jane Hamilton giving him the information he had asked for. In the last two years no-one, apart from the Parish Council, had complained about the smell.

Complaints were an important item on Lincs Water's monthly operational meeting agenda. Ian Young liked to go through each one in detail. Alan cynically thought it was because it summed up his MD's total knowledge of the industry, namely sewage smells and water mains burst. When Alan was first appointed, the northern area complaints were considerably higher than in the south. This came to a head when Alan had been in the job for about a year. Ian Young had lambasted him when his complaints for the month totalled ninety-seven compared to eight in the south. In the car park after the meeting, Charlie Swanson, old enough to be Alan's father, had put his arm around his shoulders and said, 'Alan son, let me give you some advice. In the south, we had the same problem as you, so we re-jigged the reporting procedure.'

'You can't do that; everything has to go down in the complaints register.'

'Agreed. All *written* complaints are recorded, but by telephone, it's the way you handle the call. As you know most complainants are pretty wound up, so to try and diffuse the situation we use a standard script.'

'What do you say to them?'

'First of all, after agreeing how serious their concerns are, we say, "For the avoidance of doubt, we are recording this complaint at", then state the time and date.'

'Yes, but how does that help?'

'It shows that you are going to write down every last detail. Then we ask for their name, usually not a problem, and their contact details. Address, telephone numbers, landline and mobile. We might even ask for an e-mail address. If it's a genuine complaint then you will be given the information. If it's just someone having a rant, they usually back down so you don't have to put it in the register.'

The northern area adopted the same system the next day.

Alan was brought back to the here and now by the Chairman asking if he would like to speak. As he rose to his feet, he reminded himself to use the term waste water treatment and not sewage treatment. He also wanted to mention that the sewage works pre-dated the housing estate. He limited his talk to ten minutes as he sensed a complete lack of interest amongst those present.

After his brief talk, Alan asked for questions. None were forthcoming, not even from the Chairman. He also invited those interested to visit the site after the meeting. No-one turned up. It was nearly nine-thirty when he reversed out of the sewage works. By the time he got back to Louth, his favourite takeaway had closed.

Chapter 21

'That went well boss,' Andy Potts said, with obvious sarcasm. They were stood outside the southern area office which was located on the huge new Boston Sewage Treatment Works. Andy had lit a cigarette and Alan wasn't going to let him into his car until he had finished it. They had driven down from Grimsby together to attend Jack Lumley's disciplinary hearing, the shop steward they had caught driving round the pubs of Grimsby in a company van selling vegetables and eggs. The union representative had tried everything from threats of all-out strike action to eventually pleading for clemency. Charlie Swanson, as the Southern Area Manager and an *allegedly* impartial officer, had chaired the hearing, with two of his District Managers. Alan had made it clear to Charlie, in no uncertain terms, that Jack Lumley must go.

'But he's a shop steward, Alan,' Charlie had said last week. 'Won't a final written warning be enough?'

'No, just do this for me Charlie.'

'But if it goes to appeal then Ian Young will have to get involved, and we know what he's like.'

'Charlie, it won't go to appeal, but if it does then we'll ask Gordon Reed.' Charlie had eventually agreed and, although Alan could see him wavering, he did as Alan had asked and declared a verdict of dismissal.

Just then, Jack Lumley and the union official came out of the building.

'You haven't heard the last of this Alan, believe me,' the union man snapped in a strong Scouse accent.

'Give me a call sometime Jim,' he replied. When they were out of earshot he added, 'Have you noticed how most union officials seem to come from either Liverpool or Glasgow?'

Potts ignored the question. 'Do you think they will call for an all-out strike?'

'Andy, trust me. Jim called me last night at home virtually begging for leniency, until I played Jack's taped rant you recorded. Everything you saw today was posturing; he knew what the outcome would be. The article in the Grimsby Telegraph was the final nail in the coffin. Jack Lumley's actions have brought the company's name into disrepute. Jim's problem is that he can't find a replacement shop steward. Now let's go and say goodbye to Charlie.'

§§§

Since Cheryl's funeral, Alan had been trying to get his life back on track. Samantha was fast becoming a dim and distant memory, it had been nine weeks now and he had given up hope of ever seeing her again. His shagfest with Mags two weeks ago was still fresh in his mind; however, she was starting to become a pest, phone calls, texts and e-mails being sent daily. Last weekend she had even started sexting him; sending lewd messages accompanied by nude photos of herself in provocative poses. He needed to get away.

If he was to admit it, Alan had enjoyed the short time he had spent with his parents at the funeral. They had been against him going to university, and those seven years in Newcastle meant he had broken the urge to return. He had some bridges to build. He had rung them a couple of nights ago and his mother promised to make up the bed in the spare room for him for the bank holiday weekend. He had even called his brother. Tom was the elder and the favourite. He had stayed in Sheffield, lived close to his parents, and married a local lass. It didn't matter that he had got her pregnant at the age of seventeen; he did the decent thing and married her. Alan had never liked Susie, when they were younger she had had a bit of a reputation around the housing estate. Even after their marriage, she didn't change her ways and their second child was of mixed race. To be fair to Tom, he chose to stick by her.

It had been a quiet week. Ian Young was away on holiday, giving everyone a chance to catch up with some real work. With the August Bank Holiday looming, Alan left his visit to Caistor until Friday. He had already spoken to the Water District Manager, Peter Warcup, who was based at Grimsby alongside Alan, about the possibility of employing Saul 'Paul' West as a water operative and that had been quickly agreed. Alan just needed to meet up with Andreas Demetriou to ask about Gail Swift. He headed towards the Caistor depot after lunch. He was hoping to finish there early, and then head off to Sheffield to stay with his parents. He had packed some casual clothes for the trip and was looking forward to spending three days away from the grindstone.

Andreas Demetriou was a Greek Cypriot by birth. He didn't stay in Cyprus long; he was only one year old when the Greek military junta tried to overthrow the Cypriot president, Archbishop Makarios, in 1974. The bloody coup failed but was shortly followed by a Turkish invasion which didn't, the Turks capturing thirty-seven percent of the island. With the island split into two, the Turks to the north and the Greeks to the south, families formerly living mostly in harmony side by side, fled to the safety of their fellow countrymen. Andreas's father had been a fisherman in the northern port of Kyrenia, so in 1974 the family fled south to Paphos. Still concerned for their safety, they moved to the UK, firstly staying in north London with relatives, and then moving to the fishing town of Grimsby to find work.

Andreas had learned to speak English in London and like most Cypriots living there, was bi-lingual. His Cockney accent was a complete contrast to his swarthy Mediterranean complexion, permanent five-o'clock shadow, huge girth and short stature. But what unnerved most who knew him, was his Mediterranean custom of kissing men on the cheeks. It had unsettled Alan at first, but now he just accepted it as part of the man's ways. Andreas had once sided with Alan when one of his crew told Alan to 'fuck off' and then pushed him into a sludge drying bed. Perfectly capable of handling himself in normal circumstances, that day Alan had decided to go straight home to get clean shoes and trousers, choosing to sort out the insubordination the following day. The next morning Andreas had been waiting in the area office with a letter of resignation from the wrongdoer.

In Deep Water

'Sorry about his handwriting,' Andreas had said. 'It's difficult to write with a broken collarbone.'

After catching up with Andreas's team, Alan followed the time honoured protocol. *'Andreas filos mou, ti kanies?',* 'Andreas my friend, how are you?' Then he had to endure a bone crushing handshake and hug, and the customary kisses, which had to be reciprocated. After all that, Andreas confirmed that Gail Swift would be an excellent choice.

'She can come and work with me anytime, she's worth two of any of these buggers,' he confirmed, sweeping his arm in the general direction of his crew. Alan rang Gail and told her she had been unsuccessful for the water operative position but asked if she would be interested if a position came up in a sewage team.

'Not 'arf,' she replied and Alan promised to keep in touch. With his mobile clipped into the cradle on the dashboard, he set off for Sheffield.

§§§

As he pulled onto the estate, Alan remembered why he had been so keen to get away. It looked ten times worse than he recollected. Scrap cars lined the streets; most of them had been broken into and anything of value stolen. The graffiti was worse than he recalled, and more obscene. A row of shops had all been boarded up or shuttered. The one where he used to buy a single Woodbine had been set on fire. He parked his car near his parents' house, hoping that it would be there in the morning, but more importantly, with all four wheels intact. He was welcomed home like the prodigal son. It was nearly six-o'clock and the whole family was there, even Tom, Susie and the three kids, whose names he couldn't remember until Susie screamed, *'Xenobia, Trojan, stop fighting.'*

The memories came flooding back. Last time, when Alan had been told their names, he had looked up the origins. Xenobia was named after the Greek God Zeus, and Trojan was named after a horse. At the time Alan had wondered if the youngest, Tulip Daisy Sheffield Wednesday, would end up with an inferiority complex.

Once his grip was put on what looked like a very narrow single bed, his father announced, 'Us lads are going down't club.' At nine-twenty Alan's mobile rang, caller ID *Sam*.

'Hello.'

She could hardly hear him for background noise.

'Where are you?' He didn't reply but she could hear the noise changing from raucous singing to something slightly quieter. 'Where are you?' she repeated.

'Sheffield, I've come to see my parents.'

Then she heard the sound of a flushing toilet, obviously in the gents' lavatory. She hesitated. Should she leave him to his weekend or should she test him? No contest.

'I'd like to meet up tomorrow for a clear the air meeting, OK?'

'Er. Where?'

'The Splash, shall we say twelve-o'clock?'

Does it have to be tomorrow? I've come to see my family.'

'It's up to you. I'll be there anyway.' Samantha hung up before he could say anything else.

'You bastard,' he shouted at the silent phone. 'You've just done that out of spite.'

Just then his phone pinged with an incoming text, the caller ID, *Number withheld*. It said *See anything you fancy?* accompanied by a nude photo of Margaret Vardy. It was obvious she had been crying, mascara smudged down her cheeks. He decided to wait until he was sober tomorrow morning before choosing whether to meet Samantha or stay in Sheffield.

Chapter 22

Her uncle had been away on holiday when Samantha needed him most. At first she had only wanted to seek his advice on whether to make up with Alan. After the car smashing incident, she was beginning to wonder if Alan was right, he had often told her he was 'damaged goods'. That weekend he had been on television, unshaven and scruffily dressed, obviously guilty of wrecking a car, his hair-trigger temper at work again, he was clearly drinking whisky and his language was unforgivable. In fact his use of expletives was starting to rub off on her. A week later she had seen him with another woman whom he obviously knew well. Why else would they go shopping together? That time he had been smartly dressed, black trousers, white shirt, checked sports jacket, similar to the clothes he wore for work. In Samantha's mind he was obviously trying to impress. She clearly had a rival.

Only yesterday she had overheard two girls from the typing pool talking about him in the canteen.

You'll never guess. Alan Bishop's going out with Margaret Vardy.

No way.

Yes I saw them in Sainsbury's two weeks ago. She was dressed like a tart.

What a waste, he's really fit. I wouldn't mind a rumble or two with him, but she must be twice his age.

Bit like grab-a-granny night eh?

Yeh but she's got a flashy sports car. I can't believe he fancies her.

Was that really Margaret she had seen him with? She looked completely different.

By the time her uncle had returned from holiday, Samantha had a full agenda. She was going to bare her soul to him; the funeral fight, the trashed car, his drinking and swearing, and the other woman. After three hours, her uncle had suggested she arrange a 'clear the air' meeting, somewhere he would feel uncomfortable. What better place than the pub he'd been thrown out of over two months ago.

Now sat in the beer garden outside The Splash in Little Cawthorpe, she had tried to find the same picnic table they had used on the day of the funeral. However, it was the smell of newly mown grass that made her realise that the tables had probably been moved eight or nine times since then. Saturday lunchtime at the end of August, a bank holiday weekend, should have been a busy time, but the biting wind and the threat of rain meant most customers were inside. The only others to brave the cold were a couple of small boys playing noisily around a huge multi-coloured plastic house in the corner of the garden. A man sat close by, occasionally checking on them but more engrossed in his phone, his thumbs flitting across the screen. Samantha shivered, unsure if it was from the cold, or nerves. She pulled her puffa jacket tighter and re-adjusted her college scarf to try and keep out the chill.

While she waited, her uncle's advice floated around in her mind. It had not been what she had wanted to hear. She wanted him to agree that Alan had been at fault on all counts. The words that shocked her most were, *If you're not speaking to him, ignoring him completely, why shouldn't he see someone else? He's a free agent, remember?* She had broken down and cried.

Her mother's words also came back to her. *He's nothing more than a drunken yob.*

Samantha had arrived early and had been sitting at the table for nearly thirty minutes. She had changed her mind about staying nearly as many times. She now regretted choosing The Splash for a meeting as she only knew one way in and out of Little Cawthorpe. If she wanted to leave, she would surely meet Alan entering the village, assuming he was coming. She pushed her untouched and now stone-cold skinny mocha away just as he drove into the pub, his wheels dripping water onto the tarmac, a result of driving through the nearby ford. His white Mondeo was plastered with mud and dirt. It was so unlike him to drive a car looking so filthy, even if it was nearly five years old and due for replacement. Her heart skipped a beat as he gave her a wave after parking outside the pub's front door. Although some distance from him, she heard his mobile ring as he got out of the car. He held it to his left ear, his right hand holding an imaginary glass tipping towards his mouth, signalling drink. Samantha shook her head and waited as he disappeared into the pub, taking her mobile from her pocket, remembering that her *aide-memoire* was stuck inside her phone case.

She scanned down the list, written in the order she was going to follow:
Neighbour's car
Sainsbury's car park
Alcohol
Temper
Foul language
Unhealthy food / Emily
Weight gain
SMDP lipstick photo

A list composed to put him on the back foot. Her uncle's final words came back to her as Alan emerged from the pub's rear entrance. *Start as you mean to go on. Be firm.*

As Alan walked up the slope towards her, he still had his mobile glued to his left ear. In his right hand he carried a glass of clear sparkling liquid with ice and a slice of lemon. Samantha's mind went over the possibilities, but in the end decided he didn't like either gin or vodka. She guessed it was a soft drink. He stopped some distance from her table and continued his telephone conversation. She was annoyed that he felt it was more important to continue the dialogue than to talk to her. A car driving through the village and the noisy kids in the play area meant the only words she heard him say were, 'back-feed.' Even with her limited technical knowledge of the industry, Samantha knew that it meant reversing the direction of flow in a water main. He was obviously talking to someone about work.

Alan finished the call and walked towards her. 'Sorry about that,' he said as he sat opposite her, raising his glass in a toast. 'The new me,' he added, before taking a sip then placing his drink and mobile on the table.

Samantha smiled wanly. Her resolve evaporated as she smelt his aftershave. She had lost count of the number of times she had wished she was snuggled close to him, breathing in that subtle smell. Forgetting all the advice her uncle had given her, she said, 'You look tired.' He nodded slowly. 'Family OK?' He nodded again. 'So what have you been up to then?' She mentally admonished herself; she had already gone off-script.

He raised his eyebrows and smiled. 'Well, three weeks ago I smashed up a neighbour's car, followed by a brief appearance on the local news. Then I was hauled into the boardroom and given a bollocking by Ian Young and the Chairman.' He paused as if trying to recall. 'Oh, and on Tuesday I attended a disciplinary hearing. Apart from that, not a lot.'

Samantha's eyes widened.

'Don't worry, not mine,' he said, referring to the disciplinary hearing. His mobile started ringing again. Even upside down she could read the screen. *LW Control Room.*

Alan muttered an apology and picked up his phone before heading off down the grassy slope towards his car. She was furious. It had taken all her resolve and nerve to set up this meeting and he seemed blasé about its importance. As far as she was concerned it was make or break. She decided to confront him the minute he deigned to grace her with his presence again. What did soften her attitude, however, was the fact that he looked like he had lost some weight. At the funeral he had constantly been pulling at his tight shirt collar and his trouser belt had been let out a notch, the previous position clearly showing the imprint of the metal buckle. She was distracted by three scantily clad girls who had come out of the pub for a cigarette. They were laughing and giggling, presumably talking about friends left in the bar. She hadn't notice he had returned to join her again.

'I don't suppose you know where I can get a JCB 6 fully-fuelled and ready to go?' he asked.

'Why?'

'Because we need to dig a big hole,' he replied flippantly, as he sat down again.

'Wrong answer,' she snapped. 'I meant *why*, as in why did you trash that car?'

'Sorry.' He paused to compose his reply, wanting to pick his words carefully. 'Because that arsehole of a neighbour, Cheryl's employer.' He stopped, couldn't go on, his voice quavering. Samantha leant forward and squeezed his hand. He wiped his damp eyes, then in hardly more than a whisper, added, 'He raped her then gave her £10,000 to keep quiet.'

They sat in silence for a while.

'Bish I don't know what to say.'

He looked up at her, wiped his eyes again with the back of his hands and nodded. 'He's threatening to sue me for criminal damage and attempted murder.'

'Can he do that?'

'Of course he can. He's a bloody solicitor.'

Then his mobile rang again. She still didn't know about the woman with the Mazda MX5. The girls in the office must be wrong. It couldn't be Margaret Vardy.

Chapter 23

'Mummy mummy, come quick, Alan's on the telly again.'
Samantha inwardly groaned. Up to the elbows in soapsuds and greasy pans, she had been cursing her mother's refusal to invest in a dishwasher. Now, only weeks after his last TV appearance where he hurled obscenities at the camera, Alan was back on the screen. As she dried her hands, she shuddered as she remembered her mother's words. *Complete and utter waste of space* and *drunken yob* were proof enough that her mother would never like him. She had no idea what her father thought of him, but if true to form, he would meekly follow the party line. Samantha would never forget the time her mother had once admonished her father for trying to speak out of turn.

'When I want your opinion, I'll give it to you,' she had scolded.

Fortunately only Samantha's auntie and uncle knew that she had tried to meet Alan yesterday. Even Emily had been kept in the dark and taken to a petting farm while Samantha was away.

As she walked into the lounge, Samantha saw Vanessa Redfern stood in front of a huge mobile caravan, the words 'All Day Breakfast' clearly visible over her left shoulder.

We'll now take a short commercial break and when we come back we hope to give you an update on the situation here just outside Scunthorpe.

As the camera panned back, Emily leapt from her chair.

'Mummy, I've been there,' she squealed. 'Alan took me once; he says they do the best sausage sandwiches in the world.'

The realisation of what they had been looking at dawned on all three adults.

A truckers' stop.
In a lay-by.
Somewhere near Scunthorpe.

In Deep Water

'Don't even think it mother,' snapped Samantha in an attempt to forestall another lambasting aimed at Alan. It worked, and they sat in silence until the commercial break ended.

Welcome back and for those viewers who have just joined us, I will give you a quick recap. It is now nearly thirty hours since the people of Scunthorpe have been without water. That's seventy thousand of us who cannot have a drink, boil a kettle, run a bath, or flush a toilet. Among those people are thousands of babies and vulnerable senior citizens who could die because the water company hasn't repaired the burst water main. If the camera moves to my right, you will see the men from Lincs Water sitting drinking tea, something the people of Scunthorpe can't do.

The camera turned to a group of about ten people sat beyond the caravan around two dirty and rusty, previously white, circular tables. Every one of them was wearing a yellow high-vis coat, some were relatively clean but most were covered in mud and filth. About half the group wore waders or high-vis trousers, the others just jeans and jumpers. Several safety helmets were laid on the tables amongst an assortment of disposable cups. Some of the men were enjoying a well-earned cigarette. For some unknown reason, it reminded Samantha of a group of First World War soldiers taking a break before going back into battle.

'Look there's Alan,' squeaked Emily. A chorus of shushes silenced her.

The people of Scunthorpe deserve better than the service they are getting at the moment. I think I can see Alan Bishop again, the company's Area Manager, amongst the crowd; no doubt he can give us some answers.

Vanessa Redfern walked towards the crowd followed by her cameraman husband. As the camera closed on the group, it focussed on Alan who was bent over one of his men, a gangling youth complete with a shaved head, several facial and ear piercings and some highly visible tattoos. The picture zoomed in on the man's neck. A tattoo, 'Made in Grimsby' in full view. Alan had his arm round the chap's shoulders and the microphone picked up the conversation.

Look Stu, you're all in. Go home with the others and get some sleep, OK?

Vanessa Redfern poked her husband in the ribs and the camera swung round towards her.

Well it sounds as if Mr Bishop is sending everyone home, let's see if he will answer a couple of questions.

Raising her voice to attract Alan's attention, she shouted.

Alan what do you say to the rumour that the people of Scunthorpe may not have water for another three days? Are you really all going home now? Have you been saving this work for the bank holiday weekend and overtime rates?

Alan ignored the jibes. He admired politicians for their ability to not answer questions and put across the message they wanted to. He had received similar advice as part of the media training on SMDP.

Good afternoon Vanessa. We now have nearly thirty water bowsers strategically sited around Scunthorpe. Our vans are touring the streets keeping everyone informed, distributing water bottles and helping carry water into people's homes where necessary. The repair to the twenty-four inch water main, which is the main water supply to Scunthorpe, is progressing well.

But why is it going to take three days to repair the burst main?

Alan knew it wouldn't take that long. He had a fresh team on site with Brian Price, the best and most knowledgeable water Superintendant within the company. Scunthorpe wasn't Price's normal area, he had worked out of the Grimsby depot for most of his life, but with his encyclopaedic knowledge and experience, there was no better person to finish off the repair. It should take the new fresh crew about six more hours to complete the repair, and a further four to turn the supply back on. Hopefully, somewhere around midnight the job would be complete, but Alan didn't want to commit to a deadline.

We are doing everything possible to complete the repair. This crew has worked for nearly twenty-four hours non-stop and we'll get them back tomorrow if necessary. We have a fresh team from Grimsby on site as we speak, and now if you'll excuse me, I have to get back to work.

In Deep Water

Yesterday Samantha had been livid at Alan's distractions with phone calls. He had left without really talking. Her idea of a 'clear the air' meeting had fallen flat. He had promised to ring on Saturday evening but hadn't. She certainly wasn't going to give in and ring him; he could have been with that other woman. She now understood why he hadn't called. Realising how much Emily was missing him, on the way home Samantha suggested she talk to him about meeting up next weekend. It would also give them another chance to resolve things. She was desperate to find out about the woman with the flashy sports car. Emily's joy was unconfined but Samantha wasn't anticipating her daughter's next question.

'Can we have another sausage sandwich at that café?'

Samantha's thoughts went back to her list, still stuck inside her mobile phone case. She had always tried to ensure Emily had a healthy diet; a treat for her was a piece of fruit. Samantha was appalled how much sugar, fat and junk food most kids ate. Then Alan came into their lives. More than once Samantha had said to him, '*You* may want to clog your own arteries with cholesterol, but please don't do it to Emily.' It was like water off a duck's back. Ever since his university days Alan had eaten convenience food. Twenty-four hours ago Samantha was itching for a fight with him on several fronts. Now after his disclosures yesterday, she wanted nothing more than to be friends again. In fact she wanted to be more than friends, but now it seemed she had a rival. Life was too short. Yesterday had been the first time they had spoken in nine weeks.

'I'm sure Alan will know of another Michelin star café closer to home, sweetheart.'

§§§

At ten-past-nine Alan was woken by Brian Price tapping on the car window. It was now dark and Alan had no idea how long he'd been snoozing. As he pulled himself up and got out of the car, he saw Vanessa Redfern and her cameraman striding away.

'Sorry Alan, they filmed you sleeping before I could stop them.'

'I don't care, I'm sick to death of the old battleaxe. I've been awake since seven-o'clock yesterday morning, that's . . .' he glanced at his watch but couldn't put his brain into gear, 'a long time.'

'Thirty-eight hours actually, it's time you went home, we're nearly done here.'

Alan nodded. 'OK, and thanks again Brian. Will you also thank the lads for me?'

'Sure, but before you go, what do you want to do about chlorination?'

Alan closed his eyes. 'Oh shit,' he said, loud enough for a dog walker to turn round and stare. Alan lowered his voice. 'We're damned if we do and damned if we don't.'

Since arriving at Lincs Water, Ian Young had always insisted that everyone comply with a set of emergency procedures he had brought with him, presumably from a former employer. The procedures required a repaired water main to be filled with chlorinated water, and allowed to stand for twenty-four hours before being put back into service. Everyone, except Ian Young, knew the measures were years out of date. Alan was also certain that the people of Scunthorpe would go ballistic if they had to wait for another day without water. The alternative was to overdose the main with liquid chlorine to sterilise the repair as it filled up, then put the main straight back into service. Alan was confident if anyone could take this shortcut without mishap, Brian Price could.

'Brian, are you happy to pour liquid chlorine into the main and get it back in service as quickly as possible?'

'No problem.'

'OK, let's do it.'

Chapter 24

It had been two weeks since the Scunthorpe burst main. Alan had promised to meet up with Samantha and resolve their differences, but he was still upset at her insisting he come back from Sheffield to meet her. Samantha was becoming increasingly worried that he didn't seem keen to meet. If he didn't agree to see her this coming weekend, then she would know she had lost him forever. She needed to play her trump card. She would hate herself for doing it, having read hundreds of agony-aunt column-inches about using the kids to keep a relationship alive. *Sod it,* she thought, it was time to use Emily as a last ditch attempt to win him back.

The conversation hadn't gone well, he seemed cold and distant. Samantha worried that he was now seeing someone else, but she still couldn't believe it was Margaret Vardy. In Samantha's view she must be at least fifty or sixty years old, a dried-up prudish spinster. She dismissed the idea from her mind.

'It's not for me you understand, but when Emily saw you in Scunthorpe by the truckers' café, she asked if you would take her there again.' He had agreed, reluctantly Samantha thought, but he had agreed. Next Saturday lunchtime.

§§§

Gordon Reed's office was two doors away from Ian Young's, but at five-thirty on a Friday afternoon, they both knew they wouldn't be disturbed. Reed pushed a can of soda water across the desk towards Alan, beads of condensation emphasising its coldness.

'Courtesy of the boardroom, the strongest I dare nick. I'm sure someone marks the spirit bottles with a pencil.'

'That's yesterday's technology Gordon; nowadays you just use a phone to photograph the bottles and then compare at a later date.'

Alan had found Samantha doing just that in his drinks cabinet when he had been drinking heavily. He had overcome the problem by topping up the bottles with water. The result was a lighter colour, and weaker whisky, but no nagging.

'So what's so hush hush and urgent Gordie?' Alan had heard Reed's wife call him Gordie last night when shouting for him to come to the phone. Alan had been responding to a text he got earlier, *Ring me at home tonight. URGENT.* Reed hated the name, and the angry look was quickly followed by Alan raising a hand in apology.

'I believe you know Bill Waites, Severn Trent's Chief Executive.'

Alan felt numb, his head started to swim. On his final day at SMDP, Bill Waites had peppered him with home truths. *This isn't the first time you've been drunk, - supposed to be the crème de la crème, - bloody disgrace to the good name of the industry, - completely comatose, - going to choke on your own vomit, - Daisy even had to point Percy at the porcelain.* Pick any one from six. That was before the lipstick photo. Alan merely nodded.

'Well, he wants to meet us, just the two of us. No-one else. Not carrot-top. Not even the Chairman.'

'Why?' It came out like a croaking frog. Alan cleared his throat, drank some soda water, tried again. 'Why?'

Reed took a deep breath. 'Lincs Water is in dire financial straits. We are a whisker away from breaching our bank covenants and Lloyds Bank won't extend the facility. End of.'

'End of what? The company?'

Reed nodded, got up and closed the office door. Back in his chair, he went on, 'Yes. Insolvency, receivership, administration, bankruptcy, different words but they all mean the same thing in the end.'

'Hell's bells Gordon, a water company can't go bust. You can't ask a million people to stop pissing and shitting.'

Reed held up his hands; Alan nodded, recognising the need to keep calm.

'This is entirely confidential.' Alan nodded his acceptance of the secret. 'Lloyds Bank came to see the Chairman, Ian and me last week. They told us they have been to see all three of our immediate neighbours with a view to taking over Lincs Water. Anglian and

Yorkshire Water stonewalled Lloyds' overtures straightaway. Severn Trent said they would think about it, hence the request for a meeting, but Bill Waites doesn't want to see Ian, just you and me.'

'What about the Chairman?'

'Between these four walls, his days are numbered.'

'I'm surprised carrot-top didn't throw a sickie.'

'He did, he had three days' off after the bank's visit.'

Alan snorted in derision then asked, 'Why can't we find a buyer for the company, someone with deep pockets? Venture capitalists are often keen to take on lame ducks.'

'The problem is Ofwat, our regulator, is starting to put the squeeze on profits throughout the industry. Margins will fall and dividends will have to be cut. Even some of the big boys are being touted around the marketplace, looking for new owners. Lincs Water will declare a loss this year, which means we will have little chance of finding a buyer.'

'How long?' A feeling of foreboding was starting to envelop Alan.

Gordon looked at the calendar. Friday the thirteenth. 'Well, we're in the middle of September . . . maybe two months, Christmas at the outside.'

'Hell's bells,' Alan said again.

A long silence followed until Reed said, 'I understand you studied finance at SMDP.'

'Yes, I'm a graduate of . . .'

'I know, the Wilkins Micawber School of Economics. Bill told me.' After a short pause he went on. 'So what would Mr Micawber do?'

'Well for a start I would begin charging for new house connections, we are the only company in the country who doesn't. I'd make water meter installation compulsory on new supplies, have a massive drive on leakage and then start cutting overheads. Head office staff numbers have nearly doubled since carrot-top arrived. I'd certainly give him the heave-ho together with forty or fifty others, close that bloody canteen that no-one uses, freeze wages, cut salaries by ten percent. Need I go on?'

'What about investing in the infrastructure to reduce emergencies?'

'That goes without saying. That dimwit of an MD we've been lumbered with thinks if we spend money on capital projects it will have a detrimental impact on the bottom line. He's never heard of depreciation or amortisation. We could spread capital costs over anything up to eighty years in some cases.'

Reed nodded, remembering the battles he'd had with Young since he joined the company. 'What about increasing charges?'

'As far as I'm aware, those are set by Ofwat every five years. I suppose we could always ask the question.'

After three hours and half a notepad full of scribbled ideas, they called it a day. Reed promised to keep in touch. On the way out Alan borrowed a black felt tip pen, and when walking past the MD's locked office door, on the brass sign:

Mr I F Young
Managing Director

he wrote TAPS.

On the drive home Alan's thoughts turned to Bill Waites. The last time they had met was at Cheryl's funeral, Alan remembered thinking at the time that Bill didn't have to come, let alone bring his wife. They didn't even know Cheryl so they must have come as an act of support for him. Comforted by that thought, he decided a face-to-face with Bill Waites might not be so bad after all.

§§§

It was nearly ten-o'clock when Alan got home, and as he stopped in front of the garage, a dark-coloured Fiesta pulled up outside the house. An attractive woman got out and walked up the drive to meet him.

'Alan?' she asked.

'Yes.'

'Could you spare me five minutes?'

It was only when she followed him into the hall, into the brighter light, that he recognised her. It was one of those 'I know you from somewhere, but I can't remember where' moments. Going into the lounge, wanting some thinking time, he muttered something about it being chilly, windows on night-latch. He closed the curtains, lit the gas fire and asked if she wanted a drink, and as he stood in front of her, two tumblers in his hands, he remembered. It wasn't her attractive face, shapely figure or green eyes that triggered his memory. It was the proliferation of freckles and her ginger hair, today tied back in a ponytail.

'You were at Cheryl's funeral weren't you?'

Her eyes lowered as the memories came flooding back. She merely nodded, then managing to compose herself, took the proffered glass and sipped the dark liquid.

'You must think I'm awful, I forgot my manners, my name is Alexandria Murray, but everyone calls me Alex.' She offered her hand, but he didn't take it. He started trembling, the surface of the whisky in his glass rippling. He drank it in one gulp.

'I'm sorry what did you say?' She repeated her name. 'Why have you come here?'

She sensed the anger in his voice. 'There's something you need to know, something I have to tell you.'

Chapter 25

It was nearly midday when Alan finally fell out of bed, metaphorically speaking. The unexpected meeting with Cheryl's lover last night had lasted nearly two hours and almost a full bottle of Glenfiddich. Anymore and he would have had difficulty remembering what Alex had said. He now regretted drinking the whisky. For the past three or four months he had prided himself in almost giving up drink. The odd beer or two several times a week was perfectly acceptable in his view, wine didn't count either, and that's the way it had been until last night. It was the familiar burning sensation of the whisky in his throat and stomach that brought back memories of his former life. A former life not too long ago, a life he knew he could still easily slide back into; all he needed was an excuse. Last night that excuse had turned up on his doorstep.

Things had been fine to start with, but the turning point had been when she asked if she could have Cheryl's secret journal. To say his flippant comment about serialising the diaries in the Daily Mail had not been a good idea, would have been a massive understatement. She had flown into a rage, calling him every disgusting name she could think of, talking to him as if he was something she had stepped in. Normally he would have been more than a match, able to swap insults with the best, but his slurred speech and fuddled brain hampered him.

The ringing landline brought him back to the present.

'I thought you were taking us out for lunch? Emily is looking forward to another gourmet sausage sandwich.'

His slurred, slowly delivered words, 'Something came up,' were enough to make Samantha realise he'd been drinking. When he explained that Alex had called round to his house last night, Samantha feared the worst. She hoped that he had kept his temper in check and the two of them had not been fighting. She couldn't believe it when he said, 'Alex is a woman.' Samantha suddenly had hundreds of questions she wanted to ask. She also had her own bombshell she wanted to drop. He cut across her thoughts.

'Look Sam, apologise to Em, I'll take you both for an early bird meal at Luigi's, and when she's gone to bed we can talk then, OK?'

'She's going to Lizzie's for a sleepover, but I'll talk to Sharon and tell her she'll be late. If you've been drinking wait until about four-o'clock before you drive the car.' She paused. 'Remember it'll break her heart if you let her down again.'

Again? he thought, but said nothing.

§§§

Luigi had squeezed them into a corner at the back of the restaurant. Saturday night was always busy and they hadn't booked. They had planned to arrive earlier but it was nearly six-o'clock by the time they got there, having to park in a car park some distance away. Luigi was crouched down next to his favourite customer, as low as his arthritic knees would allow.

'Emily, *mia bambina*, what would you like today?'

She was sat close to Alan, holding his arm tightly, as if to stop him disappearing from her life again. Her limpet-like grip on him hadn't gone unnoticed. 'Please may I have an orange juice and a double pepperoni pizza with anchovies, olives, mushrooms, peppers and mozzarella?' Emily was one of the few customers for whom Luigi would ask chef Gino to make something special, not on the normal menu.

'The usual size?' he asked.

She released her grip on Alan and spread her arms wide. 'No, this big, Alan and I will share.' Alan screwed up his face at the thought.

Although it was nearly eight months since Alan had visited the restaurant, Luigi recognised him. After completing the order he said, 'You are a very lucky man to have two such beautiful ladies at your table.'

Once Luigi was out of earshot, Samantha leant forward and whispered, 'He obviously can't see how thin the ice is around here.'

Her angry look worried him. He was yet to learn that two days ago Margaret Vardy had gone to see Samantha and told her everything.

Alan raised his hands in surrender. 'Whoa, let's just enjoy the meal, eh?' She slowly nodded in agreement.

After the meal, Emily spotted that one of the bar stools facing the kitchen was free. It was where customers could sit and enjoy a drink, waiting for a free table, and watch the kitchen staff at work. She asked if she could watch Gino as she loved seeing him throw pizza dough into the air with apparent abandon. Samantha nodded her agreement, happy to have some privacy. As Emily walked towards the empty stool, she exchanged a wave with Gino.

With Emily out of earshot, Alan told Samantha about Alex's visit and what she had said. Gerald Smith-Etherington had plied Cheryl with drink one Friday lunchtime and forced himself on her. Alan had asked if Alex would give evidence in court, but being a fellow solicitor, even from a rival firm, she had refused.

'She asked me if she could have Cheryl's diary and I said no, suggesting instead I sell the story to one of the papers. That's when she lost it.'

'Is it any wonder? What happened then?'

'Mistake number two. I started to remember bits from the journal and goaded her with the sordid details.' Samantha lowered her head into her hands. Uncomfortable with the silence, he went on, 'When she left . . .'

'You mean she just walked out?' Samantha asked incredulously.

Alan's hand instinctively went to his right forearm. Samantha just stared at him. Eventually her glare proved too much and he slowly unbuttoned his shirt sleeve and pulled it up to reveal several scratches and wealds.

'You seem to be making a habit of fighting with women,' she said, unable to hide the sarcasm in her voice.

'I think I'd better go,' he said meekly.

'Not before you tell me why you've started drinking again, when you assured me you'd stopped.' She paused for affect. 'Oh, and while we're in a talkative mode, you can tell me about the woman with the flashy red MX5.'

In Deep Water

§§§

Back at the apartment, with Emily safely delivered to Lizzie's for her sleepover, Samantha waved Alan towards the kitchen while she went to change into something more comfortable. When she joined him she was pleased to see he was sat at the dining table with a glass of red wine. She poured herself a large one and walked over to the table, towering over him.

She said, 'I know,' in a chilling tone.

He turned and looked up at her, his neck twisted upwards, feeling totally disadvantaged. His eyes flicked left and right as his mind spun wildly looking for answers, eventually settling on a red MX5 in Sainsbury's car park.

'Know what?' he asked meekly.

'About you and Margaret Vardy.' Her cold voice sent shivers through his body. He felt the heat rise from his neck to cover his whole face. He tried to stand up, but a hand placed firmly on his shoulder prevented him.

'Look Sam I'm sorry, it was a one-off. You weren't speaking . . .'

'One-off,' she screamed. *'One-off, you are fucking joking.'* She took a deep breath, trying to calm herself. 'She came to see me, "full of remorse", she said, told me about your trip through *Hotel Erotica*, all ten rooms. Eleven if you count Room Nine twice.'

'The bitch, the fucking bitch. Can't you see what she's trying to do?'

'Seven weeks, that's all. Can't you keep your dick in your pants for seven weeks?' Samantha yelled as she threw a punch at his head.

Chapter 26

Sharon was looking forward to her evening meal. Frank, her husband, was home on three weeks' leave and was in the kitchen preparing dinner. He was a chef on one of the oil and gas rigs off the Lincolnshire coast, and Sharon always enjoyed his spells at home when she could put her feet up. Frank even did the shopping when he was back on land, preferring to buy from the local family-run artisan bakers, butchers and fishmongers, rather than a supermarket. Sharon always took the line of least resistance when it came to shopping. Once a week at Sainsbury's. Her daughter Lizzie had eaten and was playing with Emily. Sharon picked up her wine glass and wandered through to the kitchen to see how things were progressing. Frank was busy, finely chopping spring onions for a garnish.

The noise was much louder than in the lounge. Although the penthouse above them was larger than their flat, the kitchens were in the same position for drainage purposes. With only a hard floor-covering, and no carpet to deaden the noise, they could hear almost every word.

Frank said, matter-of-factly, 'Sounds like he's been playing away from home. Several times. Lucky bugger. Not sure where Sainsbury's comes into it though.'

'The language is very crude, that's not like Samantha. I'll give her a ring, just make sure everything's alright.' Sharon returned a couple of minutes later. 'Mobile just goes to voicemail and she's not answering the landline.'

The sound of breaking glass was quickly followed by an increase in shouting, then another glass shattering.

'I'll pop up and see if they're OK,' said Frank. Sharon could hear him banging on their door, even a floor above. When he returned he said, 'They're not answering the door either. If it doesn't stop soon I'm calling the police.'

§§§

Samantha enjoyed Sunday mornings and if the weather was nice, as it was today, she would sit outside on the veranda. A week after their monumental argument, Samantha had apologised to the neighbours, and she and Alan had called a fragile truce. Since then he had rung her most nights. This morning she had laid down the law, her voice cold, calm, and measured.

'Bish, - this - is - the - last - throw - of - the - dice.' She paused between every word. 'I am sick up to here,' emphasised with hand movements above her head, 'of your constant bad language, bad tempers, continued excessive drinking and now this . . . Anymore and I will never speak to you again. Understand?'

Alan and Emily had then gone ice skating, Alan keen to escape her wrath, Samantha hoping he would realise what he might end up missing. Now armed with a cup of coffee, she reclined the patio chair and lay back to soak up the sun. Dressed only in a running vest and shorts, the heat from the sun on her skin made her sleepy. It was only when the sun went behind a cloud did it seem chilly, like a typical September morning. The hypnotic effect of the cathedral bells calling the congregation to worship added to the feeling of well-being. At eleven-o'clock she knew her peace would be shattered. Her mother would ring with her usual, 'What time will you be here for lunch?' question. Today it would be quickly followed by, 'And why not?'

For the first three years of Emily's life, Samantha's mother had refused to talk to either of them. However, realising that she had been sidelined, Karen Hyde had welcomed them back into the family as if nothing had happened. She started inviting Samantha and Emily for Sunday lunch but it soon became obligatory. Then Karen took it upon herself to start match-making, blind dates sometimes turning up unannounced. Karen had a very strict selection procedure. Only professional men, doctors, dentists, accountants or solicitors, would be good enough for her daughter. No-one else could possibly be suitable, and they must wear a suit and tie.

'And when does love come into it?' Samantha had once asked.

'It doesn't,' had been the reply.

At the age of thirty Samantha needed to break away, and if she and Alan could sort out their differences, then that would be the excuse to cut the apron strings. Today she would simply say that Emily had been taken skating by a 'friend'.

Samantha was woken by the phone ringing at eleven-fifteen, and had only been talking to her mother for a few minutes when the video system from the front entrance door buzzed. Keen to get away from the cross-examination, she quickly ended the call without being made to promise to call back.

'We're back.' Alan's voice was a lifeless monotone. Samantha pressed the video door entry to allow them into the building. She opened the apartment door and waited for them to come up the three floors in the lift. She wondered if the ice rink had been closed for some reason, although Sunday was always one of their busiest days.

'What happened? Was there a problem?' she asked.

'No problem,' Alan replied shaking his head, hoping Samantha would let it drop.

She wouldn't. 'Emily?' Tears welled up in her daughter's eyes. 'Emily, what happened?'

Emily remained silent, so Alan answered instead. 'She used the F-word so we came home.'

Samantha looked at Emily and raised her arm, pointing towards the utility room. 'Naughty corner. Now.'

As Emily sloped off, head bowed, Alan said, 'Sam, she's been punished. Once is enough, she doesn't deserve the naughty corner *as well*.' Samantha looked at him, her raised eyebrows asking the question. 'I smacked her, OK?'

'*No it's not OK*,' she yelled, 'how dare you smack my daughter when she's in your care?'

With tempers and voices rising on both sides, Alan replied, 'Look Sam, when an eight year old says, "I can't get this fucking skate on", she deserves to be slapped. It was an instinctive reaction.'

'You just can't keep your temper in check, or your hands to yourself can you?' she snarled. 'First Cheryl, then me, now Emily.'

'Oh fuck it; I'm going to the pub for another three months of silence.'

'See what I mean.' Then as an afterthought, 'Which one?'

'The Plough,' he shouted over his shoulder, heading for the door.

'So you can stagger home drunk, I suppose,' she yelled, unsure if he'd heard.

Hearing the door slam, thinking she had lost him forever, Emily screamed, '*Noooo.*'

§§§

The pub was still quiet; the football team were playing away at Leasingham, a good hour's drive from Louth. That didn't include the time the lads would spend in the Duke of Wellington before they left. As he took the first sip of his third pint, Alan wondered if the last week had really been nothing more than a dream. It had started last weekend. Reading between the lines, it looked as if Lincs Water wouldn't last until Christmas. If Lloyds Bank pulled the plug Alan had no idea what would happen.

The discovery of the company's financial plight was quickly followed by a verbal and physical fight with Alex Murray. Saturday had been fairly quiet until teatime, but only because he had been home alone. That night he had been grilled by Samantha who believed he had begun drinking again, never mind the weekend with Margaret Vardy he had been forced to admit was true.

Today he had chastised Emily and upset her. No wonder. They hadn't seen each other for three months and he ended up smacking her. During the quiet drive back to Lincoln he had tried to explain why she should tell her mother. 'It's wrong to have secrets,' he had said. 'I'll let you tell her in your own time, but you must promise me you will.' She had agreed, and then he just blurted it out himself. He had let Emily down. Another argument with Samantha, and it still wasn't yet two-o'clock.

In the event of the company going belly-up, there was always plan B. Margaret Vardy was seriously rich and over-sexed, and with £2 million, neither of them would ever have to work again. But in reality there was no plan B. He knew it had been nothing more than a one night stand. Two nights actually. During his ordeal, because that's the way he now looked back on those two days, he quickly got the impression he was being used to fulfil her fantasies.

At first he naively thought it would help Margaret, or Kate, whoever she was, exorcise her demons. After two days and nights of extremely tiring and noisy sex, totally drained of all his strength and stamina, he was glad to escape. At times, it had seemed to him that she was trying to rewrite the *Kama Sutra,* complete with soundtrack. He had once read that the appetite of a love-hungry woman far exceeded the capacity of a man. How true it had been that weekend.

He smelt her perfume before she spoke. 'Penny for your thoughts?' He blushed; turned around slowly, wondering what kind of mood she would be in. 'Look, Emily's just gone to the toilet. She wants to make up, but please be gentle with her; she's been sobbing continuously since you left.' He nodded and they waited in silence.

'Hello pet, come and give me a hug. I want to apologise for smacking you.'

Initially Emily hadn't liked being called 'pet' until Samantha had explained that Alan had picked up the term of endearment from his university days in Newcastle. It now made her feel special.

'Would you like a drink? Wine, beer or whisky?'

'An orange juice please.'

'And some crisps? What flavour?'

Emily gave Samantha a furtive look. Samantha sighed, and then nodded.

'Cheese and onion please.'

Alan turned to Samantha. 'If only *all* my problems could be solved with orange juice and crisps.'

Emily moved away to sit at a table in the bay window. Samantha took Alan's hand and asked, 'Can we start again? These last three months have been hell.'

He nodded, and locked in each others' arms, they kissed passionately. Emily watched and pulled a face. Everything was going to be OK.

Samantha pulled him close, her lips touching his ear. He could smell her perfume on her neck and hair. She whispered, 'The photo of you modelling lip gloss is doing the rounds.'

'But that was months ago,' he said, pulling away from her.

'Just make sure *that* skeleton stays in the cupboard.'

Chapter 27

Sir Bertie and George Thomas sat in a comfortable silence at opposite sides of the large oak farmhouse kitchen table. None of the eight oak and pine dining chairs around the table matched. Sir Bertie had pulled his favourite captain's chair from its usual position at the head of the table to sit facing George. At first Sir Bertie hadn't liked the informality of mismatched furniture, but he had grudgingly accepted that it complemented the themed room. The kitchen had been tastefully refurbished under Moira's supervision, three of the walls half-covered in antique tiles; the remainder roughly plastered to give a farmhouse feel to the kitchen. The floor had been laid in reclaimed York flagstones.

On the wall opposite the windows, a solid fuel Aga blasted out heat seven or eight months of the year. Close by, an electric oven and induction hob were available for cooking during the summer months. Kitchen appliances had been integrated into bespoke units, and copper pots and pans hung around the walls. In the corner of the room, a recently acquired old and sagging two-seater floral settee was awaiting collection by the upholsterer. A Belfast sink completed the overall impression that, despite being a mix of old and new, there was a strong Victorian feel to the room. On the table between the two men lay several blown up photos, an A4 folder, a decanter of whisky, and two glasses.

Since Sir Bertie met George Thomas over three years ago, George had proved an invaluable asset both to their home and Sir Bertie's business life. They had easily overcome the problems linked to Thomas's court case following his heavy-handed restraining of the One Hand Gang. The case had been quickly resolved when the local prosecution lawyer virtually threw in the towel when he had realised he was up against one of London's top QCs. Sir Bertie had kept his promise and offered Thomas a job as a gardener cum chauffeur, on three conditions. He had spelt them out.

'Get rid of the pony tail, wear long sleeves to cover the tattoos, and give up smoking.' George had protested, but Sir Bertie was adamant. 'There is no way I'm having you in my car stinking of cigarettes. It's take it or leave it George.' He had reluctantly agreed.

After a couple of months, Sir Bertie offered George and his wife, Shirley, use of the two bedroom gatehouse situated at the entrance to the Foxton Manor estate. Moira quickly discovered Shirley was an excellent cook and she soon became the Manor's cook and housekeeper. Although Moira herself had won many baking, cooking, and pickling prizes at the local WI meetings, she was sensible enough to realise that it was only since she had become Lady Campbell that the awards started to appear.

George said, 'I'm getting too old for this JB. You did say this was the last one, didn't you?'

After three years they had become friends and, in private, it was first name terms. In public it was always 'Sir Bertie', and 'Lady Campbell'.

'I am too, if truth be known,' replied Sir Bertie just as Moira walked into the kitchen. They had both thought she had long since gone to bed.

She froze in the doorway as her eyes caught sight of the photos on the table. Sir Bertie quickly scooped them up with his right arm, and roughly shuffled them into the A4 folder, out of sight.

'JB you promised me,' she hissed, unable to hide her rising anger.

'Sweetheart,' he paused, momentarily lost for words. 'This is the last one, I promise you. George is as tired of it as you are, but if we nail this, then it will nearly double the size of Campbell Homes, and then we can float it on the stock exchange and retire.'

'Bullshit, you make nothing but pie-crust promises.' She went to the drawer at the end of the table and pulled out a pile of press cuttings from a large envelope. 'Just read these, remind yourself what a ruthless bastard you can be.' She thrust the cuttings under his nose and waited. Sir Bertie didn't move. 'Right then, let me help you, this one's from the Daily Express,' she said, grabbing the top sheet.

Campbell Homes' owner, Sir Bertie Campbell, was knighted five years ago in recognition of creating one of the largest and most successful privately owned companies in the country. But at what cost? Since its formation nearly thirty years ago, Campbell Homes has grown organically and, more significantly, by acquisition. In the early days, the company's acquisitions were seamlessly integrated, every new member of staff being guaranteed a job. That, unfortunately, didn't last long and more recently a ruthlessness has come to the surface, staff made redundant, salaries slashed, benefits cut, and promises broken.

Just when we thought it couldn't get any worse, shortly after being knighted, Sir Bertie employed an ex-SAS soldier, George Thomas, initially as a chauffeur, but more recently as the company's Business Opportunities Manager. That's business speak for bully. Thomas earned the nickname 'Silent Assassin' during the Benton Builders takeover. He allegedly followed and spied on members of Benton's staff, getting whatever dirt he could for Sir Bertie Campbell to use during the negotiations. Although Jim Benton didn't register a formal complaint, he said from his new villa in Spain, "It seems strange that only five of our thirty-four full-time members of staff chose to join Campbell Homes."

'Should I go on? Do you want me to read another article?' she said as she flicked through the cuttings.

Moira was fuming. 'We have the Daily Telegraph, the Yorkshire Post, the Daily Mail, and the Lincolnshire Echo. You even made it into the Daily Record from bonnie Scotland,' unable to hide the sarcasm in her voice.

'Sweetheart I promise this will be the last,' Sir Bertie replied meekly as Moira towered over him, hands on hips.

He picked up the decanter, poured himself a hefty measure, and downed it in one as his hackles rose and his voice hardened. 'I'll tell you why I'm going for this one last takeover. It's simple. I intend to stop Clive Oglanby blackmailing and bribing Council officials.'

'What do you mean?'

Sir Bertie pulled the first photo that came to hand from his folder, and pushed it across the table to Moira. She stared at it incredulously. In black and white, it showed a young naked woman, hands tied to an overhead beam with two nude men pawing her, unable to hide their excitement. One was very thin and tall, and the other short and extremely obese. Their faces were clearly visible.

Moira's eyes widened questioningly as she looked down on her husband.

'That's how Clive Oglanby gets his planning permissions so easily. Those men are the Chief Executive and Planning Officer of West Kesteven District Council. Oglanby's blackmailing them.' Conscious that Moira was lost for words Sir Bertie went on, 'He's also bribing the officials he can't tempt into his honey pot.'

Moira felt her legs weaken and she sat down heavily. 'Who's the woman?'

'I'll not bore you with all the sordid details. Her name is Valentina Petrescu, Oglanby's common-law wife. She came to England seven years ago and worked for an escort agency in London, that's how they met. Oglanby tempted her up to Lincolnshire with the promise of £3000 a week if she "entertained" some of his friends.' Air quotes emphasised the word. 'George did some covert surveillance and soon discovered the sex parties took place on Wednesday nights. She's got a tidy sum invested offshore now which she uses to look after her eight year old daughter back in Romania. However, two weeks ago someone from London turned up on her doorstep with two heavies. They raped and beat her to a pulp for running away. She was covered in bruises; her left eye was swollen and closed, so the next day George followed her and after a cagey introduction, she spilled the beans. She wants out, and for £150,000 she has given us the full details, and all the evidence.'

'Poor girl, is she alright now?'

'Yes, she's fine and next Tuesday I'll have the paperwork ready, and the money required to buy Oglanby Land Developments. That's all I want, his land bank; he can keep the building company. We'll pick her up when we leave and take her to the airport.'

'How do you know Oglanby will agree to sell?'

'Because Valentina's visitor, Dmitri Talanov, is an enforcer for a large Russian mafia gang in London, and Oglanby had always told her to film any action in the playroom.' Sir Bertie picked up a DVD from the folder in front of him and raised it in the air triumphantly.

In Deep Water

'What about the press? Won't they hound you again?'

Sir Bertie shook his head. 'As far as they're concerned, this time I'll be the lesser of two evils.'

§§§

It hadn't taken Alan long to discover that sexting, the act of sending sexually explicit messages or images, was not illegal if both parties were over the age of consent, and willing participants. However, he had never agreed to Margaret's barrage of texts, or replied to any of them. He could make a case for sexual harassment, but with things so delicately balanced with Samantha, he had decided to keep quiet and hope that Margaret would eventually stop sending them.

At first it had been mostly innocent; merely statements about loneliness and pictures of her sad face, but that didn't last long. It soon turned into a flood of suggestive texts accompanied by sexually explicit photos, and reminders of their activities during their time together. It had been over two months since that weekend, and he wished she would tire of sending the messages. That was, until last week. The latest message had thrown his mind into a spin. Within hours he was wondering whether he wanted to spend the rest of his life with Margaret, or Samantha.

To a third party, the message would have been innocuous. For Alan, it brought all the memories bubbling to the surface again. The text simply said, *Lucky No 9*. The attached photo showed only her left wrist, with a studded leather cuff around it, tied with rope to the corner post of the bed. Room Nine had been the fantasy they had enacted twice. The second time, at her request, he had bound and gagged her. It had been the best sex he could ever remember.

Not that he had much to compare it with. The marital bed had started as predictable, soon changing to infrequent, and ending up as non-existent. Even a threesome last Christmas with an ex-employee and her oversexed daughter paled into insignificance compared to his time in Room Nine. He hadn't realised a woman could get so much enjoyment, for so long, as Mags did that night. The problem was he had no idea what he had done to satisfy her so completely.

Chapter 28

Even on the journey to Honeysuckle Drive, Samantha wasn't sure if she had done the right thing. She had accepted an invitation for herself and Alan to have Sunday lunch at her parents. Emily was away on a school trip and Karen Hyde had insisted they come for lunch.

'We need to get to know him better,' she had said. What she hadn't told Samantha was that she didn't want her to stop coming for Sunday lunch again. In order to see her daughter and grand-daughter every week, if she had to invite a 'drunken yob' into her house, then that's the way it had to be. She was sure Samantha would see the light and ditch him again. Hopefully sooner rather than later.

As they pulled onto the drive, Samantha had said, 'Promise me you won't lose your temper or swear.'

'I promise.'

'Or drink too much.'

'Sam, for fuck's sake . . .'

'There you go already.'

'Well Em's not here, is she?'

'Just behave yourself, or you can walk home.'

Alan was surprised that Samantha's parents lived in a semi. He had expected more. Karen and David Hyde were stood at the front door waiting. Samantha remembered the last time she visited her parents. *He's a complete and utter waste of space . . . Nothing more than a drunken yob.* It promised to be an interesting day.

As she entered the kitchen, Samantha saw the half empty bottle of cooking sherry. She also knew that her father liked malt whisky and would be tempting Alan. She couldn't be in two places at once. Before, and during lunch, the conversation had been stilted, almost monosyllabic.

In Deep Water

David again tried to make conversation. His wife wasn't any help whatsoever. She had spent most of the time staring at Alan, the hatred obvious in her eyes. It hadn't gone unnoticed, Samantha privately hoping Alan would behave himself, or at least try and make a good impression.

'Samantha tells us you have a doctorate, Alan,' David said.

'Yes that's right.'

'What did you study?'

'Anaerobic sewage treatment.'

'What exactly is that?'

Alan, happy to talk about his favourite subject, opened up and gave a detailed overview of how the anaerobic micro-organisms could live without oxygen, needing only food and liquid to survive.

'You mean like wee and poo?'

'Exactly,' replied Alan.

'And what did you discover in your three years studying these fascinating creatures?'

'Simply that they love yoghurt and hate bleach,' said Alan enthusiastically, starting to enjoy the conversation.

'Oh please,' interrupted Karen loudly. The room went quiet again. 'Couldn't you have studied something useful, like medicine instead of *sewage*?'

Alan's temper flared, his hands thumped the table causing the cutlery to jingle, and he half rose. He glared at her. 'It may be shit to you Karen, but it's my bread and butter.'

David laughed out loud until an angry look from his wife choked the sound in his throat. Before Alan had a chance to sit down again, Samantha stood up next to him, and, in as cheerful a voice as she could muster, said, 'Well, I think it's time *we* went home.'

Before she started the car, she turned to Alan and said, 'Well that went fucking well, didn't it?'

'Language Samantha,' he chided. They both started laughing.

§§§

'What's all this "It may be shit to you but it's my bread and butter" malarkey? Where did that come from?'

'Spur of the moment thing. I thought it was quite funny.'

'So did Dad.' They looked at each other and smiled. Samantha leaned over and gave him a quick kiss. They were sat outside a pub, close to the city centre. Samantha had just felt the need to talk and had pulled into the car park. Where better than the convivial atmosphere of a pub? Although it was mid-October, the afternoon sun was warm, away from the breeze, and the bar and dining room were still full of folks relaxing after their Sunday lunch, so they took their drinks outside. Unlike The Splash, there was no garden or playground for kiddies, just a wide paved area with half a dozen small tables and chairs, fronting onto a quiet street. Samantha felt she owed it to Alan; she wanted to try and explain her mother's outburst, most likely because of her drinking sherry before they arrived, and her comments about his previous television appearance. Her words came back to Samantha. *Utter waste of space* and *drunken yob* were going to be difficult to bring into the conversation without his temper erupting again.

'Sam, can I ask you a personal question?'

She nodded, but it took a minute or two for Alan to pluck up courage. 'Stop me if you think . . .' She leant forward across the table and squeezed his hands encouragingly. 'I just wondered if Em's father pays you any maintenance.'

She was shocked and leant back in her chair. She was expecting him to mention the disaster of a family lunch they had just left.

'Why do you ask that?'

'Well it's just . . . look, tell me to mind my own business if you like.' She shook her head. 'Well, you live in a fantastic part of town, in what an estate agent would call a penthouse.'

'It's what *I* call a penthouse as well.'

He held up his hands in surrender. 'Sorry, you live in a penthouse, with concierge service, you have a one year old car, Em goes to a fee-paying school, you are talking about sending her to a public school when she's eleven and . . .'

'And?'

'And then you lent me £4000 which you seemed to whisk out of thin air. I can only guess what your salary is but it just doesn't add up.'

'Oh I see, the Mr Micawber School of Economics at work again, eh? Annual income twenty pounds etcetera etcetera.'

'Well you can't blame me for wondering if Em's father is footing the bill.'

'No he's not. In fact he doesn't even know Emily exists.' Alan's mouth fell open in surprise. 'You always gape when you're shocked.' He shut it immediately. She went on, 'When our final year at university finished, we had a party. We all got drunk and I slept with him. We went our separate ways and I never told him I was pregnant. At the degree ceremony I wore loose clothing and kept out of his way. As far as the penthouse and car are concerned, they're not mine. My uncle's company own them, it's a tax dodge. The company's profits are in the millions, and I mean millions, so it helps reduce the tax bill.'

'Will I ever meet your uncle and auntie? I don't even know their names.' Alan was hoping Samantha would tell him about this secretive side of the family. She didn't want to because he would go straight home and Google her uncle whose notoriety was spreading day by day. She wanted to introduce them face to face before Alan found out about his much maligned business dealings.

'Of course you will. After today they're about all the family I've got left.'

Still trying to prise more information from her, he said, 'You seem a lot closer to your uncle than your auntie.'

'Yes, that's true. They got married late in life; I was fifteen before I met her.' Wanting to change the subject, after a short pause, she went on. 'Anyway, what did you think of my mum and dad?'

'Well speaking bluntly, as Yorkshire folk sometimes do, your mother has all the warmth of a slab of granite, and she's such a snob I bet she thinks her shit doesn't stink. As for your father, he's nothing more than a doormat.'

Although shocked by his candour, Samantha could only nod in agreement.

Chapter 29

The Bentley stopped 300 metres short of the house. Sir Bertie stared at it in disbelief. It had started life as a windmill which had been derelict for many years. Clive Oglanby had bought it for a song then extended it on three sides. The two sides in view were concrete and glass monstrosities, proportionally way too big for the dwarfed windmill in-between.

'If I hadn't seen it with my own eyes, I wouldn't have believed it.'

George nodded in agreement. He had spent many days, sometimes late into the night, lying under a Land Rover Defender, or in a damp wet ditch, camera in hand, watching the comings and goings of guests. They both sat in silence for two or three minutes while Sir Bertie steeled himself for the meeting. Oglanby was a big man who was known to be violent.

'OK George, let's get this over with.' George's right hand instinctively moved to his ankle to check the snug fitting revolver. He didn't expect to have to use it, but having turned forty some time ago, he was all for taking the easy option. During his time in the forces, George used to refer to such weapons as pea-shooters, which, if some distance from the target, would have insufficient power to cause an exit wound. However a member of the public would still be intimidated when looking down the barrel. One warning shot to prove it was loaded would still leave five rounds to get the job done. His weapon of choice, when in the army, had been a nine millimetre version of the Sig Sauer P226 with an extended twenty round magazine. Swiss-made, it was engineered and crafted as skilfully as the watches for which the country was famous. The Sig had mysteriously vanished when George left the army, but it was too big and bulky to hide in civilian clothing.

In Deep Water

George put the car into drive and let it roll gently forward towards the house. Once outside the double oak doors, he stopped the car. The men looked at one another and nodded. 'Once more unto the breach,' muttered Sir Bertie.

'Remember to tell Harry, England, and Saint George this is the last one,' added George caustically. Sir Bertie turned and stared at his friend in surprise. 'Shakespeare's Henry V,' he explained.

Sir Bertie Campbell stood nervously at the front door waiting for someone to answer. His unease increased when he heard a man's voice bellow, '*Whoever it is, I'm out.*' Clive Oglanby was a cigar-smoking, fist-swinging, scotch-drinking, wife-beating ogre of a man, forty years older than the sweet, timid woman who answered the door.

Immediately recognising George, she whispered, 'He in library, follow me,' in her stilted English.

Sir Bertie took a deep breath, gripped his briefcase tightly, and pulled himself to his full height. All five-foot-seven. George could sense his unease and led the way. Valentina Petrescu opened the library door and showed them in, before quietly making her exit. Although it was not yet ten-o'clock, Clive Oglanby was sat in a high-backed winged armchair with a glass of whisky in one hand and a cigar in the other.

'*What the fuck do you want Campbell?*' he yelled. To emphasise his perceived superiority, he always shouted.

Sir Bertie moved to sit in the chair opposite him, a coffee table between them. 'I've come to buy your company,' he revealed, as calmly as he could, trying to dilute the obvious anger Clive Oglanby felt towards him. His dulcet, soft, Scottish accent did little to placate the situation.

'*Fuck off out of here before I throw you and your hit-man out.*'

Reminded of George's presence, Sir Bertie turned to see him standing by the door, arms folded, and legs apart. In gangster movies, George would have been described as one of Sir Bertie's 'heavies'. Except he wasn't; he was thin and wiry with muscles as hard as steel. He had that look which said, 'don't even think about it' without a word being said. Gaining in confidence, Sir Bertie turned back.

'Actually it's not your building company I want to buy; it's Oglanby Land Developments you are going to sell me. I am willing to pay £4 million and I have already drawn up a contract.' He pushed a four-page document across the coffee table which Oglanby immediately grabbed and tore in two, his face red with rage.

Having anticipated the move, Sir Bertie took another copy of the contract from his briefcase and slid that across the table. It took ten minutes for Oglanby to calm down, during which time Sir Bertie explained that they had a video of Valentina having sex with Dmitri Talanov.

'Who the fuck's he when he's at home?'

George took up the story. 'He's Valentina's ex-pimp and an enforcer for the largest Russian mafia gang in London. If he ever finds out this DVD . . .' he lifted it out of his pocket, 'was shot in your house he would murder you. If you're lucky, he'll put a bullet through your brain. If you're not, he'll inject you with something that will take three weeks to kill you and half way through . . .' George let the sentence hang, unfinished.

A silence of almost five minutes was eventually broken by Oglanby who turned to Sir Bertie. 'What's the deal?' his voice barely audible.

'Simple, I buy your Land Development company which contains your entire land bank for £4 million, and then I sell the three huge plots back to you for £3 million. That way you continue trading and I keep the rest, all the small packages of land.'

It took Oglanby less than a minute to decide. The implications of not signing were life threatening. 'You bastard,' he muttered as he handed Sir Bertie the document. In return, Sir Bertie passed over a bankers' draft for £4 million. Valentina Petrescu was waiting outside the library door, and George invited her in to witness the signatures. The three of them then left the library and headed for the front door where four suitcases and a large grip were waiting. George loaded the baggage into the boot of the Bentley, placing the grip on the back seat next to Valentina. He then returned the copies of the DVDs she had given him over the last few weeks, together with a draft for £150,000.

In Deep Water

'What are you going to do with the DVDs?' asked a naive Sir Bertie.

'Make sure they no go on internet,' she replied.

George half-turned towards her. 'You may not get them through airport security. Do you want us to destroy them?'

She nodded. 'Thank you Mr George, you very nice man.' George started the car and headed for Humberside airport.

Two days later several local and national papers reported Clive Oglanby's suicide.

Chapter 30

Bill Waites came from a privileged background. The only child of a wealthy farming family, he excelled at everything he did. A gifted intellect, both sharp and bright, he was educated at Eton College followed by Cambridge, and then enjoyed a meteoric rise through a consultancy company. Nearly ten years ago he was head-hunted by Severn Trent Water to become the youngest-ever CEO in the water industry. It was while he was house hunting for his impending move from London to the Midlands that he came across Bertie Campbell purely by chance.

Bertie, on the other hand, came from more humble beginnings, a small-holding in Scotland. He left school at sixteen to join his father's building firm, and only after his father's death did the business flourish. Educated in the University of Life, Bertie was shrewd, savvy and street-wise. Blessed with a smooth lilting accent, people found it easy to believe and trust him. However, beneath the surface, he was a hard-headed and ruthless businessman.

Although the two men came from backgrounds at opposite ends of the spectrum, when they met nearly ten years ago, they soon gained a mutual respect for one another, which later developed into a lasting friendship. After being offered the job by Severn Trent, Bill and Sheila Waites had gone north one weekend house hunting, staying with friends in Stamford. Unable to find anything suitable, but impressed by the build quality of their friends' home, they contacted the builder, Campbell Homes. Two years later, when their new house was complete and the business relationship ended, a friendship flourished. When Bertie was knighted a few years later, the two couples toured Scotland together, Sir Bertie keen to show off the castle and estate where he had been raised.

§§§

Every time Bill Waites turned off the country lane and drove through the huge brick piers supporting the enormous wrought iron gates, which wasn't as often as he would have wished, he knew he would have an enjoyable time. However, today, a cold and overcast Friday afternoon in November, it was with some trepidation that he headed up the gravelled drive to Foxton Manor. By the time Bill and Sheila Waites reached the Manor house, some 600 yards away and hidden from the road behind a large coppice, Sir Bertie and Moira Campbell were stood at the front door to greet them. Family and staff always used the rear entrance, a boot-room adjoining the kitchen. Guests were afforded the honour of being met at the front, giving them the chance to admire the house in all its glory. Set at the top of a wide flight of stone steps, guarded by lions rampant, the oak double doors were fitted with black wrought iron furniture. The seven bedroom house was built mainly of brick, only the clock tower on the north wing was limestone. The windows were stone mullioned and leaded. All four people knew what Bill would say the moment he got out of the car.

'I can't believe you wanted to demolish this,' always with arms spread wide.

It was Saturday afternoon before the purpose of the visit was revealed. Sat under umbrellas at the side of the two acre lake behind the house, Bill and Sir Bertie were fishing, a steady drizzle making one of them wish he was somewhere else, the other knowing that conditions were ideal.

'You might as well spit it out Bill, and then we can get on with enjoying the rest of the weekend.'

'Is it that obvious?'

Sir Bertie nodded. 'And you can dispense with all the bullshit and flowery, mealy-mouthed words. Just cut to the chase.'

Waites took a hefty slug from his hipflask. Dutch courage.

'JB, I want to ask you a favour. Would you consider becoming Executive Chairman of Lincs Water?' Bill continued talking while Sir Bertie took a sip of whisky from his own flask. Bill explained that Lloyds Bank had refused to extend the company's line of credit and had been in touch with Anglian, Yorkshire and Severn Trent with a view to a merger or takeover.

'Nobody is interested. I only got involved because I know one of their senior managers. Lloyds Bank say they will only increase their credit facility if the entire board of directors is removed and they get a seat on the board. The Chairman has agreed in principle but the MD has gone AWOL.'

'And the Finance Director?'

'He's a new chap, seven, maybe eight months, sound as a pound but not yet appointed to the board, blocked by the MD.'

'What if I say no?'

Bill Waites swallowed. 'I've already given them your name. I said I would talk to you.'

'Thanks.' Bill looked suitably embarrassed. 'When were you thinking of, and how long?'

'Monday, and as long as it takes. It would only be two or three days a week.'

§§§

After four hours, the three men were exhausted. They had been sat in the conservatory, overlooking fields planted with winter barley, RAF Waddington in the distance. Formerly home to the Vulcan bomber during the Cold War, Waddington now housed some of the ugliest and ungainly looking aircraft, all adapted for surveillance and reconnaissance. A couple had taken off during the morning and it had made a welcome break to watch them claw their lumbering way skywards. If it had been warm enough, and the conservatory door had been open, at eleven-o'clock they would have heard the bugler on the airfield playing the Last Post in remembrance of their fallen comrades. Instead the predominant sounds throughout the morning had been of a crying baby and squabbling children from deep within the house.

The table between them was scattered with calculators, mobile phones, a couple of laptops, pens and various files and writing pads. Crumpled scraps of paper covered the floor.

In Deep Water

Gordon Reed turned to his two colleagues, 'Well I don't think there's much else we can do. It's all in the lap of the gods now.' Alan rubbed his eyes with the heels of his hands and Charlie Swanson sat back and exhaled deeply. Following their secret meeting with Bill Waites, Alan and Gordon had been charged with producing a plan to save Lincs Water from receivership.

Bill Waites had been blunt. 'Cut costs and increase income,' he had said. 'Easy as that. Put together a plan of action and I'll see if I can find a way of implementing it.'

As Southern Area Manager, they had invited Charlie Swanson to join the brainstorming session. Charlie had already asked for early retirement and Alan knew he would give an honest and unemotional slant to the discussions. He also knew they could trust Charlie not to tell a soul. Gordon gathered together about a dozen sheets of scribbled notes which he would type up for their next meeting with Bill Waites. The suggestions agreed today had been a huge leap forward from the outline of ideas Alan and Gordon had talked about nearly two months ago. There was also a second list, now in Gordon's pocket, of proposals too sensitive to voice in the public domain. Top of that list was, 'Get rid of MD'.

'What a way to spend a Sunday morning,' Charlie said, 'I'll be glad when next March comes and I can start enjoying life again.'

Alan said, 'Oh shut up you old bugger, you'll miss the cut and thrust.' Charlie stared back at Alan and slowly shook his head. Since last month's AGM, Charlie had been a changed man. On the day, the Chairman had announced that the share dividend had been cancelled. Charlie had worked for Lincs Water all his life, joining the company at the age of sixteen. For the last twenty-five years or so, he had invested, buying shares, and enjoyed the generous annual dividends. Now with no dividend, and little prospect in the short term of the share price getting back to its former level, Charlie was facing a retirement with less income than he had hoped. He stood up, arched his back and was about to speak when Alan's phone rang. The caller ID *Sam*.

'Shit, I promised to take Sam and Em out for lunch,' he said, as he walked to the conservatory door and into the garden for some privacy. A blast of cold air filled the room when the door was opened.

'He won't stop out there long,' Gordon said, referring to the cold. It was nearly twenty minutes before Alan returned, shivering.

'I think we'd better sit down again,' he said, his voice quavering from the cold. Charlie and Gordon looked at one another.

§§§

'But why did he ring Samantha?' asked Gordon for the umpteenth time.

Alan's reply didn't change. 'All she said was that she used to work for him.'

Charlie turned to Alan, 'Well, if he knows Samantha then you'll be in the pound seats, won't you?'

'What do you mean by that?' snapped Alan.

'Well she's bound to put in a good word for *you,* isn't she?'

Alan slammed his hands on the table, started snorting, breathing rapidly through his nose, trying desperately to control his temper. Gordon stood up; put his hand on Alan's shoulder. 'Beer everyone?' It had the desired effect. On his return, he asked Alan to once again summarise his conversation with Samantha.

Alan opened his can and took a hefty slug.

'It appears that after our meeting with Bill Waites, he went back to Lloyds Bank and suggested that his pal Sir Bertie Campbell take over the chair of Lincs Water to help get us out of the shit. And no, I haven't a clue how the two men know each other. Sam said she used to work for Campbell Homes part-time in sales when Emily was very young. She would run the sales office on various housing sites at weekends. She took Emily in the pram or pushchair. Sir Bertie mainly asked her about carrot-top and what she thought of him. She did mention that this morning, the three of us were working on a plan of action.'

'That might get us a brownie point or two then,' said Gordon.

Alan raised his eyebrows. 'From what we've just discovered on the internet, I think it'll take more than that to impress him.' All three men sat in silence for a couple of minutes, reflecting on what they had just read about Sir Bertie Campbell and his recent dubious business tactics. Eventually Alan said, 'Look we're all good at our jobs so we should have nothing to worry about. If Sir Bertie is as shrewd and ruthless as the papers make out, it's carrot-top who should be worried, not us.'

Chapter 31

After three days, Sir Bertie was exhausted. He had held meetings with each of the key team members of Lincs Water's HQ staff. Not that there were many. The Head of Engineering, Tommy Ward, seemed closer to death than retirement. He coughed, sneezed, and wheezed his way through the three hour session, Sir Bertie wondering if he would make it until lunchtime. Fred Osborne, the Admin Manager, quickly proved to Sir Bertie that he hadn't a clue what he was doing. The one-time bricklayer admitted that he had met Ian Young in their local pub and been offered a job, in Young's words, as his 'eyes and ears'. Sir Bertie quickly concluded that Osborne was so thick he didn't know what Young had meant by that.

Sir Bertie had said, 'Fred, the best advice I can give you is find another job.'

'What? How long have I got?'

'Not long, but if it's a problem I can get my assistant, George Thomas, to help you with your job search.' That was enough. Word spread like wildfire that the Silent Assassin was already in the building. No-one knew what he looked like, but everyone started looking over their shoulder.

A whole day with Ian Young was several hours too long. Sir Bertie had been armed with the notes he had from his conversation with Samantha Hyde, but more importantly, the notes given to him by Bill Waites. Within ten minutes Sir Bertie had concluded that after a three hour session with Bill Waites, he himself had more understanding of the water industry than Young did.

On Wednesday, the meeting with the FD, Gordon Reed, had started badly. Once Gordon had explained the reasoning behind the Chairman's decision to cancel the company dividend because of the rapidly increasing debt, he dropped another bombshell. He admitted that, because of the possibility of breaching the bank's covenants, when he was appointed he had been instructed to pay nothing into the company's pension scheme. When he checked back, he found that contributions to the pension fund hadn't been paid for nearly three years.

'Does anyone else know about this?'

'Yes sir, Ian Young gave me the instruction, verbally of course, and the Chairman knew.'

'And what did Young say?'

'It was something along the lines, "As long as there's enough for me, it's not important".'

Sir Bertie wondered why Young hadn't mentioned it yesterday. Young had obviously been instrumental in stopping the pension pot payments to massage company profits. By the end of the day, Sir Bertie was shattered but comforted that, in Gordon Reed, Lincs Water had a very competent FD. He looked forward to getting home, putting his feet up, and enjoying an island malt. On Thursday he merely had a disciplinary matter to attend to, and then he would get someone to show him round a water treatment works. He would leave the sewage aspect of the business until later.

§§§

'Good morning Mr Bishop, I have a message for you from our new Chairman.' Alan recognised the voice immediately and wondered why she was being so formal. Perhaps someone was within earshot. 'He would like to see you and Mr Young in the boardroom at twelve-o'clock sharp.'

'Do you know what it's about Margaret?'

'I'm afraid I don't,' then Alan heard shuffling and Margaret lowered her voice to a whisper. He guessed she was covering the phone mouthpiece with her hand. 'Be careful Alan, carrot-top is going about like a dog with two dicks, he's up to something.'

When Alan saw Ian Young outside the boardroom with a sneer on his face and a copy of the company's Emergency Operating Procedures in his hand, he knew exactly what he was up to. A chance to impress the new Chairman, and get Alan into trouble at the same time. At precisely eleven-fifty-eight the door opened and the

Chairman ushered them in, shaking Alan by the hand and saying how pleased he was to meet him. He ignored Ian Young as he walked into the room.

Sir Bertie said, 'Don't bother sitting down, this won't take long,' as he leaned against the boardroom table, arms folded. Alan was surprised how small he was. After everything he had read, he expected someone bigger, someone who would strike fear into anyone he met. Sir Bertie was dressed in a three-piece black pin-stripe suite, a pink shirt with matching silk tie and handkerchief, black leather shoes and bright red-and yellow-striped socks which Alan would have described as gaudy. Sir Bertie reminded him of a shop-window manikin.

'Right Young, what's this all about?'

'Well Mr Chairman, it has come to my notice . . .'

'How?' interrupted Sir Bertie.

'Well sir, I have been informed . . .'

'By whom?' Ian Young started to get flustered, unable to put his case forward. 'Come on man, spit it out.'

Young took a deep breath. 'Sir, recently one of our Superintendants, Brian Price, put a burst water main back into service at Scunthorpe without adhering to our company's Emergency Operating Procedures.'

Alan couldn't contain his anger. 'Oh come on, that was months ago. In fact I remember exactly when it was. August bank holiday weekend to be precise.'

'It doesn't matter when it was, these procedures were written to protect the public and ensure they enjoy a safe water supply at all times.'

'They weren't enjoying *any* water supply. Anyway it wasn't Brian's doing, I instructed him. These procedures are so out of date Noah could have written them.'

'*Bishop*,' snapped the Chairman, 'that's enough. Are you saying this maverick attitude towards our safety procedures was at your behest?'

'Yes sir.' Alan decided to put his shovel away and stop digging the hole he was already in.

'Well,' said the Chairman, 'this may take longer than I had hoped. I think we should sit down while you, Bishop, tell us what happened.'

And that was exactly what Alan did, emphasising the vulnerable, babies and OAPs, the need for water for fire-fighting purposes, he mentioned the huge carpet warehouse fire in Scunthorpe two years ago, and the fact that 70,000 people had been without water for nearly forty hours. 'If we'd waited another twenty-four hours to comply with those stupid procedures . . .' He realised, as soon as he'd said it. He held his breath, waiting for the eruption. Even Ian Young didn't respond, he too was expecting an outburst from the Chairman. An uncomfortable silence enveloped the room, eventually broken by Sir Bertie.

'Well it seems this whole episode hinges on the efficacy of these Emergency Operating Procedures.' Alan exhaled quietly. 'I'll get someone to have a look at them and give me their thoughts.'

§§§

Alan had been asked to wait in the car park for the Chairman who wanted to visit a couple of water treatment sites. While leaning against his car, Margaret Vardy came out to speak to him, a folder in her hand. Memories of how she had inundated him with suggestive texts and erotic photos came flooding back. One of them had even made him think he may be happier sharing his future life with her instead of Samantha. However, a lifetime spent between the bedroom and the pub, with little else to fill his time, had soon lost its appeal. He remembered how his marriage to Cheryl had quickly gone off the boil after the initial sexual high of the new relationship.

'OK?' she asked.

'Yes thanks,' he said nervously, remembering their two days of rampant sex. That had been three months ago, and two months since she let the cat out of the bag and told Samantha.

'Look I want to apologise for . . . you know. It was . . .'
An uncomfortable silence engulfed them.

He was determined not to call her Mags. 'Look Margaret, I've told you what I thought of your actions, it was unforgiveable telling

Samantha the way you did, the *detail* you went into, it's over now, but I promise you one thing.' He paused for effect. 'It will never be forgotten.'

'If it's any consolation it helped me, you know . . . what we did.'

'No it's *not,*' he said, emphasising the point with a shake of the head. He knew she needed help, therapy maybe, but prayed that she didn't turn to him again. Samantha was now on speaking terms, and he wanted to make a go of it with her. If she'd let him.

Margaret handed him the folder. 'These are the first few chapters of my autobiography. It's only in draft form but I'd like you to read it. I'm going to dedicate the book to you. Thanks again.' She squeezed his forearm and turned to go back into the building. As he watched her walking away, his attention was caught by movement at a first floor window. Samantha. He waved, nervously.

§§§

'Do you mind if I answer this?' Alan asked Sir Bertie who was sat in the passenger's seat, his head buried in a bundle of papers. Sir Bertie looked up at the mobile phone warbling in its dashboard cradle, caller ID *Number Withheld.* He nodded his approval and went back to reading the notes in front of him. They had just pulled out of Lincoln Water Treatment Works after spending the last hour inspecting the site.

'Alan Bishop.'

'Mr Bishop, its Joyce Green from Faldingworth. I'm sorry to trouble you but the pumping station has broken down again.' Alan wished he hadn't taken the call. Sir Bertie had only been at Lincs Water four days and less than two hours ago Alan had dodged a reprimand from him for not following the company's Emergency Operating Procedures. Now he had Joyce Green, a persistent and regular complainer, talking on loudspeaker.

'Just a minute Mrs Green, I'll just pull over and take your call.' He was determined to hold the conversation in private, but once parked on the grass verge, Sir Bertie put his hand on Alan's forearm as he was about to pick up the phone. Alan sighed inwardly, knowing there was little he could do. He had a great deal of sympathy for the

Greens, they had bought their bungalow three years ago and quickly realised that the sewage pumping station on the adjacent plot was susceptible to frequent blockages. By their very nature, sewage pumping stations are always sited at the lowest point in the village, and any problems always affected the same nearby properties. An idea suddenly struck him.

'Joyce, are our crew on site yet?' Mrs Green and Alan had spoken and met many times over the last three years and were both comfortable on first name terms.

'Yes, they are just starting to lift the first pump out.'

'OK give me two minutes and I'll ring you back.' He finished the call and turned to Sir Bertie. 'Do you have time to come with me to take a look at the problem, sir?'

'Tell me about it first. The last thing I want is to be drawn into a row I know nothing about.'

Alan took an audible deep breath, wondering where to start. 'Faldingworth is a small village; it has a church, a shop, post office, a pub, and one sewage pumping station. The Greens bought the bungalow next to the pumping station three years ago and have been plagued with flooding ever since.'

'Did it just start after they bought their property?'

'No, it's been going on much longer and the previous owner should have made them aware of the problem.'

'Haven't they got any recourse against the vendor?'

'Yes and no. After the previous owner sold, he went into a nursing home, but died last year.'

'OK, so what causes the problem?'

'Because of the proximity of RAF Scampton, many of the forces' personnel rent property in Faldingworth. This usually means young people. Young families mean babies. Babies mean disposable nappies and baby wipes, both of which block the pumps.'

'Why haven't you done anything about it? What can be done?'

'We need to put new macerator pumps into the station, preferably three instead of the existing two. They will chop and pump at the same time. If we also install OMS, our operational monitoring system, which at present is only installed at our major sites around the county, any blockages will alarm out to Lincoln emergency control room but still leave two working pumps.'

'Why haven't you done it then?'

Alan saw his chance. He took a deep breath and replied, 'Ian Young won't approve the expenditure, plain and simple. As well as new pumps we also need to upgrade the power supply to the station, the total cost is around £135,000. He refuses to spend the money for the benefit of one or two properties. All we can do is send notices around the village from time to time asking people not to dispose of nappies and baby wipes down the toilet.'

'Let's go and take a look.'

Chapter 32

If Riverside House had been a boat, it would have capsized. Just about every member of staff was peering out of all the available windows on the side of the building overlooking the car park. Alan and Margaret Vardy stood shoulder to shoulder in her office. Alan hadn't noticed that their bodies were touching, but he could smell her perfume. Two floors below, in the car park, Ian Young was in a raging temper. He was sat in his six year old Jaguar, a dirty, rusty and dented hand-me-down wreck which he had failed to get the board's approval to replace. Unable to park his car in the bay reserved for the Managing Director, he held his hand on the horn for what seemed an age. Whoever had the effrontery to park a Mini in his allotted spot was certainly going to get a piece of his mind when they came out to move it.

Only when he turned to speak, did Alan realise they had both squeezed between the filing cabinets, looking out of the one window in the office which offered a view of the car park. He didn't try to wriggle free or step away. He now saw Margaret as a lonely woman desperately seeking love. He could see a vulnerability in her he had never noticed before.

'Doesn't he know that's the Chairman's car?' he asked.

'Obviously not. How do *you* know?'

'A couple of weeks ago I took the Chairman around some sites but he wanted to collect some papers from his office first. That car was outside Campbell Homes, and the personalised MJC registration is a bit of a clue. I guess it's his wife's.'

At that moment Sir Bertie came out of the building and walked towards the Jaguar, whose horn was still blaring.

Alan said, 'I think carrot-top is just about to shit himself.'

He made to move away from the window, squeezing past her. She seemed to press herself closer to him. He went to sit in his usual chair to await his boss. There were two chairs immediately outside Ian Young's office door, known throughout the building as the 'naughty chairs'. These were where miscreants waited to be called into the MD's office for a dressing down, accompanied by spraying spittle from 'slobber-chops', a new nickname which was rapidly replacing carrot-top. Margaret remained at the window, her back to him.

He said, 'I read the start of your latest book; I couldn't put it down. I found it very sad in parts.'

She turned round to face him. 'My life story, warts and all. I'm going to leave next month and concentrate on my writing full-time.' A single tear fell from her face. She walked over and sat beside him. 'I hear you and Samantha are back together again.'

'Margaret, we've *never* been together, we've only ever been good friends, and thanks to you recently . . .' He was cut short by Young bursting into the room.

'*Meeting's cancelled,*' he screamed, as he stormed towards his office and slammed the door.

Wanting to change the subject she whispered, 'Want some more good news?' Alan nodded. 'You know he had been told to update the Emergency Operating Procedures. He hadn't a clue.' Alan nodded again. 'Well now he's got to put a proposal to the board next month to increase profitability to millions. He's shitting bricks.' Alan couldn't stop a smile creeping over his face. When he had seen the new operating procedures it meant he was off the hook for the Scunthorpe episode. Now it looked as if Sir Bertie was going to compare the savings plan he, Gordon, and Charlie had drawn up with one produced by slobber-chops. Game on.

As he stood to leave, Margaret asked, 'By the way do you know what TAPS stands for?'

'Thick as pig's shit. Why?'

'I guessed it was you,' she said with a grin.

'Me what?' he said, trying to look innocent.

§§§

It was nearly two am when the phone rang. Alan, still unable to get his drinking completely under control, groaned as he rolled over to find the phone. Although he and Samantha were on friendly terms, the telephone conversations they used to have each evening were intermittent. Last night she hadn't rung, and because he was pig-headed, obstinate and didn't want her to know he had been drinking by slurring his words, he had decided not to ring her. His head began to throb as he picked up the receiver.

'Alan, it's Dave Ramsey, we have an emergency, there's been a chlorine leak at Spilsby.'

Dave Ramsey was the supervisor of the company's emergency control room, and a nephew of Ian Young. In Alan's opinion, together with most of the operational staff who dealt with him, Ramsey was about as much use as a chocolate teapot. Young had appointed him a year ago, and within weeks had promoted him to the supervisor's role when he had complained that the salary was insufficient now that his wife was pregnant again.

Alan groaned as he tried to pull himself together and clear his head. 'Where in Spilsby?' he asked.

'The sewage treatment works. I've mobilised the standby crew and informed the duty officer. Ian said you were to be informed as well.'

'Just a minute.' Alan put the phone down, sat up in bed, and rubbed his eyes, trying to wake up. He picked up the receiver again. 'Ian said I had to be told? When?' Alan was beginning to realise something was amiss. Firstly, chlorine was never used in the sewage treatment process, and secondly, he didn't believe Ian would be involved himself.

'Last night. He rang at about ten-o'clock.'

'Ian spoke to you four hours ago about a chlorine leak and you've only just decided to tell me now?'

'Yes, it's an exercise to test our response to a real emergency.'

'*In the middle of the fucking night?*' he screamed.

'Emergencies can happen at any time,' Ramsey replied but Alan had already slammed down the phone, picked up his mobile and scrolled down to *Young*. He answered on the eighth ring, unhappy at being woken up.

'What's going on at Spilsby?' Alan asked, trying to keep calm.
'We've arranged an emergency exercise.'
'Are the emergency services involved?'
'No, not in the middle of the night.'
'Then I'm calling it off. It's not a true exercise.'
'If you do . . .' but Alan had already cut the call.

The next morning Margaret rang Alan, telling him he was to attend a meeting in Mr Young's office at three-o'clock.

'Will the Chairman be present?'
'No, he's in London today.'
'In that case Margaret, tell Mr Ian bloody Young I'm not going to turn up until the Chairman is there.'

§§§

The meeting had been arranged for the following Monday. Sir Bertie had discovered, through his spy in the camp, Samantha, that the MD always went to the pub at lunchtime. The meeting was set for one-o'clock, killing two birds with one stone. Alan had discovered that the exercise was to test the new Emergency Operating Procedures, recently written by Young. He had been so unimpressed with them, after reading three pages he had thrown his copy away.

Once they had all sat down in the boardroom, Young strategically choosing to sit next to the Chairman, the meeting started.

'I understand Bishop,' Sir Bertie began, 'that you refused to take part in the emergency exercise last week and cancelled the event.'

'Yes sir, that's right.'

'Do you realise that the exercise at Spilsby Sewage Treatment Works was planned to test the new Emergency Operating Procedures which Mr Young has just finished rewriting?'

'I didn't at the time, no sir.'

'You do have a copy of the new document, don't you?'

'I did have, but after reading two or three pages I threw it away.'

'*What?*' Young yelled, half rising, his face rapidly reddening. Sir Bertie placed his hand on Young's forearm to calm him.

'Bishop, we've been here before because of your maverick attitude. Perhaps you'd better explain yourself.'

In Deep Water

Alan could see even the Chairman was getting angry. 'Well sir, four reasons.' He started counting them on his fingers. 'For a start, the new procedures are a load of rubbish. Secondly, and I don't need to remind anyone in this room, the company's financial position can't support wasted overtime. Thirdly, the emergency services weren't involved. They would play a pivotal role in any such exercise.'

'And the fourth reason?'

'You will recall sir, when I took you round a few of our sites, I showed you how chlorine was used in the treatment process to treat *water*. It is *not* used on a sewage works. We would have looked complete idiots if the press got hold of the story.'

Sir Bertie put his head in his hands and sighed heavily. When he looked up he said, 'Alan, do you ever do anything by the book?'

'Sometimes.' He paused, and then added, 'When I think the book is right. Otherwise, no.'

§§§

'How old is she?' It had been nearly three months since Samantha had found out Alan had slept with Margaret Vardy, but she still couldn't believe it had really happened. In Samantha's eyes, Margaret was an old spinster. She always dressed in dowdy clothes, tweed two-piece suits, blouses always buttoned to the neck, and pearl jewellery. Who in this day and age dressed like that? Samantha on the other hand always dressed in smart clothes, whether for business or leisure. At thirty years of age, she considered herself trendy.

'How old is who?' Alan was laid back on the settee casually flicking through the TV channels, the volume on low, waiting for the ten-o'clock news.

'Margaret Vardy. How old is she?'

'Oh for fuck's sake Sam can't you . . .' Her angry look forced him to raise a hand in apology. He sat up but couldn't look her in the eye. 'She's the same age as me, thirty-five.'

Samantha sat back in her chair, deep in thought. Although Margaret dressed like a sixty year old, she had to concede that her facial features were a lot younger, no laughter lines, no bags under her eyes, no wrinkles.

'So what attracted you to her?'

Alan couldn't really answer her question, other than he had felt sorry for Margaret and wanted to console her. He couldn't remember how they had ended up in bed together, but once there, he knew exactly why he had stayed for so long. It had been the best sex of his life.

'Oh come on Sam, I've told you before, it was a one-off and it happened ages ago.'

'Eleven times over a forty-eight hour period between the ninth and eleventh of August is hardly a one-off, nor was it ages ago,' she snapped.

Alan exhaled loudly. 'Is it always going to be like this? Are you ever going to forget it? If not, I might as well piss off now. *Forever.*' He stood up to leave.

She knew that he always swore when he was angry and she realised she had overstepped the mark. She stood up and walked over to him, put her arms around his waist and pulled him to her.

'Bish, please don't go. I just want to understand. If we are ever going to . . . you know . . . then we can't have any secrets can we?' He looked up at her as she squeezed him tight, crushing her breasts against his chest, pulling his head to the nape of her neck. 'If I tell you about my love life, as sparse as it is, will you tell me then, what attracted you to her?' Eventually he nodded, realising he had some bridges to build, and some lies to conjure up. Quickly. She took him by the hand and steered him back towards the settee.

Just then Emily walked into the lounge. 'Mummy, my leg hurts.'

Chapter 33

Over the next two weeks Alan threw all his efforts into his work. He felt he had to do something to repair his standing with the new Chairman. After his actions at Scunthorpe had been vindicated and Young told to rewrite the emergency procedures, he had again been carpeted over the Spilsby exercise. Although he hadn't been given the bollocking he was expecting, he hadn't been able to gauge the Chairman's thoughts. He had again been called a maverick and he wondered if he had overstepped the mark by saying he often didn't follow agreed procedures.

The southern part of the county was suffering from water shortages, and Alan saw his chance to gain some brownie points, offering to help Charlie Swanson find a solution. The main problem was around the Boston and South Holland areas, where agriculture and horticulture were the main sources of employment. This had resulted in an influx of a large number of immigrants seeking work, and as a result, Boston Water Treatment Works was struggling to cope. Alan remembered his days in the engineering office where urgency was not part of the vocabulary. The Head of Engineering, Tommy Ward, like many other HQ staff, had a *laissez-faire* attitude to work. This meant there were long delays in the design of new schemes, so Alan undertook to design a quick-fix solution to upgrade the Boston plant. Until recently he would have been wasting his time as the spending would not have been approved by Young, who failed to understand that costs could be spread over a number of years. Now with a sharp FD and a savvy new Chairman, Alan was happy to spend his own time helping Charlie, knowing there was a strong possibility of the funds being found for the work.

However, burying himself under a mountain of work didn't stop him thinking about his personal life. It had been nearly four months since he had slept with Margaret Vardy, although the term 'slept with' was hardly an apt description of the forty-eight sleepless hours they had spent together. Samantha had taken it very badly when she had been told of his infidelity, just about everyone in her apartment block had become aware of his wanderings. He still didn't believe he had done anything wrong, and although she would never admit it, Samantha knew it was her own fault for locking him out of her life. His smacking Emily had been less easy for Samantha to understand, until he explained that his upbringing had included a succession of clips round the ear and leather straps across the back of his legs.

'It never did me any harm,' he had said.

'Two wrongs don't make a right,' she had snapped back. Another final warning from Samantha and a solemn promise never to raise his hands again, to either of them, had calmed, but not totally resolved the situation. Samantha was still worried his hair-trigger temper may flare up at any time.

It seemed to her that since Cheryl's death, things between them had started to become strained. He had promised to reign in his excessive drinking, but his idea of cutting down simply meant no whisky; wine and beer were still part of his regular diet. At least he had become more mindful of the country's drink-driving laws. He had slapped both her and Emily and had a short but torrid affair with a colleague. Lately he had twice been taken to task by the new Chairman who had described him as a loner, a maverick. It sometimes seemed to her that he had an inbuilt self-destruct button he was itching to press. At times Samantha felt as if she was walking on eggshells.

Then there was Emily. As an eight year old, going-on eighteen, she and Alan had become good friends. Samantha was aware Emily needed a father figure in her life and Alan seemed to fit the bill. She was a very tactile child and Alan responded in kind, making Samantha sometimes wish he would be the same way with her. He would often put his hand on the small of Emily's back, an arm draped over her shoulder or around her waist, a peck on the cheek. Samantha had never thought any more about it until a friend, stood at the school gates, watching Emily race across the quadrangle to greet Alan, had said, 'They seem very close.' It had made Samantha think about their tickling competitions and playful wrestling games on the lounge carpet. She quickly dismissed those dark thoughts from her mind.

§§§

'Sam, can I ask you a personal question?'
'Not another one. The last time you said that, I got the third degree about my financial status and you called my father a doormat.'
'Well he is. Your mother's a control freak and he just lets her . . .'
The look from Samantha was enough to stop him. She knew he was right but they were still her parents. They were sat outside The Plough, huddled together for warmth. Even though it was lunchtime, the overnight frost still stuck to the grass and the puddles were frozen. Emily had been taken Christmas shopping by Samantha's uncle and auntie, a sad reflection of her dysfunctional family.

He took his hand out of his jacket pocket and drained his near-empty pint glass. 'Let's go home, I'm bloody freezing.' He had hoped the pub would have been quiet enough for an intimate chat, but on a Saturday just weeks before Christmas, there was little hope of that. Nearly eight months after Cheryl's death, he still worried what the neighbours might say about him entertaining another woman at home, alone. Staying in the lounge, in full view of No 6 and Nosey Parker would solve his dilemma. Today he had decided to ask Samantha if she would like to go away for a weekend, just the two of them.

'So what's the question?' Samantha was sat in his favourite seat, a rocking chair he had ordered at the Lincolnshire Show a couple of years ago. He and Cheryl had never done anything or been anywhere together for years, and while wandering around the showground alone, Alan had bumped into Thomas Hotchkiss. Thomas was the founder and owner of a company which made bespoke oak furniture and was exhibiting much of their range at the show. Alan had wished he could have afforded a new made-to-order sofa and matching armchairs, but having bought a new three-piece suite when they moved to Louth three years previously, a replacement was out of the question. Instead, he settled for an oak hand-crafted rocking chair.

Cheryl had hated it but Alan had always admired the craftsmanship which had gone into making it. Two months later he had even driven down to Tutbury in Staffordshire to collect it from the showroom.

Alan was leaning against the lounge windowsill with his back to the outside world, and in full view of No 6. 'Well, as I've said before, I've finally got rid of my wedding ring and all the baggage that went with it and I'm ready to move on. I was wondering if you'd like to go away with me for a romantic weekend.'

He had hardly finished the sentence before Samantha leapt up and flung her arms around his neck, kissing him passionately, their tongues trying to entwine like courting snakes. Embarrassed at being in full view of the neighbours, he tried to break free. When he did, the chair was still rocking back and forth.

'Oh Bish I love you so much.'

'And I love you too. I can only apologise for the last year or so, I must have been an absolute shit.'

She nodded in agreement. 'I've waited five years for today, I'm so happy I could cry.' And she did. It was another hour before the subject of the weekend away came up again. Samantha wasn't too keen leaving Emily and suggested she talk to her to see how she felt. Emily hated being left out and there was always the problem of where she would stay. Staying with her grandparents was totally out of the question, and she wasn't too keen sleeping at Samantha's uncle and auntie's house. Their home was old with creaking floorboards, and in Emily's mind, ghosts.

After much discussion, Alan eventually conceded that Emily should be included in their weekend away, but as it was so close to Christmas, they would leave the arrangements until early January when hotels would be advertising some cheap deals. Instead, next weekend they would go to the Lincoln Christmas market, held in the medieval square between the Norman castle and the gothic cathedral. Lincoln City was twinned with the German town of Neustadt, and together with many local Lincolnshire traders, the market had a truly international flavour. Afterwards they would return home and have a special meal cooked by Samantha and Alan would stay the night.

§§§

On Friday morning after his shower, Alan carefully selected his clothes. A site visit was out of the question, he always seemed to get filthy when on site. He had let the paperwork on his desk build up over the week. He chose a pair of beige trousers, a brown-checked Harris Tweed jacket and dark brown leather shoes. A white open-necked shirt completed his wardrobe. He threw his old Barbour jacket, and a small case containing a change of clothes, into the boot of the car. Black clouds were threatening rain as he set off for the office.

What could possibly go wrong?

It was close to four-fifteen when Jane Hamilton brought Alan a cup of coffee. He was relaxed, staring out of the window at the dark sky, the sun had set half-an-hour ago. Thankfully the rain had eased but there was a bitterly cold westerly wind.

'I've just got a message from Lincoln; Mr Young is on his way here.'

'Shit,' muttered Alan. He knew the journey from Lincoln would take about an hour and he wanted to get away from the office by five-o'clock at the latest. He glanced at his watch. After dark and with wet roads it could be five-thirty before slobber-chops arrived.

'Did Margaret say what he wanted?' asked Alan.

'No. No-one seems to know why he's coming, she was tight-lipped.'

Alan mumbled a few more expletives before he picked up his phone and dialled Young's mobile. It went straight to voicemail.

'Typical, the man's a complete arsehole,' he said to a now empty office. He spun the mobile in his right hand, deep in thought, and then decided to send a text.

Slobber-chops on his way to GY. May be a little delayed. LOL Bish xx

We'll wait. Sam xxxx came the reply. He tried to busy himself but his mind kept drifting off, thinking what the weekend held in store for them both. Alan was brought out of his daydream when his phone rang.

'He's here,' a whispered voice announced.

'Thanks Jane,' he replied, just as Young walked into the office with his wife. Young was dressed in a white tuxedo, formal black trousers and a wide purple cummerbund. As usual his shirt buttons were straining to contain his oversized body. A loosened bowtie hung limply around his neck. He tried to fasten the centre tuxedo button, but it had been some time since it had had an intimate relationship with the buttonhole. His wife, by contrast, was slim and wore a pretty black sparkly full-length dress, petite black high-heeled shoes, an off-white faux fur stole, and held a black clutch bag to her bosom. She had beautifully manicured and painted nails, and her grey, slightly coloured hair showed signs of a recent visit to the hairdressers. They made an unlikely couple. It was the first time Alan had met Mrs Young and he thought that if he were in a TV game show, and had to pair husband and wife photos, he would never have matched these two. Alan was surprised at first but quickly recovered. He walked round to the office door to close it.

'A Rotary do? Or dinner with one of your many celebrity friends?' he asked cuttingly. Young stared at him long and hard, an undercurrent of tension filled the room, only to be broken by the ringing landline. Alan, glad of the distraction, strolled back to his desk.

Chapter 34

Jim Williams had not been looking forward to Christmas. For the last two years his wife had been wheelchair-bound. She had been diagnosed with amyotrophic lateral sclerosis, a terminal muscle wasting disease, more commonly known as motor neurone disease. She had lost the use of her legs some time ago and now she was having difficulty speaking and swallowing. Although the couple were receiving benefits, the money didn't go very far. Williams had been an HGV Class 1 driver for most of his life, a well paid job which also attracted subsistence when having to stay away overnight. By sleeping in the back of his cab and taking as many overseas trips as possible, he had been able to give his family a comfortable lifestyle. His son and daughter, now twelve and fourteen, were very supportive, helping in the house with cooking and cleaning. However, that didn't put food on the table.

When his wife was first diagnosed, Williams believed he could still hold down a full-time job and be able to cope at home. His employer had been extremely helpful, scheduling him local work so that he could get home each evening. However, as his wife's health deteriorated, he had to give up full-time work; instead choosing to work through an employment agency, where he could pick and choose the work he was offered. As well as attendance allowance, Williams was claiming other benefits, one of the conditions of which was that he couldn't work more than sixteen hours a week. Yesterday, the Montrose Employment Agency had rung him and offered him work, twelve hours a day, from Friday the thirteenth to finish on Tuesday morning the twenty-fourth of December.

The work consisted of driving a petrol tanker to help deliver fuel to stations as far north as Durham and south to Leicester. His hours would be six pm to six am for eleven consecutive nights. He briefly thought about his working hours being exceeded, but immediately dismissed those concerns. It wouldn't be the first time he had breached the benefit rules or disconnected his tachograph. Williams knew that he probably wouldn't receive any pay before Christmas, but at least he could buy his wife and kids something special in the January sales. His sister had agreed to help look after things until the following Friday when the school Christmas holidays began, and the kids could take over until he finished work on Christmas Eve.

Williams had never driven a petrol tanker before, but his years of experience told him that it would be difficult because of the high centre of gravity. For that reason, and not wanting to start off on the wrong foot, he had arrived at Barnetby oil storage depot an hour early. He had been told to approach the site from the south, off the A18, drive to the car and tanker parking area to the north, then report to the control room on site. Williams noticed that there were three petrol tankers neatly parked away from the twenty or so cars randomly scattered around the gravelled area. He pulled alongside the cars, got out, and picked up his hi-vis waistcoat, flask of coffee, and sandwiches. Gone were the days when he could afford to stop and eat in a roadside café.

'Jim Williams,' he announced timidly to a crowd of about thirty people assembled in the control room.

'From Montrose?' a voice shouted from behind the crowd. Williams nodded as the site supervisor stood up. 'Don't worry about this lot, they've been on a site visit, they'll be leaving soon.'

Williams handed over his Montrose time sheet and was given a clip board full of forms. The supervisor took him through the paperwork and told him that, because it was his first trip, each delivery point would be manned, despite the lateness of the deliveries.

'We always have a rush on just before Christmas,' said the supervisor. 'Everyone wants to get topped up before the holidays. You'll have diesel and ninety-five octane petrol to deliver tonight.' He was handed a set of keys with a tag attached showing the registration number of the tanker and told he could start whenever he wished.

The supervisor added, 'I'll give you five minutes to get your bearings with the vehicle, then I'll come over and explain the filling

In Deep Water

procedure. It's all fairly straight forward. When you're ready just reverse up to bay number two and wait for me.'

§§§

Alan snatched at the phone, keen to have a reason not to talk to his boss.

'Bishop.' He paused and listened. 'Put them through.' He listened some more then sat down, picked up a pen, making notes on his pad.

'Is it one of the refineries?' he asked.

'No it's the oil storage depot near the end of the M180,' was the reply.

'How bad is it?' He listened some more. 'OK, we'll get someone out ASAP,' he said and put the phone down. He immediately picked it up again and dialled Jane Hamilton's extension. He simultaneously scrolled through his speed-dial list of contacts on his mobile.

He pressed Brian Price's number just as Jane answered. A phone to each ear he said, 'Jane, is Peter Warcup still downstairs?' Then to the other phone, 'Brian, can you hang on a minute.' Back to the first phone, 'Can you ask him to pop up straight away and get the standby crew out onto site to the fire at the Barnetby oil storage depot?' He listened for a moment. 'They can't miss it; apparently you can see the flames from several miles away. Tell them someone will join them very soon.'

Back to the second phone. 'Brian, sorry to spoil your Friday evening plans but I see you're the standby officer. There's a fire at the oil storage depot at the end of the M180,' then he listened. Brian Price had been the Water Superintendant for the Grimsby and South Humberside area for years and he had an encyclopaedic knowledge of every water main, valve, hydrant, pumping station and water treatment works in the area. Less than two years from retirement, Alan knew it would be a huge loss to Lincs Water when he left. Brian Price gave him nothing but bad news.

Peter Warcup knocked on the office door and waited. He knew Ian Young and his wife were in the office and didn't relish joining the meeting. Warcup was one of five District Managers reporting directly to Alan. He was responsible for water supply and

159

distribution along the south bank of the Humber. He was a tall gangly youth with mousey-coloured hair which always looked out of control and infrequently combed. He sported a motley beard which Alan thought he ought to shave to thicken it. Like pruning trees and bushes to promote new growth, he used to think, but never told Peter. He was nearing thirty but looked years younger. Like Alan, he was a chartered engineer but had specialised in the mechanical side of the industry.

'Come in,' shouted Alan and Peter slowly opened the door. Alan motioned him to come in, pointing to a seat at the table in his office opposite where Young and his wife were now sitting.

Alan continued listening to Price; Brian had just told him that the water mains close to the depot were old and subject to several bursts a year. Brian went on to remind Alan that shortly after Young joined Lincs Water, the MD had decimated the capital works programme in an attempt to save money. The reinforcement and upgrading of the mains around the oil depot had been one of the many schemes axed.

'The stupid fucking idiot,' Alan said aloud, everyone in the room clearly hearing his expletives. 'OK Brian, can you pop out to site and I'll meet you there in about half-an-hour. Peter's here as well.'

Young snarled, 'What's all the fuss about, you're over reacting Bishop. It's only a fire, nothing to do with us.'

Alan gave him a long, hard, cold stare. 'Have you ever wondered how the Fire Brigade put out fires?' unable to hide the sarcasm in his voice. He picked up his mobile and high-vis coat from the back of the office door and walked out, calling over his shoulder, 'Can you lock up please, Ian?'

He was closely followed by Peter Warcup.

§§§

By the time Alan arrived, the Fire Brigade, or to give them their full title, Humberside Fire and Rescue Service, already had three appliances on site. They were quickly joined by two foam tenders, based at, and operated by the two nearby oil refineries. Barnetby oil storage depot had been built by one of the refineries in the 1970s to reduce the time and mileage spent by their petrol tankers getting into

In Deep Water

and out of the refinery, a saving of ten miles, and nearly thirty minutes, each way. The new oil depot was conveniently situated at the end of the M180 thus giving easy access to the west and south. It was less than ten miles from the Humber Bridge, gateway to Yorkshire and the north. It proved a wise investment as legislation requiring the compulsory use of tachographs was introduced a few years later.

The depot was ablaze, flames at times leaping what seemed to be hundreds of feet into the air. Black acrid smoke rose into the dark night sky, fanned towards Grimsby by the westerly winds. The glow from the flames meant Alan could easily locate the standby crew and Brian Price. The oil depot was sandwiched between the A180 and the A18, just half a mile from the eastern end of the M180. The fire appliances were lined along the road to the west of the site. The main entrance to the site was on its southern boundary and that was where both Lincs Water vans could be seen. They had parked on a concrete hard-standing in the corner of a field close to the site access road. These concrete areas were normally used to store sugar beet once it had been harvested, before being transported to a nearby factory. Fortunately there was room for several vehicles beside the piles of beet.

Brian Price and the standby crew's leading hand, Fred Jackson, joined Alan in his car, Peter Warcup arriving seconds later.

They gazed through the windscreen at the blazing inferno. They were all wearing their high-vis coats, the reflective tapes on their wrists and shoulders glowing briefly when the smoke blocked out the light from the flames. From their position it seemed as if half the site was ablaze, but from where they were sat, they couldn't see the fire engines or what they were doing.

Alan turned to Price who was sitting next to him. 'Talk to me Brian.'

Price took a deep breath. 'We have a four inch cement-lined ductile iron main running along the western boundary of the site where the Fire Brigade are now. It is fed from a six inch main which runs from Barnetby, along the A18 towards the airport. They are both of unknown age and we have suffered three or four bursts in the six inch main over the last year. To say it is paper thin would be an understatement. The quality of the four inch spur is unknown; it goes on to feed a handful of farms to the north and west.'

Alan asked a rhetorical question. 'So any surge in pressure and the six inch would burst?' No-one answered. He went on, 'So what else do we have in the area? Can we back-feed the fire without using the six inch?' Brian shook his head.

Alan said, 'Shit, could it be any worse?' A silence hung over the car's occupants like a damp morning mist. Alan turned to Warcup. 'Peter, go and find whoever's in charge and tell them about the tightrope we're walking. They must open and close any hydrant or valve very slowly to prevent a change in mains pressure.' Alan looked at the crew's leading hand. 'Fred, can you go with him and get your lads to somehow oversee any valve operations, do it for them if you can.' They both nodded and got out of the car.

Once alone, Alan turned to Brian again. 'What about Trent water?'

Brian's body language and words gave conflicting messages. He shook his head but said, 'It's possible.' A long silence followed, both men deep in thought.

It was Alan who spoke at last. 'If it comes to that, we'll have to get rid of Peter.'

This time Brian nodded in agreement.

Chapter 35

By the time Alan walked around to the western perimeter of the site, the chain link fence had been flattened to allow access to the fire. There were now five Humberside appliances as well as the two foam tenders from the refineries. Other assorted vehicles were also parked nearby, one with 'Rapid Deployment Unit' emblazoned on its doors, others unidentified but obviously necessary for carrying personnel and equipment. Alan's crew had done exactly what he had asked; assisting the Fire Brigade had avoided a burst main so far. A large van sporting EMTV in bold red letters had just arrived on site and was being shepherded away from the centre of action, back towards the A18 by a lone policeman.

Alan pulled out his mobile and rang Samantha. Emily answered, she explained Mummy was in the shower and they would be ready to go to the Christmas market as soon as he got back.

'Tell her I'm at the fire, you can watch it on the news, and I'll ring again soon.' He ended the call. He had no idea when he would get to the apartment.

Alan watched the fire-fighters at work. Some were hosing jets of water onto storage tanks to keep them cool, while others were spraying fine mists of water and foam onto the centre of the fires. Until any further fire appliances arrived, his own crew were idle, happy that everything was under control and the overtime was mounting up. Fred Jackson and one of his men were enjoying a cigarette and the other was playing with his phone. On his way back to the car Alan bumped into Tom Barker, the Station Manager for Immingham and some of the nearby fire stations.

'Hello Tom, got any information how this started?'

'Well the fire was reported by a tanker driver who was turning outside the loading bay entrance at the north side of the site. He had just started to reverse into the site when he saw and heard an explosion, then high-tailed it up onto the A180 slip road before he dialled 999. He told control there was another tanker inside the loading area and he thinks that was what exploded, probably during the filling process. I would guess there will be at least one fatality. There must be some operatives in the control room but so far we have no news. Someone is coming from the refinery with layout plans and hopefully more information.'

'Where's the tanker driver now?'

'Probably sat down somewhere with a cup of tea, or something stronger.'

'Are you going to need any more appliances as we may have a problem with water quantities and pressures if you do?'

'I don't know just yet, someone is coming down from our HQ, if only to control the overtime bill.'

Alan thought about his own overtime bill, three men kicking their heels and a Superintendant all being paid time-and-a-half. He and Peter Warcup were there for the love of the job. Alan shuddered to think what Lloyds Bank would say about the cost of tonight's emergency.

Tom Barker looked over Alan's shoulder and said, 'Looks like the vultures are gathering.'

Alan turned and saw the amount of vehicles at the bottom of the road had increased tenfold. Cars and vans were parked on both sides of the road, the vans sprouting satellite dishes like mushrooms on a damp morning. Two policemen were struggling to keep the crowd at bay. Film crews, photographers and reporters milled around, all trying to get the best vantage point. One of the film crews had a tripod mounted camera, with a soundman complete with microphone boom and grey furry windsock. Their lighting chap had set up arc lamps which seemed to be as bright as the fire itself. Others simply had shoulder mounted video cameras. Many more had digital SLRs hanging round their necks and camera bags slung over their shoulders. Alan guessed that each reporter would be recording whatever they could, desperate to get some concrete facts for their viewers. No doubt Vanessa Redfern was amongst them.

Just then a rapid response ambulance arrived, and the reporters and photographers rushed forward, thrusting their microphones and cameras at closed windows, frantic for a quote.

When Alan turned back Tom Barker had gone, so he returned to his car and sent a text to Samantha.

I could be a while, guess the Christmas market will have to wait until Saturday. xx

The reply was almost instantaneous. Samantha had always impressed Alan with the speed of her texting. Her thumbs seemed to be nothing more than a blur at times, she was so fast. *Take care my darling. Looking for you on TV. ILY Sam xxxxx*

Alan then rang Lincs Water's twenty-four hour emergency control room, asking if there had been any reports of reduced water pressure in the area around the oil depot.

The reply was comforting. 'Nothing so far Alan, but I'll let you know if anyone rings.'

Ian Young's recent words floated through his mind. *You're over reacting Bishop. It's only a fire, nothing to do with us.*

The car door opened and the interior light came on, bringing Alan's thoughts back to the present. It was Peter Warcup.

'I think you ought to speak to the Fire Brigade,' he said.

'Why? What's happened?'

'Well the chap from the refinery brought the plans and some bad news. There was a group of visitors touring the site; fortunately they were in the control room when the explosion occurred. There's a busload of them and when the refinery manager spoke to his people on the site, they reported that the sprinkler system had stopped working.'

'Drop in pressure or a burst pipe?'

'Don't know.'

Alan leapt out of the car into a steady drizzle, so he went to the boot of his car for his safety helmet. It was the only headgear he ever wore and experience had shown that it wasn't much use in keeping him dry. Water usually ran off and down the back of his neck. As he walked towards the fire tenders he noticed that more vehicles were now on site, together with an incident control van, light spilling out of its open door. He spotted Brian Price inside the van just as his phone rang. The caller ID showed *LW Control Room*. He waited outside to take the call.

'Alan I've just received a red light alarm from Brigg water pumping station, showing a power outage or a tripped pump.' Although OMS, the operational monitoring system, was several years out of date, it gave them warning of a problem long before members of the public started to complain. Alan had long since given up hope of persuading Ian Young to update the system to include some form of off-site remote control. The existing system still meant someone had to physically respond and visit the site of the alarm.

'Shit.' He paused deep in thought. 'I'll send someone down from here; it'll be quicker than getting another crew out from Lincoln.'

He motioned to Brian Price to join him outside the van. Somewhat reluctantly, he came out into the rain. Alan briefed him about the latest problem.

Brian said, 'Why not send Peter? It'll get him away from here so when we instigate plan B, as I'm sure we'll have to now, none of the brown stuff will fly his way when it hits the fan. I'll be happy to take early retirement and, who knows, he might get your job when you're sacked.'

Alan grimaced. 'Good idea, can you tell him to keep us informed then go straight home when it's sorted. Ask him to ring us around eight-o'clock tomorrow morning.'

§§§

It was nearly half-past-nine before Samantha sat down and relaxed. She and Emily had waited until seven-thirty before they decided to have dinner. The potato wedges had been in the oven for forty-five minutes and were cooked, so Samantha asked Emily to eat her starter while she seared the tuna steaks. The sweet and sour dressing had been prepared earlier, as had the starter and they both finally finished their meal at half-past-eight.

Samantha would have liked to have said she had enjoyed the meal, Emily certainly did, but *she* didn't. The whole purpose of the celebration dinner was supposed to have been a prelude to her and Alan's first time together. She had fallen in love with him nearly five years ago and had wanted to make love to him ever since. Apart from the problem after Cheryl's funeral, when she walked out of his life for three months, even during that period she had still been in love with him. She knew that it was the right thing to do as it had cured him of his excessive drinking. He had been on the slippery slope to alcoholism, and her actions had helped drag him back from the edge. Now she was the one with a drink in her hand while he was stone-cold sober out in the wind and rain.

Mentally she had now written off tonight, she had reached the conclusion that Alan wouldn't get home until sometime tomorrow. The television was on, the sound low. Sky News had repeatedly returned to the story about the fire at Barnetby, the biggest news item of the evening. Alan was there, somewhere. She sat, hoping for a glimpse of him, but water was not the big news item. The fire was. The cameras were obviously being kept at a distance, as the same shots came onto the screen every time. One of the fire officers had given a brief interview but his message was benign, no news about casualties, no idea how the fire started, no idea how long it would take to get under control.

She poured herself another glass of wine and wondered about their lovemaking. She had thought about nothing else for the last week. Once Alan had agreed that the baggage from his previous marriage had all been shed, and they had waited a reasonable time after Cheryl's death, he had told her he was ready to start a new life with her. Apart from a little hic-cup with Margaret Vardy, it was now time for the two of them to start their life together. A weekend away had been postponed for a month and Friday, the thirteenth of December at the apartment had been her suggestion, and he would stay the night. She should have known. Wasn't Friday the thirteenth supposed to be unlucky? The day when bad luck will happen, somewhere, to someone? Samantha shuddered, wondering if it was merely superstition or whether there was some basis of truth in it.

Her thoughts were broken when Sky News returned to the fire at Barnetby. She turned the sound up but only caught the last words.

. . . followed by another explosion. It is not yet known if there are any injuries as a result of blast. Friday the thirteenth.

Chapter 36

Alan climbed into the incident control van, glad to be out of the rain which seemed to be getting heavier. Inside there were three fire officers, two policemen, a paramedic and someone not in uniform, presumably from the refinery. On the table, bolted to one side of the van, was an array of plans and most of the van occupants were stood around examining them. When Alan entered the van, several heads turned in his direction.

'At last the water board's here,' said one of the fire officers. Alan's safety helmet had Lincs Water emblazoned on the front.

'We've been here for hours,' Alan said testily. 'And it's not a water *board*; we are a public limited company.'

'Whatever,' said the fire officer. 'We have spoken to the people trapped on site. The sprinkler system in the control room has reduced to a trickle. What can you do?'

'Nothing until I know why it's stopped. If you give me a contact number I'll speak to them.'

Alan was given a name, Freddie White, a Superintendent from the refinery, and his mobile number. Just then Brian Price came back into the control van followed by a fire-fighter.

The man behind Price said, 'Sorry to bother you sir, but the water pressure has dropped. We can use the booster pump but it hasn't got enough capacity for everything.'

Then Alan's phone rang, caller ID *LW Control Room*.

'Alan, I've just got another red light alarm, this time it's a low level warning at Barnetby water tower. I think you might run out of water soon.'

'We already have,' then to Brian, 'Barnetby water tower has a low level alarm going.'

Brian looked at Alan, 'Plan B then?'

Alan nodded, 'No choice, but I need to make a phone call first.'

In Deep Water

§§§

In the 1950s, the growth of Grimsby and Cleethorpes towns together with the industrial development of the south bank of the river Humber meant that water resources in the area were in danger of being depleted. Until then, Lincs Water had abstracted all of its water from the region's limestone and chalk aquifers. If the level of the water in the aquifer dropped too far, then saline intrusion would occur, polluting the supply with salt water. Lincs Water's solution had been to build a water treatment works using water abstracted from the river Trent. The chances of an accidental or deliberate discharge of pollutants into a river is considered to be higher than pollution of an aquifer, and when Trent Water Treatment Works was commissioned a few years later, the decision was made to utilise its entire capacity for industrial purposes only. The water was classified as non-potable. Not fit for human consumption. A completely separate set of water mains was installed to serve the south bank factories with process and cooling water.

Although it was nearly ten-o'clock, the phone was answered immediately.

'Trent Water.'

He recognised the voice. 'Hello Geordie, its Alan Bishop.' Although his stomach was churning with the enormity of the decision he was about to make, Alan kept calm and exchanged small talk for a couple of minutes, chatting mainly about the fire. He then took a deep breath and asked, 'Geordie what are the chlorine levels of the outgoing supply at the moment?'

Geordie looked up at the array of meters built into the control panel in front of him. 'Just over one part per million, why?'

Alan ignored the question. 'When did we last have a chlorine delivery?'

As Geordie pushed with his feet, Alan heard the wheeled-chair scoot across the tiled floor to the end of the control panel. It took less than a minute to find the answer in the daily log-book, but it seemed like a lifetime to Alan. 'It was Monday this week, the ninth of

December. We filled up to the brim because of the Christmas holidays.'

Alan breathed a sigh of relief. The factory closures over Christmas would reduce water consumption thus lowering chlorine usage, further helping the situation. He made the decision. 'Geordie I want you to increase the chlorine level to four ppm immediately.'

Geordie fell silent for a moment. 'Alan?'

'I know, I know, but there are over thirty people trapped on site, and we are running out of water. I'm going to cross-connect the mains.'

'Why increase the chlorine levels?'

'To stop people drinking it, it'll taste like a swimming pool.'

Geordie exhaled loudly. 'Alan, someone did a similar thing about fifteen years ago, way before your time and it cost him his job, he was forced to take early retirement.'

Alan's hands were shaking, his heart was racing, but his voice was calm and level.

'Geordie, I'm too young to retire.'

Chapter 37

When Alan turned round to look for Brian Price, he had already left. Alan could see Brian's, and the standby crew's vans, besieged by the reporters at the end of the road. They had swarmed round the vehicles like angry hornets. Alan waited until he saw them turn onto the A18 before he rang.

Price said, 'There are three cross connections and I think we should open all of them. I'll start with the one closest to the site but I don't think we can back-feed to the water tower. We'll have to rely on Peter fixing the problem at Brigg.'

'Talking of Peter, just remember when I face the inquisition that it was my decision, he wasn't even on site. He knew nothing about it. I will also say you and I had a terrible row because you didn't want to do it.'

'Whatever,' replied Price.

Alan wanted to mention that although the situation on site was desperate, Price needed to open the valves slowly to prevent any sudden surge of pressure in the mains, but he didn't need to. It would have been insulting. He simply said, 'See you in a couple of hours.'

Then he phoned Freddie White.

§§§

It was after one-o'clock when Price and the crew returned to site. Brian looked shattered; it had been a long day, starting at seven-thirty, his sixty-plus years telling on him.

Price said, 'I tried to stop it back-feeding towards Grimsby and Cleethorpes but the valve wouldn't shut. I'll have to get it sorted next week. Do you want us to go further down the line to the next valve?'

'No, it'll take too long, Trent water's probably half way to Grimsby by now. Anyway, our problems pale into insignificance compared to some. I spoke to Freddie White, the refinery Superintendant who was showing a group of visitors round the site. There are twenty-eight people in there with him, twenty-nine in total, and two unaccounted for. They're all in various states of panic, the mini-bus they came in has burnt out, the rear tyres were on fire and then its fuel tank exploded just before I rang him. It blew most of the control room windows out; several people were cut by falling glass.'

'How did twenty-odd people get into a mini-bus?'

'A lot came in their own cars; they're all parked off site. Last time I rang, the sprinklers were working again; at least it's keeping them cool.'

'Bloody hell; let's hope the Fire Brigade can get to them soon.'

'Not at the moment, last time I spoke to them they said it's still too dangerous. Anyway, why don't you go home and get some sleep, and come back tomorrow. It gets light around eight.' Price nodded. 'Can you bring me a mobile with a pay-as-you-go SIM card? I may want to make an anonymous phone call.'

'No problem, we've just bought one for our grandson for Christmas. Have you spoken to Lincoln control?'

'Yes, and that's another problem. The new girl Josie something-or-other is on her own. She's only been in the job eight days and when she came in at ten-o'clock she found she was unsupervised. That arsehole of a manager Dave Ramsey has taken the night off for his wedding anniversary celebrations. He should be overseeing her training. Tonight of all nights.'

'He's a relative of Mr Young's you know.'

'I bloody well know that, and just as fucking useless,' shouted Alan.

Price could see the enormity of the situation was getting to his boss. The risks they had taken for the speedy repair of the water main at Scunthorpe paled into insignificance when compared to the possibility of poisoning nearly 150,000 people.

'Look why don't we ask our Bob to pop into the control room?'

Bob Price was Brian's son, and had joined Lincs Water ten years ago. Alan had seen the same potential in Bob as he saw in Brian, and promoted him to Superintendant on the sewage side of the business, working out of Lincoln. He only lived a couple of miles from HQ.

Alan nodded his approval and thanks. 'I've warned Josie that if she gets any complaints then she should advise people to use bottled water until this is all sorted out. I've also spoken to Peter who's still waiting for an electrician to turn up. I even tried to let Ian Young know the situation, but as usual, his phone is switched off.'

Brian smiled a knowing smile. 'I'm glad he's not my boss,' was all he said before he left.

§§§

It was after two-o'clock before Alan decided to ring. He scrolled through his contact list for Young's home phone number. It rang seven times before it was answered.

'Ian, its Alan Bishop, I'm sorry if I woke you.'

'Do you know the time?'

'Yes, it's ten-past-two.' He paused. 'I need to talk to you about putting non-potable water into the potable mains.'

'Whatever. Its water isn't it?' The phone line went dead.

§§§

It was half-past-seven when Alan was woken by Brian Price getting into the car.

'Merry Christmas boss,' he said as he handed Alan a small package, neatly wrapped in Christmas paper. Alan had noticed lately that Andrew Potts' habit of calling him 'boss' was starting to spread. He wasn't sure if that was a good thing or not.

'It's a little early Brian but gratefully accepted. First I need to ring Lincoln.' As he used his own mobile, Price handed him another two bags, one containing three bacon rolls, the other, two cups of coffee. Price took one of the rolls and one of the coffees. Josie told Alan that there had been fourteen complaints around the Grimsby area about discoloured and smelly water. Alan wrote down the address of one of them.

As he ate his bacon buns and drank his coffee, Alan could see the first signs of daybreak, that time before sunrise when the sky gradually lightens. He noticed that some of the camera crews, photographers, and reporters were set up on the concrete hardstanding between his car and the ambulance. As it became lighter, he saw that they all had muddy feet. They had obviously by-passed the police cordon by walking across ploughed fields. At times he hated the press, but today he had to admire their determination to get a good vantage point.

'Show time,' he said as he tore the Christmas wrapping, screwed up the paper, and took the phone out of the box.

'I forgot to check if it was charged,' said a sheepish Price.

'Should be enough for one call,' Alan said as he switched it on. Two bars showed on the phone. They both got out of the car and walked to the end of the lane. The camera crews watched them to see if anything interesting was going to happen. They continued walking until they were out of earshot and could see the vans at the bottom of the road. Once he was sure he could see EMTV's van, Alan read out the phone number of EMTV's HQ taken from his own mobile. Price punched it into the new phone then handed it back to Alan.

He pressed send. It was answered in about ten seconds.

'Hello, this is Bernie Bryce here. I live in Westkirke Avenue, Scartho and the water here is terrible. It's gone all black and stinks like a swimming pool. You ought to get down here and take a look.' Then he switched off the phone and waited. It was five minutes before they saw movement around the EMTV van. Their camera crew had stayed at the end of the road behind the police cordon. Perhaps Vanessa Redfern didn't fancy crossing a ploughed field in high-heeled shoes and a tight skirt. The crew climbed aboard the van and the satellite dish on the roof was retracted. Two minutes later the van had disappeared from sight.

'Why?' asked Brian.

'It's the quickest way I could think of to let the public know that they shouldn't drink the water.'

'Bloody hell Alan, you're a maverick.'

'Have you been talking to our Chairman?'

A puzzled Price didn't reply. Alan handed the new mobile back to him.

'Bin the SIM card and get a new one. EMTV will try to ring it when they realise they've been duped, and make sure your expense claim is on my desk by Monday, I might not be around on Tuesday.'

§§§

Ian Young was sat at the kitchen table watching breakfast television. He was dressed in a Pringle shirt, Pringle checked jumper, plus fours and knee-length woollen socks. He was due to play a round of golf, teeing off at nine-thirty. When the phone rang he debated whether to answer it, he was already running late after a sleepless night thanks to Bishop. He wavered, but then picked up the receiver. It was EMTV wanting an explanation. They told him that they had discovered that the water supply to Grimsby had been contaminated; the water was cloudy and smelt of chlorine. They explained that one customer had told them their eyes were stinging just looking at a glass of water. They suggested he watch their latest newsflash and his quote could be added to their next broadcast.

'Give me ten minutes then I'll get back to you. You can contact me on my mobile later if you need anything else.' He gave them the number.

He walked through to his study chuckling. 'Bishop, you've just signed your own death warrant,' he said aloud, a broad smile spreading across his face. By the time he had prepared his statement, he was nearly half-an-hour late for his golf match.

§§§

Samantha was watching EMTV with Emily when the newsflash came on. Vanessa Redfern was stood in front of the camera holding a glass of cloudy water aloft.

I am standing in Westkirke Avenue, Scartho, and this glass of water has come from the kitchen tap of the house behind me. As you can see, the water is cloudy and has a very strong smell of chlorine. There are over 120,000 people living in Grimsby and Cleethorpes and it appears that this polluted water is widespread throughout the two towns. If anyone drinks the tap water, adults, old folk, children, babies, they are all at risk of becoming ill.

Or worse.

It is believed that this water, is in fact, extracted from the river Trent, a river where pollution could so easily happen, as it passes through large towns and cities like Newark and Nottingham. Lincs Water has been so concerned about pollution that they class this water as non-potable. Not fit for human consumption.

However, late last night, whilst fighting the on-going fire at Barnetby oil storage depot, this water was allegedly mixed with drinking water, a decision which has resulted in this.

Vanessa Redfern thrust the glass towards the camera.

Someone in Lincs Water is trying to poison us all.

She then handed the glass of water to someone off-camera, the same person gave her a sheet of paper. She looked back at the camera.

Earlier this morning I spoke to Mr Ian Young, Managing Director of the water company and he gave me this statement.

She looked down and read from the script.

Lincs Water plc is legally responsible for providing a pure and wholesome water supply, to all its customers, at all times. We take this matter very seriously indeed. Alan Bishop, our Northern Area Manager, is at the site of the fire at Barnetby oil depot and, if it is proved that he has indeed put raw untreated water into the drinking water mains, then he will face disciplinary action. I, as Managing Director, would like to apologise to all our customers for any inconvenience caused by this mindless action.

She looked up towards the camera again.

When I pressed Mr Young on whether Mr Bishop could face dismissal, he replied, "Of course, it seems highly likely."

This is Vanessa Redfern for EMTV at Scartho.

Samantha immediately burst into tears, sobbing uncontrollably. Emily watched her mother and squeezed her hand, not fully understanding.

Chapter 38

Sir Bertie and Moira Campbell also saw the news on EMTV.

'Good grief Moira, I'm really starting to wonder about Bishop.' She knew when Bertie called anyone by their surname, he wasn't pleased. 'I've always said he was a maverick, he rarely plays by the rules. I'm beginning to wonder why the company wanted to invest £30,000 to put him on SMDP.' Sir Bertie paused in thought, but Moira knew better than to interrupt him during one of his rants. It was best to keep quiet and nod in all the right places, he usually ran out of steam after ten or fifteen minutes. 'And that idiot Young, did you hear his statement? Old sloping shoulders. The sooner we get rid of him the better. Fancy telling the world and his wife what might or might not happen within our company. The man's a complete arsehole.'

Whilst Sir Bertie was letting off steam, staff at EMTV head office had decided to try and sell the story to the national broadcasters. Vanessa Redfern had told them that ITV, BBC and Sky News were all on site at Barnetby, and the story was inexorably linked. They managed to persuade Sky News to buy the scoop.

Sir Bertie had just calmed down when his mobile rang. He looked at the caller ID, *Number withheld.*

'Here we go,' he muttered to himself, half expecting it to be a newspaper reporter.

'Hello.' He listened while the call was put through at the other end.

'Good morning, Prime Minister.' He listened.

'Yes, Prime Minister.' He listened again.

'No, Prime Minister.' He listened some more.

'Within the week, Prime Minister.' The phone line went dead.

He sat in stunned silence with a grim expression on his face for some time. Moira tried to lighten the mood.

'Who was that, darling?'

Sir Bertie turned towards her, ignoring the question. 'He wants to make an example of Bishop. He wants him sacked.'

§§§

Alan's mobile rang for the second time in five minutes. Samantha had just rung to tell him about the EMTV report, he had explained the reasons for his decision, and she seemed a little calmer when they had finished talking.

This time the caller ID said, *Sir Bertie.*

Alan took a deep breath and exhaled slowly before answering. He knew what was coming.

'Good morning, sir.'

Sir Bertie, doing his best to keep calm, simply said, 'Tell me what's happened.'

'I'll try and keep a long story short. We arrived on site shortly after the Fire Brigade, and my Superintendant, Brian Price, told me the mains in the area had a history of bursting. If that were to happen then we could back-feed from a different direction but the only available source was Trent water. We haven't had a burst, but last night Brigg pumping station broke down, quickly followed by the nearby water tower emptying and not being replenished.

'There are twenty-nine people trapped on site, with two more unaccounted for, and without water they will be burnt alive.'

'I didn't know that. EMTV said nothing about trapped people.'

'No sir, they didn't know, the Fire Brigade gave the press an update while they were away at Scartho.'

Sir Bertie asked, 'Can you explain why the water is cloudy and smells of chlorine?'

'Yes sir, I can, but Sam tells me that Ian Young has announced on television that he is to hold a disciplinary hearing, with me in the dock. I'd like to keep my powder dry until then, if you don't mind.'

'Who told EMTV that we were using Trent water?'

'I don't know sir, it wasn't me.'

Sir Bertie sighed loudly. 'Very well, but I have to tell you the Prime Minister saw the report on Sky News, in fact the whole

country has seen it. He wants you put in the Tower of London, and the key thrown away.'
Alan said nothing.
'Have you had any sleep?'
'Last night I dozed in the car, but if nothing changes, I'll get someone to take over and pop home for a couple of hours rest.'
Alan returned to his car and steeled himself for the next phone call. He guessed that Ian would be playing golf, as he always seemed to on a Saturday. He rang Ian's mobile and was surprised when it was answered on the second ring.
'Hello Ian, can you talk?'
Ian said, 'What the fuck do you want this time?'
'I just want to update you on the events of last night.'
'Piss off you wanker, I'm on the second tee.'
Then the phone went dead.
That was quickly followed by a huge explosion.

§§§

The EMTV report had upset Samantha more than she realised. She had switched channels and waited for the reports of the fire on Sky News. Emily had got bored and was now playing a game on her iPad. Last night Samantha had wanted to hold Alan tight and smother him with love. Just talking to him made her happy. This morning she was beginning to wonder. Would they end up, like today, spending more time apart than together?

Samantha first told Alan she loved him nearly a year ago, when they had gone to Luigi's for the first time. She told him again at Cheryl's funeral. It had taken him until last week to say it. Last night was to have been something special. She had been looking forward to it ever since he had told her he had shed the baggage and doubts that had lingered since Cheryl's death. Was that just last week? She had longed for him to come home last night and make love to her. She wanted to spend the rest of her life with him. He was her soul mate. But now? Doubts clouded her mind.

She was jarred back to the present by the sound of an explosion. She grabbed her mobile and rang. 'Bish, are you alright?'

§§§

The blast rocked the car. It seemed that the whole site had exploded. Alan sat for a moment watching the huge plume of flames rise high into the clear blue sky followed by a massive cloud of black smoke. His mobile rang.

'Yes I'm fine, that was bloody close though, the whole car shook when it went off.'

'Please take care, move away to a safe distance.'

'I'll have to go Sam.'

'I love you Bish, take care.'

He got out of the car and sprinted towards the mobile incident control van. By the time he got there it was full of uniforms from all three emergency services. Half a dozen people were looking at the plans on the desk and the senior fire officer was talking on his mobile. A fire-fighter followed Alan into the van.

'Sir, sir,' he said, trying to attract his superior's attention.

The senior fire officer looked up, 'Hang on a minute Freddie,' he said as he lowered the mobile, annoyed at the interruption. 'Yes?'

'It's one of the storage tanks near the loading bay.'

'Show me,' and the fire-fighter went to the table. After a moment's thought, he pointed to one of the circles on the layout drawing. The fire-fighter left and everyone just stared at the plan. The tank in question was right behind the depot's control room.

'Freddie can I ring you back?' The fire officer hung up.

Alan said, 'Something has got to be done now to get them out.'

'The situation can only get worse,' one of the policemen said.

The Assistant Chief Fire Officer said, 'Look, our first responsibility is to save lives, but I would be putting more lives at risk if I sent anyone in at the moment.'

Alan asked, 'Can't you drive a truck in, reverse up to the building, and let them all clamber aboard?'

The question was answered with a disdainful glare.

Alan slammed his hand on the table, '*Damn it, you've got to do something,*' he yelled. Then he stormed out.

Chapter 39

'Forgot to mention, Peter rang earlier, Brigg pumping station is back on line,' Brian said.

'Good,' said Alan, 'but I think we'll leave things as they are, the damage has been done. The dirty water problem is national news; the Prime Minister has spoken to our Chairman demanding I be thrown in the Tower.' Price said nothing.

Alan told him of the argument that had taken place inside the incident control van. They sat in silence, seemingly impotent. Alan had been sitting in the car for nearly ten minutes before he rang Freddie White.

Freddie had said, 'Alan what's happening? Everyone here thinks we're all going to die. Some folks are even thinking of making a run for it, but they won't get ten yards before they're fried alive.'

It was then that Alan decided to try and help. Freddie had told him that a Transit van was too big to get through the double doors into the control room but a car might. Freddie said a car could turn round next to the burnt out mini-bus. He also warned Alan about the bund and possible damage to the suspension of a car loaded with passengers. Alan told him to sweep all the glass away from the doors. He told Freddie that he would drive his car into the building and take seven people for the first three runs, then eight for the last one.

'Two in the front, four in the back, one in the boot,' he told Freddie. Alan suggested they mix fat and thin people.

'Forget all that shit about women and children first,' he had said.

Although very uneasy at the prospect, Freddie had agreed to wait until the last trip, he would organise everything.

'Fast is the operative word, Freddie. Fast, fast, fast,' Alan had said. Then he rang Samantha. 'I love you Sam, more than anything in the world. Just remember that.'

'Alan?' but the line was dead.

The camera crews, reporters, and photographers had been curious when they saw Alan and Brian Price unloading the car and put Alan's green box into the Lincs Water van. It was where he stored everything and anything he may need in an emergency, even a spare set of old clothing. He put his Barbour jacket and his small case of clean clothes for his weekend with Samantha, into Brian's van. He also took out the rear parcel shelf from his car and put that in the back of the van. Alan took off his high-vis coat, removed his Harris Tweed jacket and passed it to Brian, then put his coat back on. They watched Alan walk over to the ambulance and saw him talking to the paramedic. They heard him say something about 'reinforcements'. They watched him walk back to the car. They watched the two men in high-vis coats shake hands. They only started filming and photographing when the car moved off and drove onto the site.

Samantha put her mobile down and sat at the kitchen table.

I love you Sam, more than anything in the world. Just remember that.

'Oh bloody hell,' she screamed, jumped up, and rushed into the lounge, switched on the television, and stood horrified.

. . . Unbelievably, a white Ford Mondeo has just driven onto the site, into the inferno. It looks as if the driver is attempting to save the people trapped in the control room.

Samantha legs gave way; she fell back, her head spinning, and passed out.

§§§

Alan soon reached the point just short of the bund, where he and Brian Price had walked, earlier that morning.

Brian had asked, 'What are you thinking Alan?'

'I'm thinking one of our Transit vans could go and pick up those twenty-nine people before they die.' Then they had had to turn back because of the heat. Alan had looked over the bund; an earth embankment built to contain any leakage, and could see the top of the control room, less than 100 metres away.

The narrow tarmac road went up and over the bund. The car's wheels left the road at the top, Alan made a mental note to take it more slowly with a full load. He saw the control room straight ahead. The doors were open, beckoning him onwards. An overhead pipeline to his left was ablaze, and he saw the main fires were behind, and to the right, of the control room. He accelerated down the slope and sped towards the building. The heat inside the car quickly rose the closer he got.

He misjudged his speed and slammed on the brakes too late. The ABS came on, the brake system chattering away as the ABS did what it was supposed to. He thought he was never going to stop. He also misjudged the width of the door opening, and his door mirror smacked against the wall, then smashed through the window and thumped him on the chest. Broken glass, each piece the size of a tiny sugar lump, was showered into the car, covering his legs, seat and foot-well. He had his eyes closed, praying the car would stop. It did, inches from the control panel.

As he looked around, the car doors were being yanked open, and people were getting in. He picked up the wing mirror nestled in his lap, and threw it out of the car. The last thing he wanted was the mirror getting jammed under the pedals. It seemed to take an age for seven dripping, wet, people to get into the car; the biggest problem was getting four onto the back seat. Eventually everyone was aboard and someone shouted, 'OK Alan,' and banged the car roof. Presumably Freddie White.

He reversed out back into the searing heat, spun the car around next to the smouldering mini-bus, and set off down the road. The scorching heat from the burning overhead pipeline, coming through the broken window, was unbearable. He raised and bent his arm to try and protect his face from the inferno. He slowed down when he approached the bund, but the car's suspension still bottomed as he went up the slope. He accelerated towards the gates and pulled up alongside the ambulance. Brian Price had been tasked with unloading the passengers as quickly as possible, and the car was soon empty. The camera crews swarmed around the car to film the discharging passengers, but soon scattered like tenpins when Alan revved the car and spun it round to go back. He felt a bump as he reversed over something.

'Get me a bottle of water next time Brian,' he shouted out of the broken window, as he sped off again. He didn't hear the reply.

The second trip was less eventful but the heat more intense. One of the television crews had launched a camera drone, and tried to follow the progress of the car as it sped towards the control room again. The loading of the passengers was just as efficient, and still without a window in his door, the heat from the burning pipeline to his right seemed to shrivel his face. Again, he held his bent arm across the side of his head to try to shield it from the intense heat. He was soon back parked next to the ambulance. He got out, spraying little lumps of glass onto the seat and floor. As he stood up and shook the rest of the glass off his trousers, he heard the sound of sirens, approaching up the lane towards the site. Reinforcements at last; another paramedic rapid response car, and an ambulance. His face was stinging. He gratefully accepted the bottle of water, and after a couple of gulps, he poured some over his head, trying to cool his burning face. He didn't have time to sweep the broken glass off his seat, so he just sat on it, figuring his trousers would protect his legs. They didn't, and he winced as he put his full weight on the seat, grinding the glass into the backs of his thighs and buttocks.

The third trip was also uneventful; if you can call driving into a firestorm uneventful.

'Two in the boot next time Freddie,' he shouted as he left. He again tried to keep his right arm against his face as he passed the burning pipelines. When he pulled up outside the gate he couldn't get next to the ambulances, as the number of camera crews and reporters seemed to have doubled. He took great delight at driving straight at them like a man possessed, horn blaring, again scattering them in all directions.

'Get out of the way you fucking morons,' he bellowed; the adrenalin coursing through his veins. The passengers got out and Alan poured more water over his head, turned the car round, and headed back, hopefully for the last time.

Chapter 40

The final trip took more than twice as long. One of the women refused to get into the car. Freddie White had been trying to persuade her ever since the first carload had left. She was crouched in the foetal position in a corner of the room, screaming and shaking with fear. When Alan saw her, he was fuming.

'Stupid fucking bitch,' he shouted as he got out of the car. Alan was so pumped up he didn't notice that water from the sprinkler system had soaked him within seconds. He didn't know it, but blood was running down the back of his legs. His trousers were dark red instead of beige. He marched over to the woman, grabbed hold of her wet hair, and dragged her across the water-soaked floor to the car, screaming. Freddie grabbed her legs, and they threw her into the boot like a rag doll. She scratched and kicked them both.

'Lie on top of her Freddie,' Alan said, which is exactly what he did. The problem was Alan couldn't shut the tailgate. He looked up at the door entrance, realising the car wouldn't get out with the hatchback open; neither could he turn the car around inside the building. When he spun round to get back into his seat, he slipped. He put out his left hand to break his fall, and a shard of glass embedded in the palm of his hand. Unwilling to pull it out as he felt no pain, he got back into the car and winced, as once again he sat on the glass from the broken window. He looked through his one remaining door mirror; the interior mirror view blocked by the heads and shoulders of his passengers, and engaged drive. Being automatic, he could move the gear lever using only his fingers. He inched the car forward to line it up with the doors. He moved as far forward as he could, nudging the control panel before engaging reverse and flooring the throttle.

The open hatchback hit the wall above the door with an almighty crash, followed by the sound of scraping metal and breaking glass.

The car seemed to hesitate as the hatchback bent forward over the roof, like the lid of a sardine can. Most of the passengers screamed, drowning out the wailing woman in the boot of the car. Alan kept his foot hard on the accelerator but the front wheels were spinning on the wet tiled floor, getting no grip. The car was wedged in the doorway. He engaged drive and floored the throttle again. Suddenly the car shot forwards and hit the control panel with a frightening thud before it came to a halt. A second attempt at reversing through the door had similar results, but the car had gone a bit further before it again became wedged. The drama was now unfolding in front of millions of TV viewers. The drone was hovering in a position upstream of the fire and smoke, and had zoomed in on the entrance to the control room.

Alan looked at his two front seat passengers, who like everyone else, were soaked to the skin, their hair plastered to their heads; their faces frozen with fear. 'Third time lucky,' he muttered quietly. Neither believed him. Unsure what to do next; he slipped the car into neutral, wondering how they could get out.

'For fuck's sake hurry up,' someone shouted, barely audible above the screams from the car boot.

An idea came to him but it may well damage the gearbox and make the car un-driveable. He realised it was their only chance. He floored the accelerator and the rev counter shot up into the red sector.

'*Hang on*,' he yelled at the top of his voice, then pushed the gear lever into reverse. The car leapt backwards like a popping champagne cork, throwing everyone forwards. No-one was wearing a seat belt. The two front passengers both hit the windscreen, Alan's chest hit the steering wheel and he nearly passed out with the pain. The rear passengers clattered against the front seats. The car was suddenly full of cries, shouts and expletives. The noise slowly subsided when they all realised they were outside the building. As he tried to turn the car around, Alan saw that he had now lost both wing mirrors. When he engaged drive there were some worrying rumbles as the car slowly lurched forward. The tailgate banged on the roof of the car, and the one remaining door mirror was hanging from its wires, and knocking against the bodywork. These noises, together with the groaning gearbox, gave the impression the car was about to expire. The passengers fell silent as the car slowly and stutteringly lurched towards the bund. As he approached the burning pipeline, Alan realised that with his left hand full of glass, he needed his right hand to steer the car. As he slowly drove past, his unprotected hair and ear seemed to shrivel under the intense heat. Moving at a snail's pace towards the bund, Alan tried to accelerate over the hill, the engine revs rose but the speed didn't. The car just managed to get to the top, and over the bund.

The cheers from inside the car were matched by those from the crowd of reporters as he stopped the car beside the ambulances. A doctor had also arrived on site and started examining the passengers as they gradually got out, unable to believe that they had escaped.

Alan heaved himself from the car, the adrenalin draining from his body. He walked to the back of the vehicle and lent against the bumper, cradling his left hand which had now started to throb. As he looked down, the terrified woman in the boot of the car began sobbing. Someone behind him shouted his name, and he half turned and looked over his shoulder as a photographer snapped away. Suddenly he was surrounded by hordes of reporters firing questions at him, as if he would answer the loudest first.

'What was it like?'

'Did everyone get out?'

'Are you injured?'

As Alan looked up, the reporters went quiet, waiting for a quote. 'I think the gearbox is fucked,' was all he said, before his legs turned to jelly and he slumped against the car. His hand was throbbing, and he now became aware of the pains in the back of his thighs and buttocks, as if a thousand pins had been stuck into his raw flesh. The pain in his face seemed to be the worst but then his ribcage began to ache where the mirror had hit him. Then suddenly everything seemed to go quiet and blurred.

Paramedics had pushed through the crowd and the doctor said, 'I think we'll use the ambucopter to get him down to Lincoln. Grimsby and Scunthorpe will have enough to do.'

After treating his injuries, ten minutes later an ambulance took him the two miles to Humberside airport where the Lincs & Notts air ambulance, or ambucopter as it is affectionately known, was waiting.

§§§

Sir Bertie and Moira had been sat in front of the television all morning, watching events as they unfolded.

'Thank God for that,' was all he said.

Samantha had recovered from her momentary loss of consciousness, and watched the drama with Emily. She had been shaking for nearly an hour, her fists clenched, and her knuckles white. The delay in him returning from the fourth trip had nearly driven her mad.

'Where are they taking you Bish?' she asked.

Sky News answered her question as its camera pointed skyward, filming the departing yellow helicopter, which circled the site to avoid the clouds of smoke still pouring from the fire. The reporter announced confidently it was bound for Lincoln.

Samantha picked up her mobile.

'Sharon, could you look after Emily today please? My friend has been taken to hospital and I want to visit him.'

'Yes, sure, bring her round whenever you want. Incidentally, have you been watching the news? Someone drove his car into the Barnetby fire and rescued twenty-nine people. Amazing.'

'Yes I saw it,' Samantha said, tears welling in her eyes, her voice trembling. 'That's my friend.'

'I'll come straight up.'

§§§

Ian Young didn't see the news until he returned to the golf club bar. 'Shit,' was his only comment, just as his wife walked in.

She said, 'Did you see that? He must have a death wish.'

'He's like a bump in the fucking carpet. You keep stamping on it until it's flattened, only to find it pops up somewhere else. Well I'm going to nail him to the mast next week.'

His wife turned and left, pleased she had come to the club in her own car.

Chapter 41

Samantha decided to walk to the County Hospital. Her apartment was situated midway between the hospital and the cathedral and less than 400 metres away, along Greetwell Road. From her veranda Samantha had sometimes seen or heard the ambucopter land in the hospital grounds, and she anxiously looked skywards for the sight or sound of it as she scurried towards her destination. She didn't have long to wait. As she entered the main entrance gates to the hospital grounds, she heard the distant approach of a helicopter to the north. After sweeping in fast and low, it banked then slowly circled until gently settling on the helipad next to the Accident & Emergency Department. Samantha had expected the paramedics to rush Alan into the building, but it was two or three minutes before the rotors stopped and the stretcher lifted out. Even then she couldn't be sure it was him, his head was in a neck brace and heavily bandaged, his body covered with a blanket. Only when she saw one of the team throw what remained of a high-vis coat over his feet, was she sure it was him. She had watched the paramedics cut one of the arms off the coat to treat his injured hand.

Fighting the urge to scream and rush forward, instead, she headed for the main A&E entrance but she never saw him again. Half expecting to be allowed to roam the corridors of the hospital, peeping through half-open curtains, it was nothing like Holby City or Casualty. Security was tight, and the building full of bloodied men and women, most dressed in motorbike leathers. The hospital department was under severe pressure because of an early morning pitched battle at a nearby concert. Fearing for her safety, she headed for the relative calm of the main car park.

Needing time to think, Samantha leaned against the bonnet of a BMW, only to set off the car alarm. Moving away as quickly as she dared without raising suspicion, she went back to sit outside the

A&E entrance, on a bench surrounded by cigarette stubs. She decided to ring him, but got no answer. Having another idea of how to find him, she went back inside to call him again, hoping to hear his mobile ringing.

The phone was answered with a tentative, 'Hello.' It took Samantha some time to realise that she was talking to Brian Price. He explained that he was putting all Alan's belongings from the car, into his van. Samantha thanked him and promised to let him know how Alan was when she had some news. Back outside and becoming more despondent, she saw a man in green overalls walking back towards the helicopter. She chased after him.

The paramedic was reluctant to say anything at first, thinking Samantha was from the press, but when she burst into tears he finally relented, 'Look, he'll be OK, don't worry. He's in good hands.' Back in A&E she was told Alan had been taken down to X-ray and advised to ring in an hour or two when they would have more details. Unable to do anything else, she reluctantly decided to walk home.

§§§

Back at the apartment, Samantha went to collect Emily from Sharon, who offered to make them all lunch. Samantha soon realised that Sharon wanted to quiz her about Alan, but she was happy to tell her friend about him. After all she and Alan had upset Sharon and her husband Frank, and many of their other neighbours, when they had had that almighty argument some months ago. They sat in front of the TV, sipping wine and watching the heroics repeated time and time again. The frequent calls to the hospital gave nothing more than 'comfortable' or 'stable'. At six-o'clock she was told he had been taken down to theatre, and would probably not be back before visiting hours ended. Despite Sharon's offer of dinner, Samantha decided to go home, albeit just upstairs, when her mobile rang. She looked heavenwards when she saw the caller's ID.

'Hello mother.' Samantha didn't need to find a quiet corner for a private conversation. Sharon knew everything about the deteriorating relationship between Samantha and her family. They were good friends; Lizzie and Emily both went to the same school. Gossip outside the school gates was often more informative than a daily newspaper. After a long silence listening to her mother, off on one of her diatribes, Samantha said, 'I'm on the second floor; I'll buzz you in when I get upstairs.'

'Has she come to apologise?' Sharon asked hopefully.

Samantha shook her head. 'You must be joking,' she replied, 'she managed to get "waste of space" and "magnet for trouble" into the *same* sentence. The only one she missed was "drunken yob" but hey, the night is young.'

§§§

'Hello darling. We were passing and saw the light on, we've been shopping in Nottingham. We thought we'd take you both to that lovely Italian restaurant you like so much.' It was as if the conversation three minutes ago hadn't happened.

'No you didn't, I was downstairs and the lights were off.'

Ignoring Samantha's comments completely Karen said, 'You need to come to your senses. That drunken yob . . .' Samantha knew it wouldn't take long, 'tried to poison 200,000 people. Tomorrow we'll start to get back to normal; I'll cook a really special Sunday lunch for the four of us. Happy families once again.'

Samantha was incandescent with rage. She couldn't control herself; four glasses of wine didn't help either. Perhaps it was Alan's regular use of bad language. She also knew Emily was out of earshot.

'You haven't got a fucking clue, have you? Where the hell have you been today?' Not waiting for an answer, she picked up the remote and turned on the TV. 'Sky News will be best,' she hissed venomously.

There have been two further explosions this afternoon at the Barnetby Oil Depot. The control room, where previously twenty-nine visitors and staff were trapped, has now been completely destroyed by the fire. Earlier in the day, Alan Bishop, Lincs Water's Northern Area Manager drove into the blazing inferno to rescue all twenty-nine people. His car, seen here arriving out of the fire for the fourth and final time, was completely destroyed.

Whilst the commentary was ongoing, the pictures showed an edited version of the first three rescues, and the fourth in much more detail, ending with a close up of the car. The tailgate was bent over the roof like a sardine can lid, both sides battered, and one wing mirror attached only by its electrical wires.

His only comment, at the end of his heroic act, was about his car. He said, "I think the gearbox is broken." An understatement, I think you'll agree. Mr Bishop seemed to have the most injuries, most of those rescued escaping with only minor cuts and grazes. He was flown by air ambulance to Lincoln County Hospital, where he is currently in theatre undergoing surgery.

We now go over to our correspondent John Westerman who is outside the hospital for an update.

'Heard enough about my deadbeat bloke,' stuttered Samantha before she broke down in tears. Her parents were lost for words. '*Just get out,*' she yelled, 'and don't come back. *Ever.*'

§§§

All three were sat in the reception area of Lincoln County Hospital on Sunday morning waiting for Alan to be moved.

'I can't believe they didn't put him in a private room straight away,' the Chairman said, 'he's a national hero.' A receptionist had had the audacity to suggest that visiting hours to the general wards didn't start until two-o'clock. Sir Bertie had gone ballistic.

'I suppose that's the NHS for you,' replied Samantha. Emily had wandered off into WHSmith's to buy Alan a treat. She secretly hoped he didn't like chocolate. Samantha had already bought almost every Sunday newspaper in the shop. There wasn't one which didn't feature Alan on the front page. Most showed the same photograph, Alan stood behind his car, half-turned towards the camera. His burnt face, shrivelled hair, bloodied trousers and injured hand all clearly visible.

One of the red-tops even had a supplementary story about a nineteen year old trainee journalist from Grimsby, who claimed he was run over whilst helping to unload the passengers from Alan's

In Deep Water

car. A photo showed him reclined on a sofa with a plaster-cast on his left foot, and a broad grin on his face.

The nurse returned to confirm that Mr Bishop had now been moved to a private room, number one-two-seven, and there were no restrictions on visiting hours.

'I'll leave you to inform all our staff. Let's see how long it is before carrot-top turns up.' Samantha was shocked at how quickly the new Chairman was picking up on the office gossip. 'Just give me five minutes alone with him please.' And before she could reply, he marched off down the corridor, as if he knew exactly where room one-two-seven was.

§§§

She sat beside his bed and squeezed his right hand, about the only part of his body she could see without a dressing. He turned his head, covered in bandages, towards her and gave a faint smile. She lifted his hand to her mouth and gently kissed it, leaving a slight impression of her lipstick on the back of it.

'Hello stranger,' she whispered. 'How are you feeling?'

'Where do you want me to start?' he said weakly.

'They'll only let me stay a minute or two. You're a celebrity now.' A faint smile appeared on his face for a second. 'What did the Chairman say to you?' The effect of the anaesthetic and painkillers took over as he drifted off to sleep.

She placed the newspapers at the side of the bed, her favourite headline on the top.

The Mail on Sunday had written:
From Zero to Hero in One Hour.
She leant over the bed and kissed him on the lips.
'I love you so much,' she whispered.
Emily blew Alan a kiss, and got to eat the chocolate after all.

Chapter 42

Samantha returned later that afternoon to spend some quality time with her hero, only to find his room full of people, many of whom she didn't recognise. Samantha had phoned Jane Hamilton and Brian Price to update them, and they had obviously spread the word. Her own mobile phone had never stopped either. Sir Bertie had given her number to the reporters outside the hospital, and told them of a forthcoming press conference tomorrow morning, which he had asked her to arrange.

'It's an ideal opportunity to showcase Lincs Water. Hopefully Lloyds Bank might look more favourably on our dilemma,' he had told her, though he didn't really believe it himself.

Shortly after she arrived, the crowd started to disperse, presumably to give the couple some time alone. Samantha hugged them all as they left, including a surprised Freddie White.

'He saved our lives, all twenty-nine of us,' he told her, his eyes moist, as the horrific memories of the last forty-eight hours came flooding back.

They sat in silence for some time, holding hands and surrounded by flowers, fruit, get well cards, and newspapers before Brian Price and Jane Hamilton walked in.

'We come bearing gifts,' Brian said cheerfully, holding up a shopping bag, a large present wrapped in brown paper and a Harris Tweed jacket. 'We left the rest in your office,' Brian added, as he handed Alan the parcel and told him to be careful as it was very expensive; all the area staff had chipped in to buy it. Samantha helped him tear the wrapping to reveal a brand new high-vis coat. They all laughed until Alan grimaced in pain, clutching his chest.

'Nothing broken, just badly bruised,' he explained. Keen to hear the latest news he asked, 'What's the state of play at Barnetby?'

In Deep Water

'Peter's there at the moment, the fire is under control but the depot is totally destroyed. The emergency services have started the search for the two missing men. Tomorrow we'll get the water supplies switched back to normal,' replied Brian. He then emptied the shopping bag onto the bed. 'Your glove compartment is the equivalent of a woman's handbag. I took everything out of your car because we couldn't lock it. Your keys and mobile phone as well.'

Alan lunged for his phone, thinking only of the nude pictures of Margaret Vardy in the midst of the text messages. Amongst the other items were two half-bottles of vodka. He had the decency to look embarrassed.

'I was having a rough time when my wife died,' he said, not really a lie as he didn't stipulate whether the bad times were before or after her death. Just then his mobile rang. Using his right hand and holding the phone to his left ear, he could just about manage. As Alan had a conversation with Bill Waites, Brian turned to Samantha.

'That thing's never stopped ringing. I'm glad to get rid of it. Mind you the battery's almost flat.'

'I'll have to go to Louth to get the charger,' said Samantha.

'How long will he be in here?' asked Jane.

Samantha answered with a shrug as Alan finished his phone call.

'I've just been offered a job at Severn Trent,' he announced to his shocked visitors.

Not wanting to discuss anything in front of relative strangers, Samantha tried to change the subject. 'Talking of good news, while we were waiting for you to move into here this morning, Emily was telling the Chairman she was going to get 100 photos of you, which you would have to sign, and then she would sell them for charity.'

'What?' said a surprised Alan. 'You're joking.'

'No, the Chairman said that it was very enterprising of her, and he'd get the photos *and* pay for them. He's ordering 1,000.'

§§§

On Monday morning at the press conference, Sir Bertie was in his element. Many of the journalists were less polite than the groups of city analysts he was used to talking to, but he handled the meeting with aplomb. Stood beside the top of the bed on which Alan lay, he had praised Alan several times before he invited questions.

'Alan, would you do it again?'

'Yes I would.'

'Did you fear for your own life?'

'No, that thought never entered my head.'

'What about the damage to your car, will the insurance company be happy paying out?'

Sir Bertie raised his hand to interject. 'Actually the Ford Motor Company has been in touch with me today. They want to use the wrecked car as a tribute to the strength and durability of their vehicles. They have offered us a new replacement car at no cost.'

'How do you feel about that Alan?' asked one of the hacks.

'It's the first I've heard of it,' he replied.

'Is it true that this is the second car you have written off in the last three or four months?' asked one of the national broadsheets. The room went silent.

'Yes it's perfectly true,' replied Alan.

'Do you care to tell us about it?' persisted the journalist.

'I'm surprised you haven't heard the saga. My neighbour, a well known local solicitor, raped my wife and got her pregnant. I also found out that he bribed her to stop her going to the police, so I went to seek retribution.'

'What did your wife say about that, Mr Bishop?'

Both the Chairman and Samantha wanted to help, but neither said anything. Alan paused for a long time. 'My wife died eight months ago.'

Sir Bertie interjected. 'Ladies and gentleman, I would very much like to stick to the script here, that being the events of last weekend.'

'Alan can you tell us how you got so many injuries and the twenty-nine others had hardly a scratch between them?'

'Oh that's simple,' he replied, 'a mixture of bad driving and a wing mirror.' There was a ripple of sniggers around the room. 'The first run I made scraped all the side of the car on the metal door frame, and the wing mirror flew through the driver's window, smashing it, then injuring my ribs. The broken glass landed on my lap, but when I got out of the car and sat down again the glass

In Deep Water

lacerated the backs of my legs. With no door window to protect me, the intense heat from the fire burnt my hair and ear. Finally, when one of the trapped women wouldn't get into the car, I went to persuade her to join us. Getting back into the car, I slipped on the wet floor and got some more glass in my hand.'

'How did you manage to get her into the car? What did you say?'

'No comment.'

'John Westerman, Sky News. What is the prognosis for recovery from your injuries?'

'My hand is the worst injury and will take four to six weeks, two tendons had been severed and ultimately repaired, but the broken bone has been plated together, and that plate may have to be removed when the bone heals.' There were some gasps as Alan revealed the extent of his injuries. He continued, 'The burns have been examined by a plastic surgeon, and she seems to think I will heal naturally, depending on how much disfiguration I can live with. My legs have numerous but not life threatening cuts which have all been cleaned and stitched where necessary. The surgeon wants to have another look in a couple of weeks to see if they have missed any bits of glass.'

The room went quiet when Alan doubled up in pain, clutching his ribcage. The short silence that followed was broken by a question from Vanessa Redfern.

'Alan, can I ask about your decision to feed untreated water into the drinking water supply? Why did you do it?'

'No comment, I'll give my reasons to the disciplinary hearing, whenever that is.'

'Well ladies and gentlemen,' said Sir Bertie, 'I think we ought to let Alan get some rest. We may see you all again later in the week.'

As the journalists were filing out of the room, Samantha handed Alan a box containing 1000 photos, and a felt tipped pen.

'Start signing sunshine, we'll collect them tonight.'

Chapter 43

When Samantha came back around seven-o'clock with Emily, his phone charger and some toiletries, Alan had completed the signings. He looked shattered. Emily gave a little squeal of delight when Alan told her he had sold fourteen to visitors and nursing staff for five pounds each.

'What's the charity Em?' he asked her.

'It's for a children's hospice in Grimsby, I can't remember the name. I went to see one of my friends there once, but she died.'

'Well that's good enough for me,' he said as she bundled the remaining photos and the seventy pounds into a carrier bag. 'Where are you going to sell them?'

'At school. Mrs Underwood says I can sell them in the quadrangle or the cloisters before and after school.'

'Your school has a quadrangle and cloisters? That's posh. We just had a school yard with a bike shed at the end.'

'And what did you get up to behind the bike shed?' asked Samantha.

'That's none of your business,' he replied. Wanting to change the subject, he asked if she had the file and papers he had asked for. She handed him the red file from his office, and the test results she had obtained from the in-house laboratory where she used to work. He looked at the single sheet of paper. 'Excellent,' was all he said.

Samantha also handed Alan a sealed envelope. 'Details of the disciplinary hearing. Eleven-o'clock on Friday. For some reason it's at Riverside House. I would have thought they ought to hold it here.' Margaret Vardy had let Samantha see a copy when she had asked her to deliver the letter to Alan. It had been a tense discussion, but more than four months down the line, they had both agreed to bury the hatchet. Margaret had apparently gracefully accepted the situation.

'No problem, I'll get discharged at ten.'

'Do the doctors know you will want to leave on Friday?'

'Not yet. Can you pick me up?'

Samantha hadn't thought through the fact that once he left hospital, he would clearly not be able to look after himself, particularly in a house with stairs. She had seen how he had struggled yesterday going to the en-suite with bandaged stiff legs. It had looked even more comical as he had been wearing a hospital gown, loosely tied at the back, his bare backside clearly visible. She had decided not to mention it.

'Of course I can. You can come and stay with us afterwards until you're better.'

'I can look after Em during the school holidays,' he added helpfully.

§§§

Ian Young had earmarked three days to prepare his case for the dismissal of Alan Bishop. After three hours he had decided it was an open and shut case, asking Margaret Vardy to type up his scant notes. Within an hour of Young leaving the office that lunchtime to frequent his favourite watering hole, Alan had a copy of the notes.

Alan said, 'These are a bloody joke.'

'Exactly,' replied Margaret. She was sat on his bed in room one-two-seven wishing they were somewhere else. Although he hadn't accepted her offer of undying love and unheard of wealth, she still had hopes. After all, he hadn't told her to stop sexting him.

Alan finished reading the half-page of notes and screwed up the paper. 'We'd better get rid of the evidence,' he said and waddled off to flush it down the toilet. 'How's the book coming along?' he shouted from the en-suite.

'Slowly. With the appointment of the new Chairman, old slobber-chops has to do some work for a change. Rewriting the Emergency Operating Procedures was bad enough, but now the Chairman wants the report I mentioned to you, highlighting how he's going to pull the company out of the mire. Sir Bertie refuses to alter the deadline and he's starting to get rattled.'

'So what are you doing about the book?'

'I've handed in my notice so I can work on it full time. With a fair bit of leave left, I plan to finish this weekend. My literary agent secured a £20,000 advance for me, but as you know I don't need the money anyway.'

'True, but won't you miss the camaraderie of office life?'

'Not really, I'm stuck up on the second floor with you-know-who. What sort of life is that? No, I'm going into writing full-time, I've made up my mind.'

They were interrupted by a nurse who had come to change Alan's dressings. Margaret stood to leave, and as she bent over him to kiss his bandaged face, the smell of her perfume brought memories flooding back. Something touched his cheek, and as he turned towards it, he saw a pendant hanging from a silver chain. He pulled his head back to try and get it in focus.

'It's my lucky number,' she whispered just as he realised the adornment was a silver hand-crafted number nine. 'Bye for now,' she added before turning to leave, a wicked smile on her face. He too was smiling as he recalled those two days and nights of unbridled sex. He may have deleted the naked pictures of Margaret from his mobile phone, but he couldn't stop the images of her body floating to the surface of his mind. As he lay back on the bed, he didn't notice that she had stopped in the doorway, still smiling and idly playing with the pendant, already plotting her next move.

While the nurse worked on his wounded legs, he tried to break free from his reverie and focus on the words in Young's notes.

Did Bishop put non-potable water into the drinking water mains? Yes.

Did he seek permission to do so? No.

Did that action endanger the health of our customers? Yes.

Did he inform the public they might be poisoned? No.

'It's going to be a doddle,' he muttered. The nurse gave him a quizzical look.

§§§

The only way he could fit into the car was to sit sideways across the back seat. Before leaving he had specifically asked for a double

In Deep Water

thickness of bandages on his legs and left hand. Nurse Gladys, in her mid-fifties, had been happy to help. Alan would have described her as squat, dumpy, rotund, or if being a little kinder, homely. Over the five days in her care, he had flirted with her constantly, something she had probably not experienced for a long time. She had also taped a huge dressing to his burnt ear, swathing it with bandages which covered his entire head and went under his chin. At the press conference on Monday, Sir Bertie had joked that he looked like a member of the White Helmets motorcycle display team. His ribs were also strapped. He carried his red file and a single sheet of paper, Samantha carried everything else.

'Why?' Samantha had asked.

'The sympathy vote,' he had replied.

The same attention to detail went into his choice of clothing, which Samantha had collected from Louth for him. A pair of old jogging bottoms, roughly cut off above the knee to expose the maximum amount of bandaging, an old shirt with the left arm removed, the hole so big the strapping around his chest was visible, and flip-flops to make walking more difficult. He hated the feel of something between his toes and always walked awkwardly, curling up his feet to try and keep them on.

During the journey Bill Waites rang him again.

'Bill,' he explained, 'this is nearly impossible, I'm using my right hand and my left ear.'

After nearly five minutes of conversation, he finished the call. 'He's still trying to get me to join Severn Trent; the offer is now up to £125,000.'

'What did you say?' The last thing Samantha wanted was for him to leave Lincolnshire when they were, in her mind, so close to becoming an item.

'You heard me. I said I wasn't interested. I like it here, despite what's about to happen.'

They arrived at Riverside House with fifteen minutes to spare. Samantha was wearing a smart navy blue trouser suit and matching shoes with a complementary sky-blue blouse. As she helped him out of the car, he looked more like a beach bum that a manager within a plc. His improper dress looked even more out of place in the pouring rain. There was no-one outside the main entrance but they soon realised the press were all congregated in the reception area. Cameras started flashing and questions bounced around the room like ricocheting bullets. Alan put his good arm round Samantha's shoulder, a little difficult as she was several inches taller in her high-heeled shoes, and then he did his best Douglas Bader walk across to the lifts. Cries of 'good luck' rang in their ears.

As soon as the lift doors opened, Major Wiltshire stepped out and held out his hand to shake Alan's. They all went back into the lift, but Wiltshire didn't press any buttons.

'Alan I have to brief you and it must be quick. Sir Bertie is going to go for you tooth and nail to start with in order to placate Young. Look at me Alan.' Alan turned his head. 'Just ignore it; it's like the Roman Emperor playing to the crowds. Do you understand me? Keep quiet please while it's going on, OK?'

Alan looked blankly at him. 'Yes,' he muttered. They arrived at the second floor and Wiltshire left them and walked into the boardroom.

'Well?' asked Sir Bertie.

'I don't know,' was the reply.

Samantha and Alan sat together outside the boardroom, opposite Ian Young, who stared at them as if he was wishing them dead. Samantha leaned over and whispered, 'Do you think he's got a voodoo doll of you with pins at the ready?'

Alan's response was to turn to her, put his good arm around her neck and kiss her full on the lips with a smacking sound effect. She took a tissue and wiped the lipstick from his lips, then looked at Young. There was steam coming out of his ears, his face looked like thunder, then the boardroom door opened and they were invited in.

Samantha stood up and hauled Alan to his feet, his rigid legs unable to bend. 'Good luck darling,' she said loud enough for Ian Young to hear.

'Don't worry, I won't need it,' he replied as he walked past Ian like a clockwork soldier, all stiff and ungainly.

Once everyone was seated, which was difficult with unbending legs, Sir Bertie introduced the panel for the disciplinary hearing. Apart from himself as Chairman, there was Major John Wiltshire, the

In Deep Water

company's Human Resources consultant and, a surprise to Alan and his MD, Gordon Reed. Young confirmed that he would present the case 'for the prosecution' and Alan said he would defend himself without the need for a union representative. He wasn't a member of a union anyway.

Sir Bertie read the charges against Alan then turned to him and said he was deeply disappointed, if this matter was proven he would face serious consequences. He told those present he even had to suffer the ignominy of the Prime Minister's wrath.

'You must understand Bishop these are very serious charges you are facing.'

'Yes sir,' Alan replied meekly as Major Wiltshire smiled encouragingly at him.

Young rose to his feet and opened proceedings by informing the panel that Alan had been on site the whole time while non-potable water had been put into the potable water mains.

'And why it took over three hours to open a valve I've no idea.'

Alan raised his good hand, and Sir Bertie nodded.

'If I may explain for the panel's benefit, and possibly Ian's as well, you have to be very careful when opening or closing valves on water mains. I don't know whether anyone has experienced a noise, perhaps a bang, when they shut off a water tap too quickly at home?'

Major Wiltshire nodded. 'Exactly,' continued Alan, 'it's called water hammer, and happens every time a pipe is in full flow and then closed quickly. A pressure wave goes surging back down the pipe causing a bang. Hopefully, Major, your copper pipes are sufficiently strong to withstand the effects, but closing the tap slowly will solve your problem. The same happens in water mains whether opening or closing valves, so the process is done slowly to prevent the shock waves surging up and down the mains and possibly bursting them. The last thing I wanted to do was burst the *one and only* water main we had close to the site.'

'Thank you Alan, that was very informative,' Sir Bertie said. 'Young?'

His face red with rage as Alan had got the better of him again, Young continued by saying that Bishop couldn't deny that he had perpetrated this heinous crime, and also completely wrecked company property in the form of a Ford Mondeo.

'Bishop has brought the good name of the company into disrepute, destroyed company property and worst of all, tried to poison hundreds of thousands of people. He did nothing to inform the public; we were made to look complete fools by EMTV who somehow got hold of the story, and not once did he try to contact me.'

Young glared at Alan. 'Not once,' he repeated emphatically. 'He should be dismissed with immediate effect and his pension rights forfeited.' By the time he had finished, spittle was raining from his mouth, and he was red with rage.

'Alan would you care to respond?' said Sir Bertie, who was now wondering if he had backed the wrong horse.

After struggling to get up unaided, unable to bend his strapped legs, Major Wiltshire came around the table to help pull him to his feet. Alan stood facing the panel with rubber legs and turbulence in his stomach. He nervously shuffled the red file and single sheet of paper on the table in front of him. Young had put forward a reasonable argument for his dismissal. He swayed unsteadily, rocking from foot to foot.

'Firstly, I'd like to apologise for my mode of dress, these are the only clothes that are comfortable at the moment and I can put on unaided. Secondly I'd like to say that Ian is lying.' There was a gasp from Gordon Reed. Alan could almost feel the heat from Young's red face. 'I did contact him, and spoke to him twice. I tried to contact him at nine-o'clock on Friday evening, an hour before we had taken any action but his mobile was switched off. I rang him at home again after "this heinous crime" had been committed, around two-o'clock on Saturday morning. I informed him of the actions we had taken, and that non-potable water was in the potable mains. His reply was, "Whatever. Its water isn't it?"

'I then rang him again at around ten-o'clock on Saturday morning to further appraise him and he said, "Piss off you wanker, I'm on the second tee". All I wanted was to keep him informed, and get a little encouragement and moral support. It was not forthcoming.' After a pause for effect he continued 'Operational management in the water industry is a twenty-four hour a day, seven days a week commitment, you cannot just provide the service from nine-to-five.'

Someone muttered, 'Dereliction of duty.'

Sir Bertie asked Young 'Is this true, you spoke to Alan twice?'

'Absolutely not, he is lying through his teeth.'

Alan was furious. Not with Young, but with himself. He had allowed himself to be drawn into an argument as to whether or not he had informed Young. He had gone off-script. He had already played his trump card. Over the last few days he had run through the speech in his mind time and time again, and now he had blown it. He bit his bottom lip, and rocking unsteadily, asked for a glass of water.

Chapter 44

After a short break, Alan nodded to Sir Bertie indicating that he was ready to continue. He began again.

'I feel it would be helpful if I could run through the events of the evening and night of the thirteenth of December. It started in my office. Ian was dressed in a tuxedo, cummerbund, the works, obviously going to some important function, when the Fire Brigade rang me to inform us about a major incident. I can't remember Ian's exact words but it was something along the lines, "What's that got to do with us?" Knowing how important water is in fighting fires, I immediately dispatched our standby crew and duty officer, closely followed by myself and the District Manager. We had a discussion on site about the possible problems we may encounter, and the Duty Officer, Brian Price, a Superintendent *par excellence*, told us the water mains in the area were paper thin and subject to frequent bursts. We had included the area in our mains-replacement programme, but Ian had rejected the proposal very soon after joining the company.

'Thinking we may have a problem, we had to find an alternative source of water. The only one available was Trent water. It transpired that we didn't suffer any bursts; once on site, our crews supervised the opening and closing of all hydrants slowly. What we did suffer though, was a catastrophic loss of water when Brigg pumping station failed and the nearby water tower quickly emptied. We were left with no alternative. It was a case of using Trent water, or letting twenty-nine people die.' Alan stopped and took a sip of water to let that sink in.

'I dispatched Peter Warcup, the District Manager, to oversee the repairs at Brigg, and Brian Price took the standby crew to organise the change-over of supply. I rang Trent waterworks and instructed them to increase the chlorine dosing to four times the normal level.'

'Why did you do that?' asked Sir Bertie.
'To discourage people from drinking it, it would taste like a swimming pool. To add to our woes, I discovered that our twenty-four hour emergency control room was not manned by a fully trained operator. A young trainee, Josie Shoreditch, had been left alone that night. Her supervisor and trainer, Dave Ramsey, had taken the night off for a family celebration.'

'Isn't he a relative of yours?' Major Wiltshire asked Young. A slight nod was answer enough.

'To compensate for the lack of expertise in the emergency control room, I sent one of our own Superintendents to help Josie. I also rang Ian but obviously, because he was at a function, his phone was switched off. At around one-o'clock Brian Price returned with the standby crew and told me the change-over was complete, but they had been unable to stop the water back-feeding down towards Grimsby. The valve they had tried to close was seized, so I decided to let the back-feeding continue. I sent Brian home for the night and asked him to bring a pay-as-you-go phone back with him the following day. At ten-past-two I finally got hold of Ian and updated him about the situation, to which he said, "Its water isn't it?" At half-past-seven Brian returned with a mobile phone and a very welcome bacon sandwich. Two actually. I then made an anonymous call to EMTV using the phone he had brought me. I told them the water in Scatho was dirty and undrinkable, hoping they would broadcast that and alert the public.'

'Why an anonymous call?' asked Sir Bertie.

'EMTV and I have had run-ins in the past and I didn't want them distorting the facts. I wanted them to broadcast a simple message, namely, the water was dirty and it stank. Don't drink it. Unfortunately they decided to add their own slant on things, and that's when Ian's comments about disciplinary action were added. I didn't tell them that Trent water was being used. Someone else did.' Alan turned to stare at Young for several seconds. 'It didn't help that it was also syndicated and broadcast nationwide. At around ten-o'clock on Saturday morning I rang Ian again and that's when he called me a wanker and told me to piss off.'

Young stood up and shouted, '*You are an out and out liar Bishop.*'

'Sit down Young, and shut up,' chided Sir Bertie. 'Go on Alan.'

'After that things got interesting.' A ripple of laughter came from all three panel members. 'I would say that I did everything I could to inform the public, I increased the chlorine levels and informed the press. I also allowed the water to back-feed towards Grimsby further warning the public of a problem.'

'How?' asked Gordon Reed.

'Our mains in the area are the old cement-lined ductile iron type, and the cement lining is not always smooth. Little pockets of mineral sediment sometimes lie behind these imperfections, like miniature sand dunes. When the flow is reversed, these mini sand dunes are disturbed and the sediment is picked up and clouds the water, making it look muddy. It's perfectly safe to drink but doesn't look it.

'In conclusion sir, yes, I put non-potable water into the drinking water supply. Did I endanger life? No. Because of the possibility of pollution in the river Trent, we test the water leaving our treatment works three times a week, every Monday, Wednesday and Friday. These are the results for the four weeks prior to the thirteenth of December,' he said, holding up the red file. 'Of the 363 tests carried out, only one failed on the fifteenth of November. One out of 363. I knew that when I decided to transfer the water into the potable mains. What I didn't know was the result of the tests carried out on the day of the incident. However,' he said, waving a single piece of paper in the air for effect, 'they also passed, making the water fit for human consumption.

'Did I seek permission from my superior? Yes I did, and I didn't get any support as you will hear.' Alan took his mobile phone out of his pocket to play the two conversations.

Ian, it's Alan Bishop, I'm sorry if I woke you.

Do you know the time?

Yes, it's ten-past-two. I need to talk to you about putting non-potable water into the potable mains.

Whatever. Its water isn't it?

'And the second.'

Hello Ian, can you talk?

What the fuck do you want this time?
I just want to update you on the events of last night.
Piss off you wanker, I'm on the second tee.

'Finally, I would say that providing a clean and wholesome water supply to one million people in Lincolnshire, is a twenty-four hour a day, seven days a week commitment. I put it to you that I have shown that commitment, and my actions have in no way endangered anyone. In this industry, we can't just put our pens down at five-o'clock and go home, expecting everything to be the same when we come back the next day. Sometimes you don't get to bed for a day or two, as was the case for me last weekend.'

A silence enveloped the room as the panel took in the seriousness of the facts. The barb aimed at Young didn't go unnoticed.

Sir Bertie eventually asked, 'Just one question before we give Mr Young the chance to respond. Do you have any proof that you rang EMTV to let the public know of the problem?'

'Yes, I borrowed the phone from Brian Price, it was . . . is, a Christmas present for his grandson. Just ask him.'

'Thank you, now Young do you wish to make a final statement?'

Ian shook his head.

'Is there anything else you want to say Alan?' asked the Chairman, who had noticed he was still standing. It was more comfortable than sitting.

'Yes, at the time I made the decision, twenty-nine lives were in danger. I defy anyone in this room not to make the same choice. Once the non-potable water was in supply, I did everything I could think of to let the public know that things were not as they should be. It is my belief I have no case to answer.'

'Would you do it again if the circumstances were identical?' asked the Major.

'Yes sir, I would. Without hesitation.'

Once again the room was cloaked in silence. It was eventually broken by Sir Bertie.

'Well I think we've heard enough to help us make a decision. Gentlemen if you will please leave, we will recall you when we are ready.'

Chapter 45

'How did it go?'

'OK I suppose, but I let myself get drawn into an argument and showed my trump card too early.'

Alan had hobbled out of the boardroom and flopped down next to Samantha again, grimacing in pain as his sore thighs and buttocks hit the hard seat. He placed his phone on an empty chair nearby. Sir Bertie had asked Alan to leave the test results in the boardroom so he could examine the evidence, although he wasn't sure what he was looking for. Ian Young had stormed off down the corridor, a slamming door announcing the fact he was holed up in his office.

'What was that?'

'The fact that this is a twenty-four hours a day, seven days a week business, so I said it again later. I even managed to mention Ian's dinner jacket and the fact he was tucked up in bed while I was out in the field.'

'Never mind, I'm sure it's going to be alright. Would you like a coffee or something?'

'I'll just have a small bottle of water please.'

They were interrupted by Major Wiltshire emerging from the boardroom. Seeing Samantha he asked, 'Do you mind if I use your office for a private phone call?'

She nodded, and he headed off towards the stairs. Samantha followed him as she set off for the canteen.

She returned just in time to see Margaret approaching with a tray of drinks and biscuits. Samantha knocked on the boardroom door and opened it for her. She received a coy look and a whispered, 'Thank you.'

Alan needed the toilet so Samantha suggested he use the ladies, that way she could help wash his hand. And that's what they did.

Five minutes later they came out of the ladies together, just as Major Wiltshire walked past.

'Medical emergency,' Samantha said, and the Major just nodded.

§§§

When Major Wiltshire walked back into the boardroom, he was shaking his head.

'Problem?' asked Sir Bertie.

'No. Brian Price would take a bullet for Alan Bishop; I've never known such loyalty. He's spent the last ten minutes trying to persuade me he should take the rap. He even suggested the entire northern area staff would go on strike if we sacked him. His story corroborates Alan's, word for word, right down to his grandson's Christmas present. He also said some disparaging things about Dave Ramsey, the emergency control room supervisor.'

'Young's nephew,' spat Sir Bertie, the venom obvious in his voice. 'Right John, pour yourself a coffee and let's get started.' Sir Bertie was keen to conclude this farce as soon as possible. He laid the blame for the entire charade clearly at Ian Young's door.

The discussions began in earnest.

'He certainly knows the industry inside out.'

'What option did he have?'

'How much would we save if we dismiss him?'

'How much would we save if Young goes? . . . *How much?*'

'He said he would do it again without hesitation.'

'What else could he have done to inform the public?'

'The man's a national treasure; did you see the Sunday papers?'

'I was speaking to the PM yesterday; he's now talking about some sort of bravery award.'

'What about Young's role in all this?'

'He's not even a good imitation of a manager.'

'Young's dangerous when he tries to think for himself.'

'You can't polish a turd.'

'He's vain and self important, reluctant to change.'

'Has he learnt anything about this industry in the last four years?'

'He envies the loyalty Bishop inspires.'

'I'm sick of the man; first he carpets Bishop over Scunthorpe, then Spilsby, now this.'

The panel waited a suitable amount of time, half-an-hour, before the foregone conclusion was agreed. Margaret Vardy was then summoned, on Gordon Reed's recommendation. 'She hate's Ian Young as much as Alan does, she won't say a word to him,' he said. He also offered to stand over her while she typed the two letters, to stop Young snooping.

On the way out of the boardroom, Margaret approached Alan and Samantha and squeezed each of their hands. Samantha assumed it was an unspoken message, saying everything was going to be alright. She didn't notice the look that passed between Margaret and Alan as their eyes locked momentarily. Nor did she see Alan's eyes glance at the silver pendant around Margaret's neck. Seconds later Gordon Reed appeared and winked at Alan.

Time seemed to stand still waiting for Margaret to type the letters, and then take them back to the boardroom for signature. Minutes later Alan and Ian Young were recalled, Samantha remaining anxiously outside. She didn't have to wait long.

Young came storming out of the room, a letter crushed in his hand, and rushed straight down the corridor towards the stairs. Alan hobbled out slowly and handed Samantha his unopened envelope.

'I'm still here,' he whispered.

She leapt up and gave him a passionate embrace; they were kissing when the Chairman came out. Alan went scarlet, Samantha not quite so much.

'Samantha, would you now please get the crowd from downstairs up here for the press conference. Alan you had better come back in and help me out.'

§§§

It took nearly fifteen minutes for the press to get up in the lift, five or six at a time, and then set up all their cameras and equipment. The boardroom was large enough for the gathered throng, but had insufficient seats, most journalists leaning against the walls of the room. Samantha had tucked herself away in a corner, out of the limelight.

Sir Bertie rose from his chair and the crowd hushed in anticipation.

'Ladies and gentlemen, before we open the floor to questions, I am pleased to inform you that the disciplinary panel found that Mr Bishop had no case to answer. It has been proved that on the thirteenth and fourteenth of December, non-potable water was allowed to enter the drinking water mains. Mr Bishop had been aware that the water used *was* fit for human consumption, and at no time were the public in danger. He also took all steps possible to inform the public. In view of the fact he saved twenty-nine lives, the charge of maliciously damaging company property has also been dropped.'

'So not even a slap on the wrist?' someone shouted.

Sir Bertie raised a hand before continuing.

'With regard to Mr Young's part in all this, his involvement will be discussed at an emergency board meeting tomorrow. The panel stresses that the operational management for the provision of water and sewage treatment, is a twenty-four hour a day commitment.'

As the Chairman sat down, there was uproar, everyone trying to ask questions at the same time. Samantha stood at the back of the room, open-mouthed. Sir Bertie brought the meeting to order, and told the assembled crowd that they should raise a hand and then ask their question when invited.

'John Westerman, Sky News. Alan, can you explain how you informed the public?'

'Yes, I let the public know in three different ways. Firstly I increased the chlorine dosing of the non-potable supply to four times its normal level, that's enough to make your eyes water. I was fairly confident no-one would drink such a revolting concoction. Secondly, I allowed the water to backflow in the mains, which is in the reverse direction to normal. When this happens mineral deposits in the pipes are disturbed and the water looks cloudy, again stopping people drinking it, although it is perfectly safe to do so. The third thing I did was to make an anonymous phone call to EMTV.'

'You bastard, you used me,' screamed Vanessa Redfern.

Alan continued, 'I used the name Bill Bryce from Scartho, Grimsby, and told them about the state of the water supply. Within twenty minutes Vanessa and her crew were broadcasting live. I didn't realise the newsreel would be syndicated nationwide; I understand the Prime Minister even took an interest in the problems. I couldn't have done anything else.'

'Alan, why an anonymous call?'

'Vanessa and I have crossed swords before; I didn't want a different slant put out on air, other than the water was cloudy and high in chlorine, making it undrinkable.'

'Alan, how did you get away with the damage to the Mondeo accusation?'

Sir Bertie cut in. 'Alan used company property to save twenty-nine lives then Ford offered us a brand new replacement free of charge. They wanted to use the car, which had been on national television, for marketing purposes. "Look at the strength of the Mondeo, it can carry twenty-nine people through a burning inferno and survive," type of thing. When I refused the offer, they bought the car off us for considerably more than the cost of a new one.'

'Alan why did you go in there for those people, it wasn't your job, the emergency services were all there, you could have died?'

'After the explosion on Saturday morning I thought the sooner they got out the better, and although I'm not a gambling man, the odds of twenty-nine to one seemed like a good bet.' The room burst out laughing.

The questions came thick and fast for a further hour, until Alan gave the Chairman an appealing look. Sir Bertie brought the meeting to a close, and everyone started to file out of the room. Samantha came forward. 'You look shattered.'

'I need my tablets and some more water please.' Samantha went to fetch them.

'You were absolutely marvellous my dear chap,' gushed Sir Bertie.

'Thank you sir, do you mind if I go, I'm absolutely whacked?'

After taking his medication, Samantha took him down to the car and back to her apartment for a rest. She undressed him down to his boxer shorts, and after another drink of water, he lay on top of her bed and immediately fell asleep.

§§§

It was nearly three-o'clock when he woke to find Samantha sitting at the bottom of the bed, her housecoat wrapped around her. Just about every part of his body was aching. He guessed the adrenalin that had pushed him through the morning, had now all drained away. He didn't know which was worse, his ribs, legs, hand, or head.

'I'm throbbing all over,' he said.

'Good,' she replied, a wicked smile on her face, as she stood up and let her housecoat slip to the floor, revealing nothing underneath.

'Oh God *please* be gentle,' he whispered, as she removed his boxer shorts and straddled him. He closed his eyes and grimaced, expecting pain that never materialised.

Afterwards, as they lay snuggled together, he asked, 'What time do you collect Em from school?'

'Oh shit,' she yelled. A minute later, the front door slammed behind her.

Chapter 46

With the apartment cloaked in silence, Alan pulled the bedding over himself to cover any embarrassment when Emily returned, and looked forward to having his dressings removed. He had asked the nursing staff, Gladys in particular, to put extra bandages on his legs and hand. His dressings were so excessive around his thighs that he couldn't put his feet together. His bandaged left hand was the size of a rugby ball. The dressings around his ear and face rubbed and scratched his raw skin. As soon as they got back, he would ask Samantha to remove them all. The only one which was not excruciatingly irritating was the strapping to his ribs.

He must have dozed off because it was dark when he heard the shout, 'We're back.' Samantha sent Emily straight to her room to change out of her school uniform, giving her the chance to check that Alan's nakedness was hidden.

'Thank goodness you're back, can we take these bandages off now, they're all sweaty underneath.'

'I think you need to talk to Emily first. She hasn't sold all the photos, and wants to go to Sainsbury's tomorrow, with you all bandaged up. She wants you to stand outside and shake her collection bucket.'

After much discussion, Alan agreed to go straight away, despite feeling terrible, but only if he could remove the bandage from his face. He argued that, seeing his burnt face and ear with half his hair missing, they would get more donations. Neither Samantha nor Emily had seen the burns to his face since the televised newsreel last weekend. It was not a pretty sight.

§§§

In Deep Water

It was nearly midnight when Samantha dialled 999. It was fortunate that an empty and unallocated ambulance was just exiting Lincoln hospital. The heavy rain, which had been falling all day, had now been replaced by snow, leaving a covering of over an inch in the uphill area of Lincoln. The medical team were only a few hundred metres from the apartment when the call came through. As soon as the crew saw the distress Alan was in, writhing on the sofa in a great deal of pain, and shaking uncontrollably, they checked his vital signs. His core body temperature was dangerously low, as was his blood pressure. Seeing his blue lips and toes, the lead paramedic questioned Samantha, who confirmed they had been out in the rain collecting money for charity, wearing only a T-shirt, shorts, and flip-flops, but had come home when the rain had turned to sleet. Samantha had wanted to get Alan undressed and into a hot shower, but his violent shivering, stumbling gait, and confusion had all meant she couldn't manage it unaided. The whisky she had offered him to try and warm him only made matters worse.

She was distraught. 'We'd have been alright if we had stayed indoors at one supermarket,' she sobbed, 'but he wanted to visit all the five big ones. We were walking backwards and forwards to the car through driving rain most of the night. Just look how wet his bandages and clothes are.'

'Samantha he's going to be OK, if you could get us some clean dry clothes and underwear, we'll take all his dressings off and have a look at his injuries.'

'We haven't got any clothes. He doesn't live here.' Then she burst into floods of tears. 'He's going to die, isn't he?'

It took one of the paramedics fifteen minutes to calm Samantha, and when he had, she gratefully accepted a cup of tea. Meanwhile his colleague was treating Alan for hypothermia, firstly removing his wet clothes and dressings. When Samantha saw his ribs she was shocked. Even a week after the accident his chest was still severely bruised, an assortment of greens, browns, blues, and reds covering an area the size of a dinner plate. She had been upset earlier that afternoon when he had removed the bandaging from his ear and face. The seeping skin was a vivid orange colour, the hair on that side of his head mostly shrivelled, just tiny pinpricks of black hair roots on his scalp. It would have been less distressing if the remainder of his head had been shaved.

After a painkilling injection and a huddled conversation, the decision was taken to remove Alan straight to hospital, wearing a borrowed pair of fleece jogging pants, a foil blanket inside several others, and strapped to a folding ambulance evacuation chair. Because of Emily, Samantha couldn't go with him.

§§§

It wasn't even eight-o'clock and Samantha had been talking to her auntie for ten minutes, all the time wanting to say, 'Shut up, it's him I want to talk to,' but she didn't.

At last her auntie said, 'I'm sorry sweetheart but I'm going to have to dash, there's so much to organise with Christmas just around the corner. I'll tell him you rang.'

'Do you mean he's not there?'

'No, he left at seven, in such a rush. He even forgot his mobile.'

Samantha put the phone down. 'Shit.'

'Mummy where's Alan?'

Samantha blushed, embarrassed she had sworn within earshot. 'Sorry sweetheart, he's been taken back to hospital.'

'Why?'

Samantha had spent half the night blaming Emily. If only she hadn't had that crazy idea to raise money. If only she had sold all the signed photos at school. If only she hadn't asked to go to the supermarket to sell the rest. If only customers hadn't wanted to stop Alan in the car park for selfies in the pouring rain and sleet. If only he had at least tried to put on a coat. If only they'd waited until Saturday morning.

'Because he got sick after we got home. Are you alright?'

'Yes, can we go and see him after we've counted the money?'

Samantha had completely forgotten about the money, still in the boot of her car, in the bucket and four supermarket bags-for-life. Not only were people generous enough to buy the remaining signed photos, they were throwing handfuls of loose change into the bucket

In Deep Water

at every stop. For security reasons, they had started each visit with an empty bucket, leaving the previous collections in the car.

'I'll go and bring the money up here while you have some breakfast. We'll count it when we've seen Alan, OK?'

Emily grudgingly agreed. Because of the fear of the supermarket bags splitting, Samantha used the bucket for all the money, eight trips in total. She hadn't realised how heavy loose coins were.

§§§

As Samantha had suspected, when she enquired at the main reception desk, Alan was no longer in a private room. He was stuck in the Medical Emergency Assessment Unit, and it gave her hope that they may only keep him for a short time, discharging him later, rather than send him to a general ward. To fill in the time, she sat in the car park and phoned the hospital asking to speak to him.

'Not possible,' a stroppy receptionist told her. 'MEAU don't have the facility to receive incoming calls.'

A second phone call was answered by someone else, who whispered, 'He's in MEAU, and it's on Lower Level One near Burton Ward. I'm sure someone will let you see him for a minute, after all he's a hero.' After the fiasco last weekend following the helicopter ride, when she never got to see him until the next day, she had devised a strategy. Leaving Emily with strict instructions not to move, she took her old white laboratory coat out of the boot, and locked Emily in the car. She hadn't worn the coat for nearly a year since getting her new job. Leaving it undone, she dug her hands deep into the pockets, and marched into the main hospital building confidently. She breezed down the stairs and followed the signage.

'You have Mr Alan Bishop here?' she asked a stunned nurse at the nursing station.

'Yes,' she replied looking down at the paperwork in front of her, 'bed four.'

Samantha had no idea how the numbering worked, but strolled into the unit confidently. She spotted him immediately, he was the only patient covered in bandages. His mouth fell open when she walked over to his bed.

'Mr Bishop, how are you feeling this morning?'

'Fine . . .er . . . fine.'

'Good, it was a silly thing you did yesterday wasn't it.' He merely nodded, unable to think how she got in. 'Well I'm sure we'll have you out of here soon, your family are worried so I've brought your mobile. Give them a ring when you feel well enough, OK?' He nodded again as Samantha handed him the phone, spun round and walked out without another word.

When passing the nursing station she turned and said, 'Keep up the good work.' She could feel her heart pounding in her chest as she picked up speed, anxious to get back to Emily. Her mobile rang just as she opened the car door.

'How the hell . . . ?'

'Matey, I've got more balls than Wimbledon,' she replied, and they both laughed. 'Any idea when you can come home?'

'They said it may be this afternoon, but there'll be strict conditions.'

'Good, I'll go and get you some more clothes and bits and pieces, just remind me what your burglar alarm code is, I've forgotten already.'

'The month and year I was born.'

'Of course. I'll talk to you later.' She held the phone to Emily's ear.

'Bye Alan,' she shouted.

'Bye pet, see you soon. Love you both.'

Chapter 47

Alan was 'home' by four-thirty, just in time for Final Score. Although not a great football supporter, he had seen one game at St James' Park while attending Newcastle University. Since then he had always kept an eye on their results and progress. He left hospital with a list of do's and don'ts. Do stay in a warm house for the next few days, don't drink alcohol for three or four days, don't remove the dressings, do go to the Monk's Road walk-in medical centre on Tuesday to get the head and hand dressings checked. They had told him he had suffered moderate hypothermia, and possibly septic shock. His exposed burnt ear had also got an infection after its soaking in the rain. The problem was when someone said don't do something, he always took that as a challenge. They had given him several injections, he presumed painkillers and antibiotics, and because of the imminent Christmas holidays, a goody-bag full of medication. Samantha had been to Louth and collected an assortment of clothing and footwear. His biggest problem now though was Christmas shopping. Because of his hospitalisation, and habit of shopping at the last minute, he hadn't bought either Samantha or Emily any presents.

Samantha, preparing dinner in the kitchen, shouted, 'How did they do?'

'They lost one-nil.'

Just then the doorbell rang, followed by Emily squealing. 'Can you get that please, Bish?' shouted Samantha. He got up and walked down the hall, his legs now free of any bandaging. Because the video entry system from the front entrance hadn't buzzed, Alan expected it to be a neighbour at the door. His mouth fell open in shock when he saw Sir Bertie.

'Alan my dear chap, how are you? Can I introduce you to my wife Moira?' Alan closed his mouth and leaned forward, looking right and left, up and down the corridor, wondering if a neighbour had let them in.

'I'm fine thank you sir,' he said, regaining some, though not all, of his composure. He offered his hand. 'I'm pleased to meet you Lady Campbell.'

'Oh *please*, call me Moira,' she said smiling, and shaking his hand warmly. After an uncomfortable silence, she raised her eyebrows in question. Still Alan stood frozen to the spot, so she prompted him. 'Aren't you going to ask us in then?'

Feeling uncomfortable about inviting strangers into someone else's home, he looked over his shoulder for help. There was none.

'Er . . . yes, come through to the lounge,' he said, and led the way. In the lounge all three stood uncomfortably in a triangle, facing each other. It reminded Alan of the final showdown in the spaghetti western, The Good, the Bad and the Ugly. Even a jingle on the television added to the surreal situation.

Sir Bertie broke the silence. 'I see your legs have made a miraculous recovery.'

Embarrassed that his ruse had been rumbled, Alan's face reddened. 'Er, yes sir, they found another piece of glass this morning and removed it,' he replied, trying to justify the need for bandages yesterday, but not today. 'They patched the cut with butterfly tapes.'

'Good, so tell me why you ended up in hospital again.'

Alan rocked from side to side, praying Samantha would appear to help him out, but the rest of the apartment was cloaked in silence. He recounted the events of Friday night, how Emily wanted to continue collecting money for the hospice, and how they went to visit all five of the large supermarkets.

'But I was told Emily suggested you just go to Sainsbury's. Was the idea to visit the others yours? Was it because you might bump into Margaret Vardy at Sainsbury's?'

Alan was speechless. His legs turned to jelly and his knees gave way. He caught the edge of the armchair to steady himself. He could feel his face burning with embarrassment. Samantha meanwhile, still stood in the kitchen with her hand clamped over Emily's mouth, released her grip. Emily dashed into the lounge screaming, 'JB, JB,' and threw herself airborne at Sir Bertie. Alan's mouth refused to close; his eyes widened and looked as if they were on stalks. His head moved from side to side, looking first at Sir Bertie and Emily, then at Lady Campbell.

'Emily, how many times have I told you? One of these days you are going to send me flying.'

The spell was broken when Samantha came into the room, kissing both her auntie and uncle. 'Well, now we've all met, who would like a drink? Talisker JB? Red wine Mo?'

'Thank you,' replied Moira as they sat down, 'but just a quick one; we've got a table booked at Luigi's. We had hoped you could join us, but with Alan confined to barracks, another time perhaps. While I remember, we'd like to invite you all for Christmas. As you know Samantha, we will be having our usual all-day soirée on Boxing Day, but we'd like you to come across on Christmas Eve and stay a few nights.'

'That would be lovely, thank you Mo. Alan can go fishing with JB, and Emily can hunt for ghosts.'

'But I've got nothing decent to wear,' objected Alan, having regained his composure after the shock.

'Alan my dear chap, anything will be better than yesterday's attire,' retorted Sir Bertie. 'Flip-flops indeed.'

§§§

'What about your mother?' asked Alan. 'I assumed you always went there for Christmas, just like the Sunday lunch routine.' Peace and quiet had now returned to the apartment after the 'surprise' visit. Samantha had admitted she had set the whole thing up, she had hoped to keep it quiet until Christmas, but with Alan moving into the apartment, she just couldn't trust Emily to keep the secret any longer. As they were leaving, Sir Bertie and Moira had welcomed Alan into the family, an act which had touched him, then swore him to secrecy in the workplace.

'I'm afraid after last weekend mother is now *persona non grata* as far as I'm concerned.'

'Isn't she jealous of Sir Bertie?'

'Yes, on two counts. When I was a baby and Piers was three or four, JB offered mother a chance to join the company. She refused, thinking it would go belly up. A few years later he asked her again and she was too proud to admit she'd been wrong. Her pig-headedness has cost her millions.'

'And the second?'

'When I was a young girl I always sat on JB's knee, cuddling him, the way Emily did tonight, sharing all my worries.'

'Hence his remarks about Margaret Vardy. Have you told him everything?'

Samantha nodded then went on, 'Dad was always away in the Middle East, and JB effectively became my surrogate father. Remember JB didn't marry Mo until I was fifteen. He gave me the love I lacked from my parents and we became very close. It has always rankled mother, that's why she tries to tie me down to Sunday lunches and Christmas dinners, to stop us going to see JB and Mo.'

'And now?'

Samantha shrugged. 'Now you're here and that's made it worse.'

'How?'

'You're a vulgar, foul-mouthed, beer-swilling, abrasive, coarse, crude, unrefined northerner and mother's a stuck-up snob.'

'Sam, that's a bit harsh,' he said, a hurt look on his face.

'Why, I always thought Sheffield *was* a northern town.' He smiled, acknowledging her joke. 'You said yourself that she thinks her shit doesn't smell, didn't you. It didn't take you long to work things out. With your sharp and perceptive mind you'll go far.'

'How about bed?'

While lying in bed, waiting for Samantha to ablute, his mind went back to Margaret Vardy. He smiled as he recalled the knowing look they gave each other outside the boardroom yesterday, Samantha only inches away.

'What are you grinning about?' Samantha asked as she emerged from the en-suite.

He merely shook his head.

§§§

On Sunday morning Alan was still trying to catch up with the reports of his disciplinary hearing in the papers. The broadsheets had moved on, and even the tabloids were tiring of the story. Samantha and Emily were sat on the kitchen floor surrounded by a mountain of coins. They had separated the paper notes and dried them in the utility room, the new plastic five and ten pound notes were unaffected by the soaking on Friday night. They had also split the coins into eight different groups when the phone rang.

'I'll get it,' said Emily, as she leapt up.

Samantha sighed, 'Emily sweetheart, it's eleven-o'clock.' Even Alan understood the unspoken explanation.

'Oh,' Emily said as she sat down again, and started counting the penny coins into a plastic bag.

Five minutes later Samantha returned.

'I don't believe it,' she said with rising inflection. 'She only wants us to go for Sunday lunch.'

Chapter 48

'Alan says I can, so I want the sign *now.*' Emily was in a strop. Buoyed by her success with the hospice collection, she had suggested that she wanted to make another at the Boxing Day soirée, this time for the air ambulance that took Alan to hospital. She wanted her mother to make a sign to put on her bucket, but so far Samantha had resisted.

'Sweetheart, there will be over 100 people there, the Chief Constable, leaders of industry, financiers, everybody,' Samantha had pleaded.

'Yes, they'll all be rich, I'll get loads of money,' Emily had retorted. She had been confined to her bedroom for arguing.

As Alan was passing the partially open door, he eased it open, put his mobile on the nearby table and mouthed 'Sir Bertie.' Emily took the hint. When Sir Bertie heard the plea, he couldn't say no, and he had agreed that the previous collection couldn't be split as it was collected solely for the hospice. He was very impressed that she had already collected over £4800 for the children's wing of St Andrew's Hospice in Grimsby.

§§§

The sun was just setting on Christmas Eve when they arrived at the entrance to Foxton Manor. Samantha stopped between the two huge brick pillars at the end of the drive. Each supported a large wrought iron gate, neither of which had been closed in years. To the left stood the original two-storey gatehouse, with a new three-bay oak-framed garage behind. A Mini, a Bentley, and an old Land Rover Defender were parked in the bays. On the right of the drive, there was a similar and almost identical house. Apart from the moss on the roof tiles of one, it was difficult to tell them apart. Only the owners, and the

In Deep Water

locals from the nearby village, knew that one house was 200 years younger than the other.

'Because of the cars, I guess it's the one on the left,' volunteered Alan.

Emily started giggling. 'No silly,' she chuckled, 'that's George and Shirley's house, he's the chauffeur.' Samantha set off up the drive, the tyres crunching through the gravel as they moved forward along the winding road. The headlights came on automatically as they entered a large wood; it seemed as if they were driving through a black tunnel. As they emerged at the other side, the Manor came into view.

'Holy shit.'

'Language Bish,' Samantha chided as she braked the car to a stop. He apologised. 'We have to use the tradesman's entrance at the rear, but the guests on Boxing Day will all be greeted on the front steps over there.' Alan couldn't fail to be impressed, Samantha commentating on the features. 'Seven bedrooms, many en-suite, stone mullioned and leaded windows, clock tower on the north wing, a *pied-à-terre* in London and a villa in the Algarve.'

'A *pied-à-terre* in London?'

'Well, a three-bedroom penthouse apartment in St John's Wood, overlooking Lord's cricket ground. It's probably worth more than this.'

Alan couldn't stop himself. 'Holy shit, does he need an assistant?'

'You'll have to ask him now you're family.'

'What's the format for the next few days?'

'Tonight will just be the five of us, tomorrow George and Shirley will join us for the day. It's their day off, so Mo does all the cooking and serving. On Boxing Day George and Shirley will do most of the work, but we will all end up helping.'

'And no farting or burping?'

'Bish, behave yourself,' she chided, slapping his thigh. Emily giggled away in the back seat.

§§§

'You know Fred, it's been three days since they frogmarched me out of Riverside House, and still no-one has had the decency to tell me when I'll get my pension, or how much it'll be.'

'Well *it is* Christmas.' Fred Osborne was sat in Ian Young's warm kitchen, gratefully drinking his wine and whisky, even if it did mean having to listen to him ranting on. Mrs Young had been so sickened by her husband's moaning she had gone to their daughter's for Christmas alone. As a single man, Fred had little else to do on Christmas Eve. Ever since Young's sacking last Saturday, they had met every evening in the local pub to plan their next moves. Osborne had been told weeks ago by Sir Bertie that he needed to find another job. Young, however, had a bigger problem. He needed to get some vital documents from his office, incriminating papers which would prove he had fraudulently forged his letter of appointment to enhance his annual salary. After his sacking at the board meeting last Saturday, George Thomas had escorted Young off the premises, forcibly removing the office keys from his jacket pocket, ripping it in the process. Fred had reported that on Monday joiners had changed the locks on the MD's door.

'That's not a problem,' Young had said, thinking his ex-secretary would come to his rescue. 'Margaret Vardy will have new keys.'

'She finished work last Friday,' Fred had told him. 'She's going to be a full-time author you know,' he had added helpfully.

'Well if it comes down to it Fred, you're going to have to break in and steal those papers. While you're on, you can get details of my pension payments.'

Fred Osborne had first met Ian Young five years ago in their local pub. A former bricklayer, redundant at the time, Young had appointed him as Admin Manager on a salary of £40,000 to be his 'eyes and ears'. They used to meet every lunchtime in the pub next to Riverside House to discuss what Fred had learnt, which was very little, as the staff soon realised he was spying for the MD.

'I can't do that,' protested Osborne. 'Didn't you say you had to go back for your photos and certificates?'

'A lot of bloody use they are now.'

No matter how long they talked, both men knew their futures looked bleak.

§§§

After unloading the car of luggage, presents, and Alan's new high-vis coat to keep him warm if he went out, they ate a light supper in the kitchen before Alan was given a tour of the property. Samantha meantime laid the presents out under the Christmas tree. Alan had sought the help of the internet to buy gifts for Samantha and Emily. Unfortunately, some had yet to be delivered. Once back downstairs, Sir Bertie guided Alan towards the library. Free standing bookcases stood against one of the walls, in a random, but not untidy way. Opposite, was a large leather-topped desk with a captain's swivel chair. The French doors onto the patio outside were flanked by heavy brocade curtains, and the inglenook fireplace had a log-burning stove set into it. The kitchen had been warm with the Aga churning out heat, but the library was even warmer. Someone had banked the stove high with logs, and an assortment of wood was piled at both sides, larger logs to the left, and smaller to the right. Alan surmised there was an art to burning wood. His face felt on fire, and he used one of the linen cloths he had been given earlier at the walk-in medical centre to mop the sweat from his brow and burnt raw skin. He had been told he could start shaving again using an electric razor. Two weeks' worth of facial hair would disappear on Christmas morning.

'At least you don't look like a member of the White Helmets motorcycle display team anymore,' Sir Bertie quipped, as he poured two good measures of Talisker. Alan had thought they would sit in armchairs at either side of the fire, but instead Sir Bertie thankfully chose to sit near the cool French windows. 'I thought we could have a chat about the company for a few minutes. Gordon showed me the list of proposals you all came up with, and I was impressed. Unfortunately Lloyds Bank has a concern about timescale, how long before you think we could start to turn the company around?'

'Well sir.' Sir Bertie's raised hand stopped him mid-sentence.

'I told you on Saturday, you're part of the family now, and in private its JB, stands for Jamie Bertram.'

'Sorry. If Charlie looks after some of my operational duties and you can somehow control Ian Young...'

Another raised hand. 'Don't worry about Young; he left on Saturday after our emergency board meeting. Not happy, but George helped him decide.' Sir Bertie waited for that to sink in, Alan thought, *the Silent Assassin helped him decide.* How he wished he'd been a fly on the wall. 'How long?' Sir Bertie prompted again.

Alan swirled his untouched whisky around in the glass, giving himself some thinking time. 'Twelve months to see a bottom line improvement, the shoots appearing after six.'

'What about redundancies?'

Alan hadn't expected this at all, but he had to show decisiveness. 'Inevitable I'm afraid.'

'Talk me through the redundancy programme.'

'Well sir . . . sorry, JB, you have to be ruthless in the decision making, compassionate in the execution.'

Sir Bertie repeated Alan's words. '"Ruthless in the decision making, compassionate in the execution". I like that. Go on.'

'You've seen our initial thoughts; we would work through that list taking the most obvious first.'

'What about the Press and Public Relations post? That was on the list.'

Shit, Samantha's job. If he said yes, she may never speak to him again, if he said no, he would seem indecisive. He hadn't slept with her when that list had been produced. He merely nodded, then added, 'We need the post, especially now, but we can't afford it.' Sir Bertie nodded in reply. A long silence followed during which Alan assumed he had said the wrong thing. He swallowed his whisky in one gulp, his eyes lowered, focusing on the glass, even when Sir Bertie spoke.

'Look, I like what you've said, would you be interested in applying for the MD's job, or have you anything else in the pipeline?'

Alan suddenly straightened, and looked Sir Bertie in the eye. *He knows something,* he thought. *Best tell the truth.*

'No nothing, and yes, I'd like the chance to apply. Before the disciplinary hearing, one of our competitors had been suggesting I join them, but I've heard nothing since.'

'I know,' Sir Bertie replied, fixing his glare on Alan. 'I just wanted to test your loyalty. I've known Bill Waites for over ten years, and he and Sheila will be joining us on Boxing Day. We can talk about my little deception then.' Alan's mouth fell open. 'You're agape again,' from Sir Bertie cured the annoying trait.

Alan couldn't stop himself. 'You bastard,' he muttered. Sir Bertie heard it, and smiled.

'Right here's what we are going to do. You will have until the thirty-first of December to persuade Samantha that, if she accepts redundancy, I will put you on the shortlist for the MD's job, OK?'

'You bastard,' louder this time, produced another smile.

By the time they rejoined the ladies in the kitchen, Emily had gone to bed. Still not sure about the ghosts, Samantha had put her in their bed for the moment. Alan asked Samantha if she would like to take a stroll around the grounds, so they both put on warm clothing and walked out hand in hand. Suddenly night became day, as floodlights sensed movement and bathed the house in light.

'What did JB say?'

'Two things, we can leave the rest until we get back into the warm house.' Foxton Manor's heating had been cranked up for Alan's visit, log burners lit in several rooms, the Aga going full blast in the kitchen, as was the air-source heat pump for the central heating. The difference in temperature outside was noticeable. 'Firstly, after a board meeting on Saturday, Ian Young left the company, sounds like he was pushed rather than jumped.'

'We all wondered if something had happened, his company credit cards and phone bills were cancelled on Monday.'

'Secondly, and I'm not sure how you are going to take this, but JB said if I can persuade you to accept redundancy, before the end of the year, he will put me on the shortlist for Ian's job.'

'The bastard,' she spat.

'That's what I called him, and he just smiled.'

'He's up to something,' Samantha said, as they walked on in a comfortable silence, both deep in thought. 'I think he's bluffing; he pays half my household bills anyway. If I don't have a job, he'll end up paying them all.'

Five minutes after leaving, they were back in the house. Alan asked, 'JB, could I have a word in private please?'

'No need, we are all family, say what you have to here,' and waved his hand towards the empty chairs around the kitchen table.

After they had removed their coats and sat down, Alan looked around the table then took a deep breath. 'Sam and I have spoken, and she has agreed to accept redundancy, on condition that you put me on the shortlist for the MD's job.'

Samantha added, 'I don't like the job anyway, I'll find something else, I'm sure.'

'No need,' replied Sir Bertie, 'I want you to come back to Campbell Homes and work for us. Mo and I are going to start taking a less active role, and we want to offer you a twenty percent share of the company, with a similar amount going in trust for Emily.'

'But it's worth millions,' Samantha gasped.

'Yes, and that's on top of your salary.'

'Why?' she asked, feeling dizzy at the thought.

'Well, we've no-one else to leave it to, have we? We are also going to give key members of staff a small share. As for you Alan, the shortlist was a ruse, you can have the job as MD of Lincs Water, but we'll keep it a secret, and only announce it on Boxing Day. We've invited some of your colleagues to the soirée. Now I think we'll have a drink to celebrate, you can read this while I'm away,' and he pushed a typed statement towards them before leaving to get some wine, whisky and glasses.

The directors of Lincs Water are sorry to reveal that, with immediate effect, Mr Ian Young has resigned as Managing Director to pursue other interests, and we wish him well. We are pleased to announce that Dr Alan Bishop has been offered the job of MD, and will commence after the Christmas break. Dr Bishop's key tasks are to return the company to profitability, and reinstate the generous dividend that shareholders have always enjoyed.

Sir Bertie Campbell
Executive Chairman

Alan turned to Mo and said, 'He's a ruthless bastard isn't he?'

She answered with another question. 'You've *only* just realised?'

§§§

Sir Bertie picked up his ringing mobile, the caller ID *Bill Waites*. On the kitchen table was the evidence of a satisfactory end to an enjoyable celebratory evening, an empty whisky decanter and two empty bottles of wine. 'JB can you talk?' Sir Bertie was taken aback by the abrupt question from his friend and total lack of small talk, particularly so late on Christmas Eve. He rose from the kitchen table, nodded his apologies to the others and headed for the study. Only when he was behind the closed door did he answer the question.

'What's so urgent at this time of night Bill?'

'It's the test results you sent me last Friday, I've only just managed to get someone to look at them, with the holidays a lot of our scientific staff have taken time off.' Sir Bertie had photographed half-a dozen sheets of the tests Alan had tabled at the disciplinary hearing and sent them to Bill for his comments. He had never expected to hear any more about the matter. Bill went on, 'The test taken on the thirteenth of December, the day of the incident, was very high in phosphates.'

Sir Bertie sat down heavily at his desk, the colour rapidly draining from his face. 'What does that mean?' he asked with some trepidation.

Waites took a deep breath. 'It means one of two things. Either Bishop lied to you . . . or he hasn't realised the significance.'

Sir Bertie's hands started to tremble. 'What could happen to anyone who drank the water?'

'Vomiting and diarrhoea, babies and young children are the most susceptible.' Sir Bertie exhaled loudly. Waites went on, 'On the plus side if you haven't heard anything so far, it's been ten or eleven days since the incident, you may be lucky.'

'I bloody well hope so. I've known from day one about his maverick and unconventional approach to things. Two hours ago I appointed him as our new MD. Next week he'll be responsible for the water supply to over one million customers.'

'Oh shit JB, what are you going to do?'

About the Author

Peter Goldsbrough was born in the north-east of England. After obtaining his degree in civil engineering, he worked in local government for a short time, before joining the water industry in 1976. His career included time in engineering design and operational management, where his experiences gave him the ideas for his writing.

His first novel of a proposed trilogy, *In Deep Water*, is set in Lincolnshire where he lived and worked for many years. After a brief spell in the private sector, he took early retirement in 2001, and relocated to Cyprus for 16 years. Now back in the UK and living in North Yorkshire, he has already started writing his second novel.

Peter is a relative of Alf Wight, the author of the highly successful James Herriot books, and he hopes he has inherited some of his family's writing genes.